ANGELICA'S GROTTO

ANGELICA'S GROTTO

RUSSELL HOBAN

BLOOMSBURY

Grateful acknowledgement is made to HarperCollins Publishers for permission to quote from *HMS Surprise* (1996) by P.O. O'Brian; to Northwestern University Press for permission to quote from Jerzy Ficowski's Introduction to *The Drawings of Bruno Schulz* (1990); to Channel Four Television for permission to refer to the film *The Last Navigator*, an Independent Communications Associates Production for Channel Four, WGBH Boston, ABC Australia, Directed by André Singer; to Dover Publications, New York for permission to quote from *London Labour and the London Poor, Volume III*, by Henry Mayhew (1968); to the group Garbage for permission to quote from 'Only Happy When It Rains' by Shirley Manson, Steve Markes, Duke Erikson, and Butch Vig; to International Music Publications Ltd for permission to quote from 'Windmills of Your Mind', words and music by Michael Legrand, Marilyn Bergman and Alan Bergman, © 1968 EMI Catalogue Partnership and EMI U Catalog Inc., USA. Worldwide print rights controlled by Warner Bros Inc, USA/IMP Ltd; to EMI Music Publishing, London, for permission to quote from 'Everybody's Somebody's Fool', words and music by Jack Keller and Howard Greenfield © Screen Gems/EMI Music Inc, USA. Every effort has been made to trace the copyright owners of the songs quoted.

First published 1999

Bloomsbury Publishing Plc, 38 Soho Square, London W1V 5DF

A CIP catalogue record for this book
is available from the British Library

ISBN 0 7475 4611 8

10 9 8 7 6 5 4 3 2 1

Typeset by Palimpsest Book Production Limited,
Polmont, Stirlingshire
Printed and bound in Great Britain by
Clays Ltd, St Ives plc, Bungay, Suffolk

ACKNOWLEDGEMENTS

For accuracy of detail I am indebted to the following people, listed here in alphabetical order: Jo Barnardo; Gordon Beckmann; Isabelle de la Bruyère; Michael Hardwicke; Ben Hoban; Ruth James; Sion Lewis; F. J. Lillie; John Naughton; Doris Patterson; Thomas Seydoux; and Linda Wheeldon.

I am grateful to Dominic Power and Phoebe Hoban for comments and encouragement on the manuscript. Lastly, my special thanks to Rebecca _____, whose face I borrowed for Melissa. The George III Mental Health Centre is imaginary.

To the memory of Leon Garfield

CONTENTS

'Black is the most essential of all colours. Above all, if I may say so, it draws its excitement and vitality from deep and secret sources of health . . .'

Odilon Redon, *Journals*
Cited by Alfred Werner in *The Graphic Works of Odilon Redon*, Dover 1969

'The wolf can hide in a dream. In the dream it will be a bird, or a woman you want to couple with. But when you do, the wolf will come out of the dream and open your throat.'

Larry McMurtry,
Commanche Moon

1

BREAKAGE

'What happened to your nose?' said Dr Mzumi in his beautiful lilting English. He was handsome, he was fit. His mountain bike leant against the wall behind him and above it were his framed certificates and degrees. On the other walls were photographs of Kenya and a red, black, and yellow *kikoi*. 'You look as if you've been in a fight.'

'Oxbridge wogs,' said Harold Klein. 'Oh shit.' He fanned the air in an effort to make the words go away. 'Terribly sorry, Dr Mzumi. That's not me, really – words come out of my mouth and I don't know what they're going to be until I hear them.'

Dr Mzumi tilted his head to one side. 'If it isn't you, who is it?'

'What I mean is, I'm the one who said it but it's not the sort of thing I'd ever say. Or think. I'm not that kind of person.'

'Of course not. Was it something like this that got your nose . . . what, broken?'

'Yes. Two ribs as well.' Klein was a small man of seventy-two with a small beard, no moustache. He was not fit, not handsome. 'I was on my way to the shops when I saw this big guy coming towards me, total stranger. Union

Jack tattoo on his right arm and a dragon with a banner that said MOTHER on his left. H-A-T-E on the knuckles of his right hand and the same on the left.' Klein touched his nose carefully.

'What happened then?' said Dr Mzumi.

'I heard myself say, "Ugly lout." He stopped and said, "You what?" and smashed my nose. H-A-T-E. I broke the ribs when I hit the pavement. Spent most of the day in Casualty at Chelsea & Westminster. I must learn to fall better.'

'Better if you can learn to avoid falling. This inability to know what you're going to say – when did it begin?'

'Three weeks ago after I read this piece in *The Times*.' He gave the doctor a cutting headed 'Listening to the censor inside our heads' by Anjana Ahuja. Dr Mzumi read:

Imagine arriving at a party and spying an attractive guest across the room. As you snake towards him or her, your brain is rapidly calculating how to make an introduction. In the space of a few steps, a voice inside your head will have dismissed most chat-up lines as too bold, too ghastly or too clichéd. As a result, the phrase that eventually falls from your lips is likely to be a crafted piece of wordsmanship – concise, sophisticated and socially appropriate for a first meeting.

The writer went on to describe 'the cognitive skill that allows us to "talk" to ourselves' and a projected three-year study of the phenomenon.

'So you read this,' said Dr Mzumi. 'Then what?'

'As I was reading it I began to get a leaden feeling down my left arm and an ache at the back of my throat. Next there came some really heavy angina. I'd had a myocardial infarction back in 1977 and this felt the same so I dialled 999.

'In the ambulance the paramedics gave me oxygen and did a one-lead ECG and we were chatting so I didn't notice anything until I was in Casualty again on a trolley and a nurse with a really wonderful rear view walked past. I said to myself, "If the Good Lord made anything better he kept it to hisself." That's a quote from *A Walk on the Wild Side*, Nelson Algren. Have you read it?'

'No.'

'Anyhow, when I said it I thought I was talking to myself but I heard myself speaking out loud. The nurse turned and shook her head and said, "Never say die, eh luv?" I said, "Jesus, let's pull ourself together," and I said that out loud too. That's how it's been ever since, and it's such an embarrassment! Once I've started talking I can follow what I'm saying and I can say appropriate things. But I never know what my first words will be so I never know when I'll come out with something that'll get me into trouble.'

'You could be a regular visitor to Casualty if this keeps up,' said Dr Mzumi.

'That's why I'm here. Can you send me to someone who can help me get my inner voice back?'

'I'll arrange for you to see Professor Slope.'

'Slippery?'

'Psychiatrist. He's Consultant at the George III Mental Health Centre and he's very likely come up against this sort of thing before. I see in your notes that it *was* a myocardial infarction. How're you . . .'

At that moment Klein had in his mind the image of an hourglass with all the sand in the bottom. 'It doesn't get turned over,' he whispered into his hand. 'It's a one-way trip.'

'Feeling now?' Dr Mzumi had said. He noted the hand over the mouth. 'Are you all right?'

'In places.'

'I was thinking of your heart.'

'No problems at the moment. Evidently it wasn't all that serious. They upped my Adizem and perindopril dosage and lowered the Imdur.'

'How's the angina?'

'Not too bad. I only had to stop and take glyceryl trinitrate once on the way here.'

'Diabetes under control?'

'Yes.'

'Legs?'

'The claudication's not as bad as it was. I think what I'm getting in the drug trial is bezafibrate and not a placebo.'

Dr Mzumi turned to his computer, updated Klein's prescription, printed it out, signed it, and gave it to him. 'When's your next appointment at the Cardiology Clinic?'

'Two months.'

'When was your last angiogram?'

'Some time in '93, I think.'

Dr Mzumi made a note in Klein's folder. 'When you see Dr Singh he might want you to have another one. And I'll get a letter off to Professor Slope today.' He shook Klein's hand. 'Mind how you go.'

Klein was looking at Dr Mzumi's bicycle. 'I had to give up cycling last year,' he said.

'Because of the vertigo?'

'Yes. Broke two ribs on the other side.'

Dr Mzumi made another note in Klein's folder. 'A CT brain scan and a carotid angiogram might be a good idea. They'll send you an appointment.'

4

'Thank you. One day you'll be old and pissing in two streams too. Sorry. Bye-bye.'

Klein went to the 14 bus stop in the Fulham Road. Although he'd walked from his house to the surgery by way of Eelbrook Common, Novello Street, Munster Road and Mimosa he didn't feel like going back that way. Novello Street always seemed unlucky to him; the terrace of little houses looked at him in a way he didn't like.

Klein's relationship with the 14 bus was a complex one: the old doubledecker Routemasters often kept him waiting for much too long and he could never be sure of their moods: sometimes, small and inconsequential in the distance, they suddenly loomed large and implacable like a Last Judgement; at other times they were quite docile. Their redness of course was variable, on some days sweet to the eye and on others threatening. Today the bus arrived reasonably quickly and seemed tame enough; the people who had clustered at the stop without queuing pushed ahead of Klein but he found a seat next to a very large man full of elbows and rode to Fulham Broadway with one buttock seated and the other tense.

From there he walked to his house that looked across Eelbrook Common towards the District Line. The Underground was Klein's favourite means of transport; in the end-of-September dusk the trains were poignant as they rumbled westward to Wimbledon, eastward to Tower Hill, Barking, Upminster. *Look at our golden windows*, they said. *Ride with us; we are the safe haven between the troubles at either end.*

2

ESCHER, FOR CHRIST'S SAKE

The George III Mental Health Centre was a squarish brick building in World's End. Automatic doors opened when they saw Klein coming. 'I don't like to be taken for granted,' he said, but went in.

The waiting room had five chairs, two small round tables, six magazines, and a receptionist behind glass who was busy on the telephone but indicated by gestures that Klein should take a seat. All of the magazines had beautiful half-naked women on their covers and their titles were *GUILT*, *SHAME*, *DREAD*, *HORROR*, *DESPAIR*, and *SUICIDE FOR SINGLES*. 'Don't try it on with me,' said Klein, and looked away. When he looked back the magazines were *DIY WORLD*, *CAR BOOT JOURNAL*, *GAY CUISINE*, *SWINGING SENILES*, *BIPOLAR GARDENING*, and *THE PRACTICAL DEPRESSIVE*. 'Still not quite right,' he said, and didn't look again.

A pear-shaped deflated-looking man tending towards the lachrymose slumped into the room and sat down heavily.

'I hope you're not going to start a conversation,' Klein whispered into his hand.

'Why are you so withdrawn?' said Pear-Shape.

6

'Strangers always start conversations with me when I don't feel like talking.'

'My name is Arbuth,' said Pear-Shape.

'Not?'

'Arbuthnot is what it used to be. I had it changed by deed-poll. Nothing helps. What's yours?'

'Klein.'

'Means little.'

'Nothing means much these days. When you changed your name you should have covered your tracks and changed it to Cholmondely or Featherstonhaugh.'

'Oh yes, it's all right for some.' Arbuth sniffed and pretended to read THE PRACTICAL DEPRESSIVE as Professor Slope appeared and said, 'Mr Klein?'

'Here,' said Klein, and stood up.

'How do you do,' said Professor Slope.

'Badly, thank you.' They shook hands, during which Slope seemed to be looking over Klein's shoulder.

'My office is just down the corridor,' he said, and led the way. In the office he motioned Klein to a chair and sat down behind his desk. Slope was sixtyish, had a neat little beard, rimless spectacles, French cuffs. Before him on the desk was Klein's file. On the wall to his left was an Escher print, *Three Worlds*, with a carp lurking dimly in a leaf-strewn pond in which black and leafless trees were reflected. The other walls were bare.

'Escher, for Christ's sake,' said Klein.

'You don't like Escher?'

'Escher in a psychiatrist's office is like a Pirelli calendar in a garage.'

'Why is your arm in a sling? Have you been discussing art with anyone else?'

'Very funny. Haven't you got my notes?'

'Yes,' said Professor Slope, without referring to the file, 'and I know about the cholecystectomy and appendectomy, the prostate resection, the hydrocele operation, the triple bypass, the cataract surgery, and the right-lung lobectomy; I know about about the diabetes, atheroma, ischaemia, both myocardial infarcts, the hiatus hernia, and the vertigo. I know about the broken ribs and nose but there's nothing in your notes about an arm.'

'How did you do that without looking at my notes?'

'I do memory exercises. How's yours?'

'Terrible.'

'Let me just get a couple of details down. Date of birth?'

'Four, two, twenty-five.'

'Are you married?'

'I was, twice. My second wife died in 1977.' He whispered her name into his hand, 'Hannelore.' He tried to see her face but saw instead that of the Meissen figure on his mantelpiece at home. 'You never look at me,' he whispered.

Whispers into hand, Slope wrote. 'Are you retired?' he said.

'No. I'm an art historian. I write books, did the *Innocent Eye* series on BBC2.'

'Oh, yes – Sister Wendy sort of thing, eh?'

'No.' Klein whispered something into his hand again.

'Right. Let's get back to your arm. What happened?'

'Woman ahead of me at the checkout counter in Safeway: she bent over and I said something I wouldn't ordinarily say aloud. She hit me in the shoulder with a jar of pickles and I broke the arm when I fell. She didn't hit me that hard – it was my vertigo that made me fall.'

8

'You haven't had that sort of encounter with women before this?'

'Do I look as if I've got a Union Jack tattoo?'

Slope directed his eyes to Klein's forehead which for him was transparent. He considered Klein's frontal lobes and wondered if they might be breathing a trifle hard. 'Try to remember, Mr Klein, that I'm only gathering information. A straight answer would speed the process.'

'The straight answer is that I'm not always in charge of my answers; that's why I'm here. Haven't you read Dr Mzumi's letter?'

Professor Slope stroked his beard. 'Give me a moment, Mr Klein, while I have another look at your notes.' He opened Klein's file, a very thick one, and went through some of the loose sheets at the top of the stack. 'They don't always put things in the right order. Hmm, hmmm – here we are. You read something in a newspaper, you had an MI, and you lost what you call your "inner voice".'

'I really don't know what else you'd call it.'

'Can you clarify this inner-voice thing a little for me?'

Klein clarified it a little, citing the *Times* article and describing what followed the reading of it.

'This voice –' said Professor Slope, 'where did it seem to be coming from?'

'From me. I could feel it in my vocal cords. At the post office while I waited in the queue I'd rehearse in my head what I was going to say, like "Fifty first-class stamps, please" and I'd feel it in my throat. Isn't that how it is for everybody?'

'People vary. Did you hear this voice as your voice or was it somebody else's?'

'It was my voice but I didn't actually seem to be hearing it – it was just there.'

9

'And how have you been feeling in yourself since it stopped being there?'

'Lost, cast adrift. Frightened.'

'Frightened of what?'

'What I might say, what I might do.'

'Like your remark to the woman in Safeway with the result that we see.'

'Yes.'

'Looking back on that, how do you feel about it?'

'Embarrassed.'

'What were you feeling at the moment when the words came out of your mouth?'

'Embarrassment.'

'Nothing else?'

'Like what?'

Professor Slope looked again at Klein's frontal lobes. Coloured lights twinkled here and there, as on a model railway. 'Elation?' he said.

'No, she was a total stranger.'

Professor Slope raised his voice. '"Elation," I said.'

'What about it?'

'Did you perhaps enjoy getting this woman's attention with what you said?'

Klein smiled. 'Well, she certainly got *my* attention when she bent over.'

'Did you feel any sort of relief or release when you said what you said?'

'I was shocked, and I was even more shocked when she hit me with the pickles. The queue behind me were very impatient and they were making angry crowd noises. I had to put back half my groceries because I only had the one usable arm, then I slunk home like some sort of pariah, unloaded the shopping, and headed for Casualty again.'

Professor Slope took off his spectacles, wiped them with his handkerchief, and imagined the scene in Safeway. 'Couldn't have been very pleasant for you,' he said.

'She had curlers in her hair,' said Klein, shaking his head.

'Apart from that, how've you been feeling lately? Any big ups or downs?'

'No big ones. I had a medium up a while back when I made potato pancakes and they didn't fall apart.'

'Downs?'

'Well, I always feel a little low when I haven't got a book going and right now I'm between books.'

'Any plans for the next one?'

'I've been thinking about Klimt, just the nudes. Do you know his work?'

'No.' Professor Slope contemplated the Escher. 'Can you remember, perhaps when you were young, any sort of incapacity – not an injury but a loss of function?'

'Loss of function! Catriona Moriarty, when I was fourteen – O God! she was like an Irish Aphrodite, and I . . .'

'Not that kind of function – that's autonomic nervous system. I'm looking for something ordinarily under your control.'

'That's a laugh. How much in life is under our control?'

'Let's not stray from the matter at hand. Try to remember some loss of function other than sexual.'

'When I was nine I had to take piano lessons. My teacher, Mr Schulz, always smelled of bananas. I never practised but his pupils were giving a recital and I was to play *Für Elise*, which I'd never once got through successfully. On the afternoon of the recital all the strength went out of my wrists – they just went all floppy and my mother had to take me to the doctor.'

11

'And what did the doctor say?'

'He said it was nervousness and he gave me a tranquilliser.'

'What then?'

'I became tranquil.'

'And your wrists?'

'Stayed floppy till evening; when the recital was over they were all right again.'

'That sounds to me like what we call a dissociative disorder.'

'What's that?'

'It's when there's nothing physically wrong but the body isn't taking orders from the brain.'

'What's that got to do with the loss of my inner voice? That *is* the brain talking, isn't it?'

'The boundaries in this sort of thing aren't as clear-cut as one might like. Before we can help you with your problem we need to have a better idea of what it is. I'm going to arrange for you to have some tests, then we'll proceed from there.'

'What kind of tests?'

'Psychological ones.'

'Just what I need,' Klein whispered into his hand – 'something I can fail at.' To Professor Slope he said, 'Who's going to do the tests?'

'One of our psychologists – I don't yet know which one.'

'And after that I come back to you?'

'No, my job is to make the first assessment, then I pass you along to whomever is the best person to get you sorted.'

'*Whoever.*'

'Whatever,' said Professor Slope. 'I'll put the wheels in motion and you'll be hearing from us shortly.'

'From whomever?'

'I'm sure your grammar is impeccable, Mr Klein, but more importantly we need to address deeper issues. Good luck.' He picked up a microcorder and began to murmur into it, meanwhile extending his hand which Klein shook.

'Why do ungrammatical people love to say "more importantly"?' said Klein. 'Thank you.'

3

THE MEISSEN GIRL, THE PAXOS STONE

When Klein got home he poured himself a Glenfiddich, sat down at his desk, and looked across it to the mantelpiece and the Meissen figure of a girl about to bowl a golden ball. Leaning forward with her knees bent and her right arm extended she stood thirteen and a half inches high on a round gilt-bordered base one and three-quarter inches high. Her feet were bare and she wore a classical pale-green gown that was tied with a pink ribbon below the breasts and left her right breast and shoulder bare. She was made in 1890 and the sculptor, Schott, had signed the base.

Every part of her was beautiful and shapely: her body and her limbs, her hands and feet, each individual finger and toe. Her long blonde hair framed the exquisite oval of her face. Full of sweetness, her face was, her rose-petal mouth all virginal, her eyes entranced and dreamy.

Her face was the face of the beloved who takes no notice, the beloved who passes by, chatting with her friends, with never a glance, never a thought for the one whose heart lies at her feet. Had Schott intended that face or was it that the very clay under his hands had refused him the response he craved?

14

Klein had bought that figure in Hannelore's home town, Celle in Lower Saxony. 'She looks like you,' he said to her.

'No, she doesn't,' said Hannelore. 'I was never that young, never that pretty.'

'Yes, you were, and the youth and prettiness are still there.'

'You wish.'

'I wish,' said Klein twenty years later as the girl, intent on her bowling, passed him by with never a glance.

The objects in his workroom, apart from their relationship with him, had relationships with one another: some harmless, some not. From a long-ago trip to Paxos with Hannelore, Klein, an inveterate collector of beach pebbles, had brought home one that he thought big enough to be called a stone. It appeared to be some kind of conglomerate, a pale warm grey, smoothly rounded, ovoid, weighed eighteen ounces, and felt good in the hand. On it Klein had written in black ink, in Greek letters, KINESIS/ANAPAUSIS: MOTION/REST.

Holding this stone in his hand, he saw the beach and the large mystical rocks shaped by the sea, heard the lapping of the tide and saw, magnified by the clear water, a polychaete worm, black and many-legged, like a warning to the curious. He saw the road to the villa and the olive trees on either side that flashed silver in the warm wind. There was a particular olive tree, ancient and wrinkled and still bearing fruit: in its hollow trunk was an opening that looked as if a naked goddess, Persephone perhaps, had emerged from it into the green-lit grove. Klein tried to remember the moment of balance when he had written those words on the stone, caught only the scent of Hannelore's sun-warm hair.

Sated with ANAPAUSIS, the Paxos stone longed for KINESIS. Klein had once placed it on the mantelpiece near the Meissen girl, then quickly removed it before it could jump up and smash her to bits. From then on he kept it on his desk, handling it as he would a dangerous pet.

4

FOUNTAIN OF YOUTH

It was ten days before Klein received a letter giving him an appointment with a clinical psychologist, Mrs Lichtheim. In the interval he began to make notes for a study of the nudes of Gustav Klimt and he attended diabetic, eye, cardiology, vascular, and foot-health clinics at Chelsea & Westminster Hospital.

On these visits he passed and repassed the fish in the lobby. They lived in a long, narrow, green and bubbling world and had been listed, Klein assumed, in the builders' manifest:

So many thousand bags cement
So many thousand cement blocks
1 No. 12 assortment XL Matissoid Mobile Atrium Shapes
1 world (long, narrow, green, bubbling)
16 lobbyfish (assorted)

While appearing to take no notice of Klein and the rest of humanity the fish explained to their children, 'What you see on the other side of the glass is an ichthyocentric world: it is as it is only because we are here to observe it.' Klein sensed this and avoided eye contact.

There were not very many young people queuing up for the clinics Klein visited; mostly they were others of his age group in wheelchairs and on sticks, many of them limping and halting in sandals, slippers, trainers, and divers bandages and offbeat bespoke surgical-appliance footgear. He spent half-days waiting to see registrars and consultants while nurses of many ages, weights, and shapes marched, ambled, and frisked past him. He mentally undressed the good-looking ones down to their lissome and beautifully articulated skeletons as, like a greyhound in a walking-frame, he followed with his eyes the nimble rabbits of his desire.

When his name was called he popped as required. He popped himself on to and off tables; he popped on and off his tops and his bottoms, his shoes and his socks, always 'for me'. 'Just pop yourself on or off for me,' said registrars and consultants. Nurses and house officers also required him to pop in one way and another for them. Eventually he popped into the street and made his way home to the word machine that silently asked what he had popped for it lately.

During that time he also reported to Charing Cross Hospital for his monthly visit in a drug trial for the use of bezafibrate in arterial disease of the lower extremities. The nursing sister counted the number of tablets remaining, took his blood pressure, and asked him whether he had experienced headaches, nausea, impotence, or ennui since taking the tablets which were either placebo or active. When she finished with him he was bled a little by the turbanned phlebotomist while they talked about world and local news and weather.

He had a thallium scan at Royal Brompton Hospital and a femoral angiogram at Chelsea & Westminster. He wrote a prescription request to his GP for more insulin, diltiazem, Imdur, captopril, frusemide, omeprazole, and aspirin. He bought a new bottle of glyceryl trinitrate tablets for angina and a new bottle of trisilicate of magnesium for oesophageal reflux. He stocked up on pine bark extract for his lower vascularities, green-lipped mussel extract for his knees, extract of gingko biloba for circulation in the brain and other extremities, and multivits just in case.

'I have no inner voice and must speak my thoughts aloud,' he said, 'but I feel pretty good actually. I represent a triumph of the medical arts and the never-say-die spirit of the NHS. In clinical circles all the receptionists have a smile for me and I am known to consultants and other golfers as "he who declines to hop the twig". In operating theatres I have more than once topped the bill; I am accomplished in nil by mouth and there is talk of getting me a permanent locker for my dentures. Life isn't what it was but it's a lot better than it's going to be.

'Now there comes to me a memory and I can smell the trees, feel the hot sun through the leaves. It was on the Appalachian Trail or it might have been somewhere else: my best friend Jim and I, hot and sweaty, pushing our bikes up a woodland road over a little mountain. At the top of the slope was a spring. I remember a stone trough and the clear cold water. There were leaves in the bottom of the trough and tiny crayfish. The water gushed from the pipe and it was a foreverness of itself, the endless quenching of all thirst. We drank it like an elixir and stuck our heads in the trough among the leaves and the crayfish and became new and strong and untired, for ever refreshed by the magic of that clear cold water that sparkled in the sunlight and the shadows on the mountain.'

19

5

WORTH WRITING UP?

'Actually,' said Professor Slope to Nathalie Lichtheim, 'I haven't come across anything like this inner-voice loss before – it might even be worth writing up.' They were having coffee in Slope's office where Escher's carp lurked dimly on the wall.

'You're telling me this poor man has completely lost his mental privacy, his *Selbstgesprach*?' said Mrs Lichtheim.

'He whispers into his hand when he wants to be private. He presented like he was about to blow all his fuses and my first thought was hypomania and the usual bipolar thing. Then I began to wonder about his frontal lobes but I doubt that there's anything organically wrong – his general irritability makes me think that his mental drains are blocked and he's got a lot of sewage backing up on him.'

Mrs Lichtheim shook her head and sighed a little. 'I'm surprised that it doesn't happen more often. Year after year we don't say all kinds of things that could get us into trouble, we keep an internal watch on the words about to come out of our mouths: we monitor the prearticulatory speech output code during speech production by means of an internal loop to the speech comprehension system. So here's this guy of yours who's been not saying things for about seventy years which is quite a long time, really. He hears these unsaid things in his head but they never come out of his mouth. Finally the monitor, the voice in his head, says, "The hell with this, I quit. You want to say something, say it out loud." You think it could be something like that?'

'I hope he survives long enough for us to find out,' said Slope.

6

A PERSON, ANOTHER
PERSON, A TREE

Nathalie Lichtheim M.Sc. AFBPsS. C. Psychol. was in her mid-forties, tall, with black hair, a luminous bespectacled face, and an abstractly motherly air. There was nothing in her office to lie down on but Klein whispered into his hand, 'It would be nice to fall asleep with her sitting nearby.'

'Can you tell me something about yourself,' she said, 'maybe something about how things are with you now?' She spoke softly and with a slight accent, perhaps Viennese.

Klein told her about the loss of his inner voice.

'Yes,' she said, 'but apart from that?'

'I'm not in very good shape. I live about a mile away and I walked here. I had to stop four times and rest because of angina. Life seems more of a struggle than it used to be; often people coming towards me don't give me room to pass, as if I'm invisible. When I take a bus the people who should be queuing behind me shove past me to get on – that sort of thing . . .' He trailed off into whispers.

She asked him what medications he was on and he told her. 'Now we'll begin with the Bender Gestalt Test,' she said. 'I'll show you nine cards and I'll ask you to look at them and copy them.'

'How does that bear on my inner-voice loss?'

'This problem doesn't come out of nowhere; we need to look at what's underneath it.' She showed him the cards and one by one he copied the various arrangements of lines, dots, and geometric shapes, whispering, muttering and singing into his left hand while his right hand was drawing. He sang 'Stormy Weather' and 'Nobody's Sweetheart Now'. '"*Oh no,*"' he said, '"*it wasn't the airplanes, it was Beauty killed the Beast.*"'

'". . . Beauty killed the Beast"', wrote Mrs Lichtheim. 'Is that a quote?'

'From the film *King Kong*,' said Klein as he continued his copying, 'when Kong's lying dead in the street. I notice that I shorten everything. I wonder if tall men elongate.'

'". . . if tall men . . . ?"'

'Elongate.' When he had copied the nine cards Mrs Lichtheim removed them, asked him to sign the sheet with his drawings, gave him a new sheet of paper, and asked him to draw the cards from memory. '"*Far and few, far and few, are the lands where the Jumblies live . . .*"' he said as he set to work. '"*The very thought of you makes my heart sing, like an April breeze on the wings of spring . . .*"' he sang, no longer hiding his mouth with his hand. He was able to recall seven of the cards more or less but not in the correct order; his attempts at the eighth and ninth were only guesswork. Again he signed his name and she collected that sheet and gave him a fresh one.

'That was the Bender Recall,' she said. 'Now I would like you to draw a person, any kind of person.'

Klein drew a young woman seen from the rear.

'Sign it, please,' said Mrs Lichtheim, 'and now a person of the opposite sex.'

Klein drew himself seen from the rear.

Mrs Lichtheim took the drawing and placed the first one in front of him. 'Could you tell me a bit about this one?'

'She's a young woman I saw in the Underground a couple of summers ago; I don't believe I ever saw her face. She had long fair hair, was wearing a broad-brimmed hat, straw or maybe canvas, black cotton vest, tight white denim trousers, tennis shoes I think. She was very attractive, very appealing; her figure was shapely and girlish, she was graceful in the way she moved. She looked the very essence of youth and beauty. Walking away from me.'

Mrs Lichtheim wrote down his words. 'Anything about her state of mind? What she could be feeling, what she could be thinking about?'

'She looked as if she might be going to meet someone she liked. She seemed well-pleased with life.'

'Anything about her future?'

'Years and years ahead of her, full of good things.'

'How old would you say she was?'

'Twenty-two or so.'

'And this other person you've drawn?'

'Well, that's me. I'm seventy-two years old. I've drawn this man from the rear in pretty much the same pose as the young woman. His posture – he looks hesitant, as if he's been brought to a halt, come to a pause. He's wearing a rucksack because I don't feel right unless I'm burdened to some extent. I think somewhere in Sholem Aleichem somebody says something like, "God doesn't ask how far you can carry your burden, He just says to put it on your back."'

When Mrs Lichtheim finished taking down his words she offered him another sheet of paper. 'Now I'd like you to draw a tree, please.'

Klein drew the olive tree, smelling as he did so the

24

warm summer wind and hearing the distant braying of a donkey.

'Do you draw?' said Mrs Lichtheim. 'You have an artistic touch.'

'I went to art school but I haven't done any drawing for a very long time.'

'What can you tell me about this tree?'

'It's an olive tree I saw on the island of Paxos the last time my wife – she's dead now – and I had a holiday there. Olive trees flash silver in the sun when the wind stirs the leaves. They look as if they're personally acquainted with gods and goddesses. This tree is very old but it still bears fruit. There's a hole in the trunk and it looks as if the naked Persephone might just have stepped out of that darkness into the green-lit shade of the olive grove. Naked Persephone in the green-lit shade.'

'When did your wife die?'

'In 1977.' Klein was looking at the olive tree in his mind, listening to the wind in the leaves, feeling the Ionian sunlight on his face. 'Hannelore,' he said.

'That was your wife's name?'

'Yes.' He put both hands over his mouth and whispered, 'She killed herself.'

Mrs Lichtheim allowed a little pause to happen, then she said, 'If you feel ready we can now do the Rorschach Test.'

'Yes,' said Klein. 'Let's do it.'

'I am going to show you ten cards with inkblots. The original blots were made by dropping inks on pieces of paper and then folding the paper in half. There are ten standardised inkblots that have been in use since the Rorshach was introduced in the forties. When I show these to you I'd like you to tell me whatever you can see on the card.'

The first inkblot looked to Klein like a motorcycle seen endwise from the rear. There was no one in the saddle but there was a person on each side with both feet on one of the footrests, one hand gripping a handlebar and the other flung out behind. Both of these people were in silhouette and wore loose black garments that fluttered in the wind.

'Anything else?' said Mrs Lichtheim.

'Only that the motorcycle would have to be going fast enough not to lose its balance and fall over.'

Mrs Lichtheim wrote down his description and in this manner, very slowly, Klein made his way through the Rorschach blots. He described the two jolly fellows wearing conical red hats who, undeterred by being legless and footless, were congratulating each other with a high-five handslap. They might be genies, he thought, just out of a bottle and still trailing smoke.

He described the two black dancers, a man and a woman, evidently romantically involved because of the two red hearts hanging point to point in the air between them. Although the idea of dancing was reinforced by musical emanations from their heads they seemed at the same time to be picking up their luggage or perhaps their shopping.

He described the full-frontal head of a wild boar, pointing out the tusks, the snout, the eyes and ears. *Schwarzwild* was the German name for this animal, and he told Mrs Lichtheim about infant *Schwarzwild* he and Hannelore had seen at the Berlin Zoo: they were striped like vegetable marrows.

He described the bat that was pretending to be a butterfly, how its wings were messy as if it had fallen into some muck.

He described the bottomprint made by some woman who had inked her naked bottom, then sat down on white paper and rocked back and forth a little to leave an impression of her buttocks and vulva.

He described what at first appeared to be the lower jaw of a shark which then became the heads and shoulders of two women with topknots, facing each other in profile.

He described some kind of angel seen from below, bearing aloft two animals, one at the tip of each wing. This one, with its delicate pinks and greys and greens, had a transcendental feeling, as it might be the higher nature lifting up the lower nature and becoming ever more distant as it rose.

He described two young women, possibly princesses, dancing and changing, as they danced, into deer with antlers.

He described two magicians at the end of a party, maybe a child's birthday party, magically making fireworks before everyone went home.

'Now,' said Mrs Lichtheim, 'I will need to show you the cards again and ask you what you see and where you see it so I can make notes. This is part of the usual procedure.' She had monochrome copies of the cards, and on these she circled and labelled the various parts of each blot according to his description. She was very painstaking about this, questioning him closely so that she was absolutely certain about what he saw and where in the blot he saw it.

'This one, the transcendental one,' he said when they came to it again, 'I didn't say it before but when I saw it I thought of Lucifer, the fallen angel. But even though he's fallen he appears to be going up, way up, far away above me. Almost I hear music, looking at this one – the *Dies Irae* theme.'

'Would you spell that, please,' said Mrs Lichtheim.

Klein spelled it. '*Days of Wrath*,' he said.

When Mrs Lichtheim had completed her notes she asked Klein to pick out the cards he liked the most and those he liked the least. He liked Lucifer and the two genies and the two dancing princesses best; he liked the bat and the bottomprint and the shark's jaw least.

'I'll evaluate these and you'll be hearing from us about your next appointment,' said Mrs Lichtheim.

Klein thanked her and walked home, still seeing Lucifer in pinks and greys and greens.

7

FINGERS AND FINS AND WINGS

With Lucifer still soaring in his mind, Klein found himself cruising his bookshelves. He saw his hand go up and return with one of his own titles, *Darkness and Light: the inner eye of Odilon Redon*. He turned to No.14 of the third series of lithographs illustrating Flaubert's *The Temptation of Saint Antony*: Oannes with his serpentine body, human face, and pharaonic headdress, hovering in a blackness.

He took the French edition of Flaubert from the shelves, turned to the Oannes page, and read his translation that was inserted there:

Then appears a singular being, having the head of a man on the body of a fish. He advances upright in the air by beating the sand with his tail; and this patriarchal figure with little arms makes Antony laugh.

'Redon's Oannes,' said Klein, 'is not laughable; he is of the darkness, he is between the times of one thing and another.' He read on:

OANNES
In a plaintive voice:

Respect me! I have been here from the very beginning. I have lived in the unformed world where hermaphrodite beasts were sleeping under the weight of an opaque atmosphere, in the depths of the dark waters – when fingers and fins and wings were mingled, and eyes without heads were floating like molluscs, among bulls with human faces and serpents with the paws of dogs.

'Yes,' said Klein: 'a world of undifferentiated matter where nothing has found its final form and function and doesn't know whether to swim or fly or walk. That's how it is with me.' He read on:

Over this muddle of beings, Omoroca, bent like a hoop, extended her woman's body. But Belus cut her clean in two, made the earth with one half, the sky with the other, and the two equal worlds contemplate each other.

'Is there a sky in me?' said Klein, seeing Lucifer high, high above him in pinks, in greens, in greys. 'Is there an earth?' He read on:

I, the first consciousness of chaos, I have risen from the abyss to harden matter, to regulate forms, and I have taught humans fishing, sowing, writing and the history of the gods.

'"Fishing, sowing, writing and the history of the gods,"' Klein repeated, and read on:

Since then I have lived in the pools that remain from the deluge. But the desert encroaches on them, the wind fills them with sand, the sun dries them up; and I am dying on my bed of mud, looking at the stars through the water. I must return.

He leaps, and disappears in the Nile.

'No!' said Klein. 'Oannes should stay and Antony should go! Poxy old Saint Antony. What did *he* ever teach that was any use to anyone?' He looked again at Oannes hovering in the black. Was Oannes looking back at him? Were his eyes open or closed? So dim, his face! Klein thought of Oannes dying on a bed of mud, his pools filled in, his blackness gone, and shook his head. 'But,' he said, 'but! Oannes didn't die; his original self, his old self, his powerful self, moved into the head of Odilon Redon and compelled him to create a *noir* for him to live in. Oannes lives! Perhaps he will yet harden my matter, regulate my form, teach me to fish, to sow, to write. Perhaps he will teach me the history of the gods. Or something else. Are there pinks in the black? Greens and greys?'

8

ANGER, FEAR, VIOLENT FANTASIES?

'Well,' said Mrs Lichtheim, 'it's now two weeks since you did the Bender and the Rorschach tests. Looking back on that session, how do you feel about it?'

'I still see Lucifer soaring high above me in pink and grey and green.'

Mrs Lichtheim consulted her notes. '*Days of Wrath*,' she said. 'You said you almost heard that music while looking at the fallen angel far above you. Are you wrathful? Is there anger in you?'

'Of course there is.'

'Why of course?'

'I don't like being invisible, I don't like being pushed off the pavement.'

'You're talking about now, but this anger in you, I think it goes further back than that; and it seems to me that you have to exert very strong control to keep it from bursting out.'

'Well, you know, in seventy-two years a lot of resentments accumulate: the whole world changes, and every change I've seen has been for the worse. The only exception is residential parking in our street but I haven't got a car.'

'How do you feel about your mother?'

'Why do you ask that?'

'Because in you there seems to be fear of women, as well as anger and guilt.'

'I think all men are afraid of women.'

'But we're talking about you.'

'All right, I'm afraid of women. But I already know that and I'd like us to start dealing with the present problem.' He was beginning to resent being steered by Mrs Lichtheim.

'I think your fear of women is part of the present problem,' she said. 'Your inner voice is the superego; sometimes it keeps you from saying what you really think. Now it shuts down, maybe it's tired of concealment; maybe now you are forced to hear yourself say what you really want to say. I think there are violent feelings in you, maybe violent fantasies.' Again she looked at his folder. 'You're an art historian. Are you working on something now?'

'I'm always working on something; I'm doing a study of the nudes of Gustav Klimt.'

'Naked women.'

'You can't be nude without being naked.'

'What's the title of your study?'

'*Naked Mysteries: the Nudes of Gustav Klimt.*'

'Are naked women a mystery to you?'

'They're even a mystery to themselves; that's why the Greeks celebrated those mysteries at Eleusis.'

'Do you believe that work is the way to understand a mystery?'

'Play won't do it.'

'Do you ever not work, just do nothing?'

'When I knock off for the day around midnight I put my feet up and watch a video.'

'You remember the first Rorshach blot, the motorcycle

33

with a man on either side but nobody in the driver's seat? It didn't fall over because its forward speed maintained its equilibrium.'

'What about it?'

'Do you think you'll fall over if you stop working for a week or a month?'

'Why should I stop?'

'Just for the pleasure of being without producing anything.'

'I picked the wrong parents for that.'

'How so?'

'Jewish immigrants from Russia, hot for self-improvement and offspring achievement. I drew well from the age of five so they laid it on me that I was going to be a great painter. I didn't produce great paintings but I write well about Art, so maybe they're partly easy in their graves.'

'Did you like your mother?'

'No.' Encouraged by Mrs Lichtheim he let himself go and talked about his mother and her faith in enemas; he talked about his father, about his school days, his first love, his army time; he talked about Francine, his first wife, and Hannelore, his second.

'Do you fantasise about women?' said Mrs Lichtheim.

'Certainly; I should think that all men do.'

'What kind of fantasies are yours?'

'All kinds.'

'Can you describe one?'

'Maybe when we get to know each other better.'

Mrs Lichtheim looked at her watch. 'This is the last time I'll be seeing you – I haven't got a vacancy so I'll be referring you to another psychologist for therapy.'

'Just when I was beginning to feel comfortable with you.'

'I believe you'll be comfortable with him as well.'
'What's his name?'
'DeVere.'
'DeVere: of truth.'
'Is that what you're looking for?'
'Maybe it's looking for me.'
'He'll help you find each other.'

9

ALL AT SEA

Feeling a powerful hunger for Willem van de Velde the Younger, Klein entubed at Fulham Broadway, emerged at Charing Cross, and made his way to the National Gallery.

Trafalgar Square, hugging a greyness to itself, had nothing to say to him. Nelson on his column turned a blind eye to mortal concerns. The stairs and porch of the National Gallery bore with stony indifference the shuffling feet of visitors from everywhere, each pair of feet terminating in a head that required to be filled with images of beauty, history, war and peace, sacred and profane love and various states of mythical, real, royal and common domesticity. Once inside, the visitors walked purposefully, dawdled randomly, collapsed on to benches, consulted floorplans, guides, maps, gallery staff and one another, and stood in front of paintings.

Klein went to the information desk, had his floorplan marked by the woman there, climbed the stairs, turned left through Rooms 29, 28 and 15, turned right through Room 22, went down the stairs, and arrived at Lower Gallery A, Screen 24 and a goodly array of the paintings of Willem van de Velde the Younger: seventeenth-century

36

Dutch ships and boats of various kinds in fair weather and under stormy skies, in calms and in stiff breezes.

'Quite a remarkable thing,' he said, 'to miniaturise the sky and the sea and the ships to a size and perspective convenient to the eye and readily absorbed on dry land by land-lubbers.' He particularly admired the paintings in which small craft met with strong winds and rough seas. One of these, No. 876, *A Small Dutch Vessel Close-hauled in a Strong Breeze*, about 1672, showed a gaff-rigged boat, a *galjoot*, on a larboard tack under a dark and threatening sky, pointing as close into the wind as possible, her weather vang bar-taut, the leech of the mainsail fluttering, the spray rising high over her bows as the seas swept her fore-deck. Klein could feel the spray, smell the salt, hear the wind in the rigging and the poom! as she rose and fell with the chop. The man at the tiller was pointing to larboard, probably shouting something to the rest of the crew, only one of whom was visible in the spray. Some way ahead a man-of-war on the same tack streamed its pennant.

'Dirty weather,' said Klein, 'but they're not afraid, they're used to this sort of thing, they're born to the sea and they know what to do.' The sea continued in his mind as he left Lower Gallery A, went up the stairs, through Rooms 22, 15, 28 and 29 without looking at anything but a few Rubens bottoms, down the stairs, out to the porch, and down to the street, the grey October afternoon, and the Underground. All the way home he heard the boom of the sea and the wind in the rigging as the bows of the Wimbledon train rose and fell with the chop.

10

FIRST SESSION

Dr DeVere was in his early forties and didn't wear a tie. He had short hair, no beard, and nothing on the walls of his office but an unframed laser copy of the Redon pastel, *Roger and Angelica*. It was stuck to the wall with Blu-Tack and it moved with DeVere from office to office in his professional travels.

'You're the first doctor I've seen with a Redon on his wall,' said Klein.

'And you're the first visitor who's commented on it. You like Redon?'

'I've done a monograph on him.'

Dr DeVere struck his forehead. 'Of course! You're *that* Harold Klein: *Darkness and Light: the inner eye of Odilon Redon*. I've got it at home.'

'At last,' said Klein, 'a reader. Have you read *Orlando Furioso*?'

'Parts of it.'

'The part where Ruggiero rescues Angelica from Orca the sea monster, yes?'

'That's why Redon's up there on my wall.'

'Have you got it there for aesthetic or professional reasons?'

'Both. It seems to me that each of us contains an Angelica chained to a rock, threatened by an Orca, and waiting for a Ruggiero. Would you agree?'

'I would. You're my kind of shrink. Am I going to be with you for a while?'

'As long as it takes. Still no inner voice?'

'No. I've started whispering into my hand or talking to myself under my breath before I say anything to anybody, so I've kept out of Casualty for a while.'

'That's very sensible. I'm trying to imagine how it must be for you.'

'Very strange. Most of my thinking is in words, and until this happened the words were spoken by my mental voice. Now I still hear music and see pictures in my head but the only way I can do word thoughts is by speaking out loud or writing them down. When I'm at my desk it's not a problem because my words appear on the computer screen. When I'm elsewhere I go about muttering to myself or scribbling in a notebook or both, which makes me feel a little crazier than usual.'

'The words you mutter, the words you write – are you hearing or seeing anything unusual?'

'Unusual compared to what I ordinarily say or write but nothing remarkable – mostly rude words and sexual thoughts of the sort that might slip out when I'm drunk; it's pretty much what was described in the *Times* piece: there's no censor on duty.'

'Would you say, Mr Klein, that when your inner censor's working it has to work pretty hard? Or not?'

'What would be your guess, Dr DeVere? Would you expect the inner censor of a little old man to have to work harder than that of a large young man? Or not?'

'I see your point but I'd like to hear you spell it out for me if you would.'

'All right. I have a certain reputation in the world of the arts but in the streets of daily life I am an object of no significance to anyone.' He told DeVere what he had told Mrs Lichtheim about his apparent invisibility. 'I won't bore you with more examples,' he said, 'but my inner censor used to be kept pretty busy.'

'So you've got a lot of anger in you. What about the rude words and sexual thoughts?'

'I sometimes think a dirty old man might be the only kind of old man there is.'

'Go on, please.'

'My interest in women has become obsessive; one of these days I'll be hit by a car while crossing the road with my eyes on a female bottom. I marvel at the action of hips and thighs, the articulation of knees and ankles. I love to see good flesh over good bones, women walking around in really classy skeletons and moving like thoroughbreds. The streets are full of beauties and I can't stop looking and wanting.'

'Are you married?'

'I was. Her name was Hannelore. She was eighteen years younger than I when she moved in with me in 1970; I was forty-five; she was twenty-seven. She'd been my editor on the Daumier book I did for Hermetica. She was with me for seven years, then one day when I was at the British Library Reading Room she set the timer clock to start *Die Schöpfung* on the record player about the time I was expected home. Then she emptied a bottle of Tomazipan tablets and half a bottle of gin. When I got there she'd been dead for about three hours and the chorus were belting out '*Und es ward Licht*'. She was a very methodical person.'

40

'I'm sorry.' Then, after a few moments of silence, 'Do you know why she did it? Was there a note?'

'No. She was a mystery to me, and as time passes I know less and less about her. I think about her all the time; now that I have no words in my head I see her face and I talk to myself. I was never her kind of person; she liked to go out and I like to stay in; she liked parties and I like to work. I got her by being a good wooer but I never properly recognised the uniqueness of her. She was a handsome woman and tall. People wanted to be thought well of by her.'

Dr DeVere paused for another sympathetic silence, then he said, 'Any children?'

'No. She had two miscarriages, then a hysterectomy.'

'Was she very depressed after the hysterectomy?'

'Very. Actually she never got over it.'

'You've been alone since she died?'

'There've been women from time to time but nothing that lasted. I've never been a whole lot of fun to be with except at the beginning when I was courting Hannelore. What I had with her only happens once.'

'How do you feel about your life right now?'

'I'm afraid I might lose control altogether.'

'And do what?'

'Touch the woman ahead of me on the escalator in the Underground, or start making indecent proposals.'

'Do you think you're a danger to the public at large?'

'More to myself. As you see.'

'I know this is a difficult time for you, Mr Klein. I can't really imagine what it's like to live without the constant companion of an inner voice but it must be a terrifying kind of aloneness. And I can understand how frightened you are of what you might do or say. What we categorise as normal behaviour is an unbelievably complex and fragile system of

41

the most intricate checks and balances. I'm always amazed that it doesn't break down more often than it does. Let's go back to the moment when you lost your inner voice: can you remember the very last thing it said? After you read the *Times* piece, did it say something before it went silent?'

'It said, "O God, what would happen to me if I lost my inner voice?"'

'Some might say that your It wanted to plunge you into inner voicelessness.'

'My It?'

DeVere opened a desk drawer, took out *The Book of the It* by Georg Groddeck, and handed it to Klein.

Klein held the book in his hands. It was a hardback, small and compact, heavy for its size. There came into his mind the Big Little Books of his small-town childhood in Pennsylvania. He used to buy them at the local Woolworth's, called 'the five-and-dime'. They were perfectly square little hardbacks about six by six inches and three inches thick with board covers. They were printed on coarse paper with text on one side and a black-and-white picture on the other of each spread: *Mickey Mouse at Blaggard Castle*; *Terry and the Pirates*; *Dick Tracy*. Unlike modern comic books, they had only the occasional speech balloon. He recalled the feel of them in the hand: pleasantly chunky.

'Have you read this?' said DeVere.

'No, I haven't.' He turned the pages, came to *LETTER II*, and read:

I hold the view that man is animated by the Unknown, that there is within him an 'Es', an 'It', some wondrous force which directs both what he himself does, and what happens to him.

'OK, I'm animated by the Unknown,' said Klein as he closed the book. 'What else is new?'

'Groddeck was contemporary with Freud and Freud was so impressed by the It idea that he developed his theory of the Id from it. It's the sort of book that got passed around when Ronnie Laing was doing his thing and lecturing barefoot in the seventies. A lot of what Groddeck says is utter bollocks but this idea of the mysterious It is a useful one, I think.'

'What're you leading up to, and should we burn some incense?'

'I'm leading up to asking you if you've been friends with your It.'

'I've been friends with my head, or I thought I was.'

'All right – forget about Groddeck for now; do you think of your inner voice as coming from you or is there another entity that speaks those words?'

'There's nobody in my head but me, and the me in my head has gone silent.'

DeVere found nothing to say for a few moments while he rubbed the back of his skull as if to stimulate that part of his brain. Presently a light bulb appeared over his head.

'What?' said Klein.

'If you were now to visualise a speaker in your head other than yourself, who or what would it be?'

Now it was Klein's turn to rub his head. After a time he said, 'I've just been looking at Oannes. Do you remember Number 14 in Redon's lithographic series. *Tentation de Sainte-Antoine*? The god who's half fish and half human: "I, the first consciousness of chaos, arose from the abyss to harden matter, to regulate forms." He's hovering half-seen in a sea of black, wearing a pharaonic headdress, observing us from the dimness. I think he's the one I'd like to hear from.'

'Oannes was the Babylonian god of wisdom.'

'That's what it says in the mythology books – science, writing, the arts, all that sort of thing, but Redon's Oannes, the one that I visualise, is deeper and darker than wisdom – he's nothing safe, nothing explicable.'

'Is it possible that you've already heard from him?'

'I don't know.'

'Can you remember anything your inner voice said in the time shortly before it said, "O God, what would happen to me if I lost my inner voice?"'

'OK, the afternoon before that morning I was walking down the Fulham Road and a good-looking young woman passed me walking a lot faster than I was: statuesque, classy walk, black suit, short skirt, great ass, wonderful legs, black stockings, shiny black high heels. I say stockings rather than tights because I imagined a suspender belt. I tried to keep her in good viewing distance but she kept pulling farther away and I was getting angina; so I had to stop and do some glyceryl trinitrate and rest a little while she got smaller and smaller and finally turned a corner and disappeared. And I said to myself or it said or he said, "One day you'll drop dead while something like that walks away from you and out of sight."'

'What do you mean by "something like that"?'

'I mean everything that I can't have. I'm an old man but I want what I wanted when I was young and I want it maybe more than when I was young. And there's not a lot I can do about it.'

'Did the inner voice say anything more after that first observation?'

'It said, "Well, that's life, innit."'

Dr DeVere scratched his head, massaged his face, cleared his throat. 'Might that have been a more Oannes sort of utterance?'

'Maybe; I don't know. I hadn't really been thinking about an Oannes voice until you asked me about a speaker in my head.'

'Things change, you know. The fact that you visualised Oannes makes me think there might be an Oannes element in you that wants to be heard, an aspect of you that you haven't been in good touch with. Maybe you're going to have to meet it halfway. What do you think?'

'I think,' said Klein, 'that if I hang out with you too long I could get more confused than I am now. Just tell me, do you think I'll ever have an inner voice again?'

'I doubt very much that the shutdown will be permanent. You can borrow Groddeck if you like.'

'Thanks, but I'll stay on standby for Oannes.'

'That'll have to be it for today. Good luck, mind how you go and watch your mouth.' He made a note in Klein's folder: *Inner-voice shutdown – buffer lost?*

11

ANGELICA'S GROTTO

'*Evening shadows make me blue,*' sang Connie Francis, '*when each weary day is through. How I long to be with you, my happiness.*' The honey of her voice, the sweet sadness of the words and melody made his throat ache. Pictures riffled in his mind: rain streaming down windows; night roads unwinding in the headlamps' beams; sunpoints dazzling on the sea; nakedness and firelight, glimpses, sounds and smells of youth and love and sorrow.

'Everybody's Somebody's Fool' was the next track on the CD. Klein sang along with it as he went to the bookshelves and took out *Darkness and Light: the inner eye of Odilon Redon*. He turned to the Oannes lithograph with its caption, '*I, the first consciousness of chaos, arose from the abyss to harden matter, to regulate forms.*' In the blackness where he hovered Oannes coiled and uncoiled the serpentine length of himself. Under his pharaonic headdress his face was dark in the dimness. Were his eyes open?

'Oannes,' said Klein, 'can you see me? I know you can hear me because you live in my mind. Are you a god or are you something else? Will you speak to me?'

No answer.

Klein went back to his desk, where he sat facing the

bookshelf-blocked fireplace. On the white wall above and to the left of the Meissen figure on the mantelpiece hung one of the few original works of art that he owned, a 1910 *Pegase Noir* by Redon, oil on canvas, 76 x 102 cm. Thirty years ago he'd brokered several profitable deals for a Swiss collector and this painting had been his fee. In earlier works Redon had shown his winged horses variously as captives and victims, unable to fly, defeated by forces that drained their energies and crippled their wings; but this Pegasus was a triumphant creature whose primal darkness contained the light of its resurgent vitality. Its black was suffused with purple, ultramarine blue, cerulean, crimson, subtleties of rose, and it reared up in an effulgence of reds and oranges, its wings full of lift and the gathered power of its haunches recalling Redon's sun horses and hippogriffs. Hannelore had said, looking at it after the making-up that followed one of their rows, 'It's like our marriage – full of darkness but it flies.' Klein shook his head and went to pour himself a drink.

Returning to his desk and the computer he called up:

NAKED MYSTERIES
The Nudes of Gustav Klimt

No additional words had appeared since the last time he'd looked at the screen. He opened one of his Klimt books and looked at the painting of Pallas Athene wearing the mask of the Gorgon on her breast. 'Wisdom,' he said. He considered Medusa's dread rictus and her loosely hanging tongue. He quit the word processor program, switched on the modem, double-clicked on the Internet icon, and clicked once on Connect. The modem chirped its dial-up and trilled, twanged, and roared through its connection sequence. He watched impatiently as the computer logged on to the network, and when he arrived at the Internet homepage he went to the Yahoo search engine.

'Everybody's somebody's fool,' he said. 'There's no fool like an old fool and there's a first time for everything.' He took a deep breath, typed SEX in the box, and clicked on Search. Scrolling down the results he clicked on Sexuality, clicked again on Oral Sex, and found a page of text with instructions for performing cunnilingus. 'Give me a break,' he said, and closed the page. Ignorantly but determinedly he pressed on until he found websites with free samples showing a whole range of sexual activities in clinically detailed photographs. Videos, live performers, telephone fantasists and other services and goods were also available, demotically described and payable by cheque or credit card, sometimes to be invoiced under names like Opticom and Allegro and sometimes more straightforward ones.

'Oannes, you strange fish,' said Klein, 'is this your kind of thing?' Website after website offered free samples and previews and promised the earth if he would sign up. The women were young and pretty, some of them beautiful; many of the men were heroically endowed. Several times he was on the point of signing up but shrank back at the thought of giving his credit card details and e-mail address to whatever might be lurking out in cyberspace.

Eventually he stumbled on to a website called Angelica's Grotto. The homepage, to Klein's astonishment, featured the Ingres painting, *Angelica Saved by Ruggiero*. 'I don't believe it,' he said, responding as always to the Ingres Angelica's blonde attractions. 'O God! the tastiness, the marzipan, the utter confection of her goodies and her sweeties and her rosebuds. Angelica, yes! Her nudity and her bondage – what more could a hero ask for! The tight little crease of her firm young flesh where her right arm crosses her bosom! "How long?" says her expression. "How long must I await the hero's pleasure?"'

Turning away from the chocolate-box Angelica on the screen he got one of the Redon books off the shelf and looked at the *Roger and Angelica* pastel, so intense in colour, so full of danger and unknowing. He took a magnifying glass to the tiny figure of Angelica who seemed more than a story, who seemed the heart of a mystery, chained to her rock and awaiting death or rescue.

'Lost and helpless,' he said. 'Lost and helpless and seductive in the darkness and obscurity, in the purpureality of her rock, her body glistening with spray as the sea-wind moans, the waves crash on the rock, the monster bellows, the hippogriff shrieks. The rock is like a face islanded in darkness; Ruggiero on the hippogriff is almost lost in the murk, battling against the darkness and the monster Orca. So much lostness!'

He went back to the computer and Angelica's Grotto. CLICK HERE TO ENTER, said the screen. Klein clicked and got a beautiful naked young woman with long dark hair crouching in the shadowy opening of a cave by the sea. 'Another naked Angelica,' said Klein. 'No chains, but is anyone without chains? Her face – what is it saying? Is she waiting in her grotto for a rescuer?'

YOU HAVE FOUND ANGELICA, said the screen. THIS SITE IS ABSOLUTELY FREE. ENJOY IT! BROWSE MY GALLERIES TO YOUR HEART'S CONTENT. RING ME UP AT THIS NUMBER IF YOU WANT TO CHAT.

There were seven galleries in Angelica's Grotto, each containing twenty to thirty thumbnail photographs which could be enlarged by clicking on them. Klein scanned them thoroughly, entranced by Angelica's beauty, the suppleness of her body, and the expressions on her face as she was penetrated in every orifice. From picture to picture she was by turns pensive, shy, coquettish, dreamy, surprised, but always submissive and eager to please. She looked no more than eighteen, with little pointed mermaid-breasts and the face of a Waterhouse nymph. 'How can she want to do this?' demanded Klein. 'Can she possibly enjoy it? Has she read Ariosto? Does she want to be rescued?'

In the first gallery Angelica and her colleagues performed in rocky and sandy places by the sea but after that they moved indoors. Sometimes she was nude, sometimes in white knickers and bra, suspender belt and stockings. She was active with single partners of both sexes and with groups, using her hands for whomever she could not accommodate more intimately. Klein regretted that she had removed her pubic hair; the baldness of her genitalia seemed degrading. He examined each photograph carefully, looking at many of them several times, but the one he returned to most often was the one on her homepage where she crouched alone in her shadowy grotto, her face thoughtful.

'Angelica,' he said, 'what are your chains and what is your rock?' With his eyes inches from the screen he went over the pictures hour after hour. 'Probably I'm on the edge of madness,' he said. 'On the other hand,' noting the counter that showed him to be Visitor No. 973,472 to the site, 'I've got a lot of company.' Lamenting that he was no longer a player, he consoled himself manually. '*And there are no exceptions to the rule . . .*' sang Connie Francis (afraid of silence, he had put the CD on REPEAT) '*Yes, everybody's somebody's fool.*'

12

THE GORGON SMILE

Many of the views of Angelica in action were confined to the sexual organs, seen from only a few inches away and suitable for gynaecological study. After a time these images became abstract; a kind of visual dyslexia set in, and Klein didn't always know what he was looking at. He was confused, disoriented, and baffled in his quest for solitary satisfaction; nonetheless he persevered, achieving tiny climaxes that were little better than footnotes referring him to the *op. cit.* of his youth. '*Ibid*,' he said. '*q.v.* Call me Ozymandias.'

In photographs of anal intercourse Angelica was often seen sitting or lying supine on her partner and spreading the lips of her vagina while he sodomised her. In that view her genitalia and anus seemed an ancient and savage face from which protruded the curved penis 'Like the tongue of the Gorgon,' said Klein. 'Hundreds of thousands of fools like me are staring at screens where this face laughs at them. Hundreds of thousands of pounds – no, millions! – are spent on this demonstration of . . . what? A mystery?

'Her genitals (he knew them intimately now) no longer seem firm and fresh. The monster that menaces Angelica has by now mounted her many times. Maybe she never wanted to be rescued, maybe she lusted after the monster. What will she give birth to? What is the mystery behind the Gorgon face? Why do I sit here for hours with my nose up the bottoms of strangers? Bottoms in cyberspace, for God's sake, slick with lubricant! Surrogates, stuntmen and women for the stunts I can't do any more. Or never did in the first place. I wonder what her voice is like? I wonder if she's read Ariosto? Not likely. Am I going to ring her up?' He picked up the telephone, put it down again.

He noticed that he was still connected to the Internet. 'Lucifer,' he said as the name came into his mind. He put the Yahoo search engine on it and went down the list of matches until he came to a painting with that title by Zdenek Polach. He clicked on it and got something bluish-white, blurred and spinning, tilting on its axis. 'Confusion,' he said. Unlike the soaring Lucifer in the Rorshach blot it made him uncomfortable. He clicked on Next Painting and got *The Confusion* in which a dim and malevolent face looked out of a noxious yellowish-white bafflement. 'I'm sorry I asked,' he said.

Klein disconnected from the Internet and switched off the modem and the monitor. It was quarter past nine on a rainy evening in September. Across the common a District Line train rumbled towards town. His mind gave him the red telephone box outside the block of flats in Beaufort Street where he and Hannelore had lived from 1970 to 1972. 'The red telephone box in the rain under the drooping white blossoms of a chestnut tree,' he said, 'the red telephone box all fresh and juicy in the rain with the white petals scattered on it.' He'd never made a call from that telephone box but he'd always passed it going to and from the flat and it stood in his memory like an illuminated gatehouse to his love. '*Ein feste Burg ist unser Gott*,' he sang: her favourite hymn. 'All gone,' he said. He went down to the kitchen, poured himself a large Glenfiddich.

13

NIGHT SIDE

'When the world was young,' he heard himself saying, and his voice woke him up. 'What?' he asked himself, trying to hold the fugitive thought. 'When the world was young the movies were black-and-white, the people in them spoke in short snappy sentences. At restaurants and getting out of taxis they paid with banknotes and never received any change. The big gangsters used electric shavers in their cars as they were driven downtown. At home they were massaged by ex-prizefighters who called them Boss. When they got shot there was no blood. The chorus girls had beautiful rounded legs, not thin. The money in those films was only stage money; no wonder they didn't bother with the change. There was an organist at the cinema of my childhood, spotlit and sparkling; we followed the bouncing ball and sang but later, much later, last night I was thinking of the red telephone box in Beaufort Street, I can see it now. In 1970 Forbidden Fruit was the shop at the corner of the King's Road. 'The Windmills of Your Mind' was a song we listened to. Hannelore gave me a copy of Jung's *Archetypes and the Collective Unconscious* and I still haven't read it. New flowered sheets on the bed for our first night. Minutes and hours that will still be there when I'm long gone.

'I want to speak in black-and-white,' he said. 'I want not to bleed when I'm shot. I want to part the slats of a venetian blind and look down at the street and say, "I'm tired of running." From what? Everything. "*Keys that jingle in your pocket, words that jangle in your head. Why did summer go so quickly? Was it something that you said?*"'

Although Klein's self-discipline had slackened of late he was hoping to get back to a solid work routine with *Naked Mysteries: The Nudes of Gustav Klimt*: opening one of his Klimt books he turned to the plate of Danae being entered by the shower of gold that was Jupiter. He studied the picture intently, marvelling at the magnificence of Danae's haunches lifted to the downrush of the god, the pearly paleness of her breast, the surrender in her flushed enraptured face, eyes closed, red mouth open. From the opulence of Danae he went to a book of drawings, ghostly sketches of naked and half-naked women sitting, standing, lying in each other's arms or playing with themselves, Klimt's faint and snaky lines stroking every curve and savage flaunt of hip and thigh, buttock and breast, lustful lines enclosing volumes of indolent and eager female flesh. 'He was as woman-hungry as I am,' said Klein. 'I wonder if he ever got as much as he wanted.'

'Others have appreciated women,' he wrote, 'but Klimt is unique in the astonishment with which he perceives the essential mystery of the female.' He stopped typing.

'What he does,' he said, 'is fuck them with his eyes.' He saved the page, switched on the modem, went to the Internet and put Angelica's Grotto on the screen.

He skipped from picture to picture in the various galleries, shaking his head and following the anatomical permutations eagerly. Returning to the homepage, he looked long and earnestly at Angelica's face. 'Haunted,' he said. 'She looks haunted; there's no other word for that look. What is the rock she's chained to? Is it the money she gets for posing? Is she a prostitute? Does she want to be rescued? Is she waiting for Ruggiero?' He saw himself mounted on the hippogriff, felt the wind on his face and the beating of the great wings, heard the shriek of the animal as it battled through the murk towards the incandescent nakedness of Angelica.

When he reached the end of Gallery 7 the screen suddenly went black, shuddered a little, then came up with the home-page picture of Angelica in her grotto. Below her a dialogue box asked: *WOULD YOU LIKE TO TAKE A WALK ON THE NIGHT SIDE?* YES/NO

'Yes!' he said, and clicked on it. On the left side of the screen appeared a block of text under the title, MONICA'S MONDAY NIGHT. The right side was a photograph of the Strand near the Aldwych on a rainy night, the wet road and pavement reflecting the darkness and the lights. Walking towards the viewer was a very pretty young woman with long red hair, very chic in a black suit with a short skirt, black stockings, and shiny black high heels. She was carrying a leopard-spotted umbrella.

'Clip-clop,' said Klein, imagining the sound of her heels. He read the text aloud:

'It's quarter past ten on a rainy Monday night. Monica, an English lecturer at King's College, is on her way home from a meeting. The Strand is still lively but when she turns into Surrey Street heading for Temple tube station there is very little traffic and her heels make a lonely sound on the wet pavement.

'Monica feels good in her little figure-hugging black suit. As she walks she feels her silky red bush rubbing

56

against her silk knickers, feels her skirt tight against her thighs and buttocks. She feels the nakedness of her body under her clothes and her nipples stiffen.

'She's thinking about the weekend just past, remembering the feel of Gerald's body against hers. He's a terribly nice man who makes love as if he's done an A level in it. Unsatisfied but not wanting to seem ungracious, she's always faked orgasms and he's convinced that he's wonderful in bed.' NEXT

'I know the type,' says Klein. 'He probably considers himself an expert on wine, too.' The next picture showed Monica from behind in all her shapeliness and tightness and clip-clopping shiny black heels. 'Yes!' he said. 'So sweet!'

'It's so quiet, thinks Monica. The tube station seems far away. She looks back over her shoulder and sees no one. Were there footsteps behind her? She stops to listen, hears only the distant traffic on the Strand and the rain pattering on her umbrella. She finds herself recalling newspaper stories of women dragged into cars and taken away to be raped. She sees her thighs being forced apart; she makes an O with her lips, imagines the taste of semen on her tongue and the sweat of brutal men on filthy mattresses in evil-smelling rooms.' NEXT

'O God,' said Klein, 'it's going to happen.' He clicked again and got a close-up of Monica's face under the street lamps, her mouth open, her eyes closed:

'Monica finds strange pictures in her mind, strange stirrings in her body, feels a wetness between her legs.

57

I want to get home, she thinks as a van draws up beside her. As she turns, a powerful hand is clamped over her mouth and she's pulled inside.' NEXT

'I knew that was going to happen,' said Klein as he clicked. The new photograph was a close-up of Monica face-down on a mattress in the van, her skirt pulled up to expose her little black silk knickers and suspender belt, the whiteness of her thighs above her black stockings. Klein read:

'Her captor's hand on the back of her neck forces Monica's face down against the musty mattress. "Don't scream," he says as the van pulls away. "If you scream I'll hurt you."

'"I won't scream. Please don't hurt me." She trembles as he pulls up her skirt and she feels his hands on her.

'"You've got a sweet ass," he says. "I've had my eye on it for a while. Have you ever been ass-fucked?"

'"No."

'"I'm going to have your asshole cherry then. That's nice, I like that. But first we have to get acquainted. Turn over and give me a kiss."

'Monica was expecting rape but not kissing. She doesn't know how to prepare herself for this.' NEXT

In this picture Monica was kissing a black man.

'Monica closes her eyes and turns her face towards his. "Open your mouth and suck my tongue," he says. She obeys. His breath is clean; he tastes as good as Gerald. This is like a dream, she thinks. How will it end? His hand is inside her blouse, inside her bra, playing with

58

her nipples. His touch is rough but she feels her body responding to him. She reaches between his legs, feels him huge and hard, feels herself wet and ready, thinks of what he's going to do and is afraid.' NEXT

In this picture the man, naked from the waist down, was kneeling astride Monica who was naked from the waist up. His thighs were pressing her breasts, his penis was in her mouth.

'"I think you want it," he says, "but I'm not ready yet. I need you to lick my balls and suck me ready." Monica obeys, wanting the spurt of his semen in her mouth but he withdraws and turns her over.' NEXT

In the next picture Monica was face-down again with her torn knickers around her left thigh. Her legs were apart and her own hands were spreading her buttocks to expose her anus.

'Monica feels the man's hands on her naked bottom, on her thighs and between her legs. "Spread your cheeks," he tells her, "and open your asshole for me."
   'Monica obeys. "Please be gentle," she says. 'I'll do whatever you say.'
   '"I know you will, baby. I know you want it." He puts his hands over her hands, spreading her cheeks further apart, then his face is between them and she feels wet kisses on her anus and his hot tongue squirming in her. Gerald has never done that. Her captor changes position and she cries out, feeling herself almost torn apart as he thrusts into her.' NEXT

The picture showed the man mounting Monica whose

face was turned towards him, mouth open, eyes closed as he impaled her. His penis was as thick as her wrist.

'Monica's whole body seems to be on fire; she reaches behind her and clasps his buttocks, holding him close to lessen the pain. But now the flame of arousal has burnt out the pain and she feels an urgency in her that's new. With her right hand she reaches down between the wet lips of her vulva to stroke her clitoris as she meets each thrust of his with a backward thrust against him. As he rides her he smacks her bottom, enjoying the bouncy ripeness of her flesh while he urges her on, mastering her.' NEXT

The picture showed Monica and her partner in action. Monica's face was ecstatic.

'"You like this, don't you, bitch? Tell me how you like it with me deep in your sweet white ass, lemme hear you say it."

'"I like it with you deep in my sweet white ass."

'"Say more!"

'"I like it when you mount me like an animal, I like it when you ride me hard, I like you to be my hard master." Monica hears the words coming out of her mouth as this stranger sodomises her and she knows she's really saying them, knows it isn't a dream, thinks she might be going mad.

'"Oh yes, I know you like it. You're going to come with me when you feel my hot spunk shooting into you, yes? Going to do that for your hard master?"

'"Yes, yes!" With her free hand she pulls his bottom hard against her. "Give it to me, give me your hot spunk and make me come with you." She feels the spurt of his

60

semen inside her and she screams and faints as her own orgasm sweeps over her in a giant wave. She regains consciousness with her master still inside her. She sees his right hand near her face and presses it to her lips and tongue. "Thank you," she whispers.' NEXT

NEXT was a message: *DO YOU WANT TO TALK WITH ANGELICA ABOUT 'MONICA'S MONDAY NIGHT'? YES/NO*

Klein clicked on YES.

HI, said the screen. *WHAT'S YOUR NAME?*

Klein paused for a moment, then typed RUGGIERO.

WOW. THAT'S A HEROIC-SOUNDING NAME. ARE YOU A HERO?

NOT SO FAR.

YOU NEVER KNOW WHAT THE FUTURE MIGHT BRING YOU, RUGGIERO.

He imagined her standing close to him, lightly touching his arm, her sweet body smelling good. I'LL KEEP THAT IN MIND, he typed. HAVE YOU READ ★ORLANDO FURIOSO★?

I WANT TO TALK ABOUT 'MONICA'S MON-DAY NIGHT'. DID YOU LIKE THE STORY?

YES.

DID THE PICTURES EXCITE YOU?

THIS CONVERSATION – IS IT ON PUBLIC VIEW?

NO, IT'S JUST BETWEEN YOU AND ME AL-THOUGH IT'S NOT SECURE. NOTHING IS.

HOW DID YOU PICK ME?

BASED ON NUMBER OF HITS AND TIME SPENT AT WEBSITE.

HAVE YOU DONE THIS WITH OTHERS?

NO, YOU'RE MY FIRST.

61

WHY ARE YOU GATHERING THIS INFOR-
MATION? ARE YOU DOING A DISSERTATION,
WRITING A BOOK, CONDUCTING A SURVEY?

THERE ARE THINGS I WANT TO KNOW. I'M
NOT READY TO SAY MORE THAN THAT JUST
NOW. CAN WE CONTINUE?

YES.

DID ANY WORDS PARTICULARLY EXCITE
YOU?

YES.

WHICH ONES?

I LIKED IT WHEN SHE CALLED HIM HER
'HARD MASTER'. I LIKED IT WHEN SHE KISSED
HIS HAND AND THANKED HIM.

WHAT ABOUT THE PICTURES?

I LIKED THE SHOT OF MONICA FROM
BEHIND, BEFORE HE PULLS HER INTO THE
VAN. I LIKED THE EXPRESSION ON HER FACE
WHEN HE'S MOUNTING HER AND SHE'S LOOK-
ING BACK AT HIM. I LIKED THE WAY HE'S PULL-
ING HER TO HIM AS HE PUSHES INTO HER.

HOW WOULD YOU RATE THIS STORY? MARKS
OUT OF TEN.

EIGHT.

CRITICAL COMMENTS?

YOU COULD HAVE SPUN IT OUT A BIT
LONGER: MORE DETAIL; MORE DIALOGUE;
MORE PICTURES.

DID YOU LIKE IT THAT IT HAPPENED AT
NIGHT?

YES.

WHY?

THE NIGHT IS DARK AND SECRET. THERE

IS FEAR IN IT. THERE ARE THINGS HIDDEN IN THE DARKNESS. ONE FEELS THE BEATING OF THE HEART, SEES LESS, SENSES MORE. PERCEPTIONS AND RESPONSES ARE HEIGHTENED.

PERCEPTIONS OF WHAT? RESPONSES TO WHAT?

THE UNKNOWN THAT LURKS AHEAD, THE STRANGE THAT IS BEYOND ONE'S CONTROL. WHAT IS FEARED IS ALSO SOMETIMES HOPED FOR.

DID YOU LIKE IT THAT MONICA WAS AFRAID?

YES.

DID IT EXCITE YOU?

YES.

WHY?

MONICA'S NAKEDNESS UNDER HER CLOTHES, HER SILKY RED BUSH RUBBING AGAINST HER SILK KNICKERS, HER WHITE THIGHS, HER RIPE AND BOUNCY BOTTOM, HER NIPPLES STIFFENING WITH HER THOUGHTS – ALL OF HER SWEET FLESH WAS VULNERABLE TO THE STRANGER WHO WAS STALKING HER. WHY THE IDEA OF A WOMAN AS PREY IS A TURN-ON FOR ME I CAN'T SAY, BUT JUDGING BY THE NUMBER OF FILMS IN WHICH A SEXY WOMAN IS AT THE MERCY OF A MAN OR MONSTER, IT'S A TURN-ON FOR A GREAT MANY: A WOMAN POWERLESS AND FORCED TO SUBMIT.

DID YOU PARTICULARLY ENJOY HER SUBMISSION?

YES. DID YOU?

I'M NOT SAYING. YOU SAID THAT WHAT IS FEARED IS SOMETIMES HOPED FOR. DO YOU THINK MONICA WAS HOPING TO BE RAPED?

WHEN SHE THOUGHT ABOUT IT SHE FOUND 'STRANGE PICTURES IN HER MIND, STRANGE STIRRINGS IN HER BODY', SO IT WOULD SEEM THAT THE IDEA EXCITED HER.

WHY WOULD THE IDEA EXCITE HER?

WELL, SHE HADN'T BEEN GETTING SATIS-FACTION WITH GERALD, AND THE STORY SEEMED TO HINT THAT SHE WAS READY FOR A BIT OF ROUGH; SHE WANTED A STRANGER TO TAKE CONTROL OF HER, TO BE HER HARD MASTER.

DO YOU THINK SOME WOMEN ACTUALLY FEEL THIS WAY?

I THINK ANYONE CAN FEEL ALL KINDS OF WAYS AND THIS IS ONE OF THEM.

YOU THINK SOME WOMEN WANT TO BE RAPED?

NOT ALL OF THE TIME BUT I BELIEVE THAT ANYONE WILL CONSIDER ANYTHING SOME OF THE TIME.

HAVE YOU EVER CONSIDERED RAPING A WOMAN?

NOT VIOLENTLY – I'VE NEVER HAD THAT MUCH CONFIDENCE.

HOW THEN?

IN FANTASY ONLY, WITH THE WOMAN MADE HELPLESS IN SOME WAY.

THE WOMAN AS A HELPLESS VICTIM.

AS I SAID, FANTASY.

WHAT ABOUT THE BLACKNESS OF THE RAPIST IN THIS STORY?

THAT DEFINITELY HEIGHTENED THE STORY. THE FACT OF HIS BEING *THE OTHER* ADDS TO THE EXCITEMENT. ONE CAN'T HELP THINKING OF BLACK MEN AS BEING MORE POWERFUL SEXUALLY THAN WHITE MEN.

WHAT ABOUT THE ANAL INTERCOURSE? DID THAT ADD TO OR DETRACT FROM YOUR PLEASURE?

WHAT DO YOU THINK?

YOU TELL ME.

'This woman that I'm talking to isn't the one in the photographs,' Klein said to himself. 'In my mind she doesn't look like her or smell like her and she's not naked or in her underwear.' The woman he imaged now was short and stocky, wearing jeans and a sweatshirt and horn-rimmed spectacles; her hair had grown shorter and her smell was not quite as seductive as before.

WE WERE TALKING ABOUT ANAL INTERCOURSE, said the screen.

WELL, THE ANUS IS NOT QUITE THE APPROVED ORIFICE FOR INTERCOURSE, IS IT. SO PENETRATION THERE HAS THE APPEAL OF THE FORBIDDEN AND IT'S MORE INTIMATE, MORE EXCITING TO THINK ABOUT, ESPECIALLY IF THE WOMAN IS UNWILLING. MONICA DIDN'T SEEM ALL THAT UNWILLING, ACTUALLY. BY THE WAY, WHAT ARE YOU WEARING?

THIS ISN'T THAT KIND OF CHAT. THIS PORNOGRAPHIC FANTASY THAT YOU'VE JUST WATCHED, WOULD YOU SAY IT WAS EVIL?

I'VE HAD FANTASIES LIKE THAT OFTEN ENOUGH – I'M SURE OTHER MEN DO AS WELL. I'D NEVER WANT TO ACT THEM OUT EVEN IF I WERE ABLE TO. BUT WHEN YOU PUT SUCH WORDS AND PICTURES ONSCREEN FOR THE GENERAL PUBLIC THERE'S NO KNOWING WHOM YOU'RE REACHING. AND IT COULD WELL BE THAT NAMING AND SHOWING A FORBIDDEN ACT IS LIKE CALLING UP A DEMON BY SPEAKING ITS NAME. SOMEONE JUST ON THE EDGE OF ACTING OUT HIS FANTASIES MIGHT LET HIMSELF GO ALL THE WAY AFTER SEEING IT. SO I'D HAVE TO CALL IT AN EVIL THING.

THEN BY VISITING THIS WEBSITE ARE YOU SUPPORTING EVIL?

WHAT ABOUT YOU? IN OFFERING THIS MATERIAL WHAT DO YOU THINK YOU'RE DOING?

CONTRIBUTING TO THE EVIL IN THE WORLD THE SAME AS YOU BUT I'M DOING IT IN AN EFFORT TO UNDERSTAND PORNOGRAPHY AND THE ENORMOUS DEMAND FOR IT, OK? I HAVE MORE QUESTIONS.

SO ASK THEM.

DID MONICA'S MONDAY NIGHT AROUSE YOU SEXUALLY?

IN A MANNER OF SPEAKING.

WHAT WILL YOU DO ABOUT IT?

TAKE MYSELF IN HAND.

HOW OLD ARE YOU, RUGGIERO?

SEVENTY-TWO. HOW OLD ARE YOU?

*TWENTY-EIGHT. ARE YOU STILL A PLAY-
ER?*

ONLY WITH MYSELF. IF I HAD AN INNER
VOICE I WOULDN'T BE TELLING YOU ALL
THIS.

EXPLAIN PLEASE.

THE VOICE IN YOUR HEAD THAT CENSORS
WHAT YOU'RE GOING TO SAY, I HAVEN'T
GOT ONE ANY MORE.

*THAT COULD GET YOU INTO ALL KINDS OF
TROUBLE.*

IT HAS. NOW I'M TRYING TO MEET UP
WITH MY IT. (He didn't want to bring Oannes into
the conversation.)

*AREN'T WE ALL? I FEEL FOR YOU, RUG-
GIERO. MAYBE I CAN BE YOUR INNER VOICE
FOR A WHILE. YOUR WORDS LOOK LONELY.
HAVE YOU GOT A PARTNER?*

NOT ANY MORE.

WHY NOT?

MY WIFE DIED TWENTY YEARS AGO.

HOW?

SUICIDE.

WHY?

TIRED OF LIVING, I GUESS.

WHAT MADE HER TIRED OF LIVING?

CAN WE TALK ABOUT SOMETHING ELSE?
ARE YOU MARRIED?

GOD FORBID.

WHY DO YOU SAY THAT?

*MARRIAGE IS FOR PEOPLE WILLING TO GIVE
UP THEIR FREEDOM FOR SOMETHING THAT IN
MY OPINION IS NOT WORTH HAVING.*

WHAT MY WIFE AND I HAD WAS WORTH HAVING. 'What exactly *did* we have?' he asked himself.

WE MUST COME BACK TO THAT SOMETIME. ANYBODY SINCE HER?

NOTHING THAT LASTED VERY LONG, AND THERE'S BEEN NO ONE FOR A LONG TIME. The Angelica in his imagination, though no longer the beauty in the homepage photograph, was not unattractive, he decided, mumbling his thoughts. 'Good ass, heavy thighs and a lot of coarse pubic hair. Her smell is strong and funky; I like it. She probably tastes a little acidic.'

DO YOU MISS HAVING A WOMAN? she was asking.

YES, AND THERE'S THE DISMAL FACT THAT A MAN WHO CAN NO LONGER GET IT UP IS NOT IN A STRONG BARGAINING POSITION WHEN LOOKING FOR A NEW WOMAN.

MAYBE IT'S TIME FOR YOU TO HANG UP YOUR TACKLE AND PUT ALL THAT BEHIND YOU.

ALL THE SAME, I'D STILL LIKE TO HAVE SOME OF IT IN FRONT OF ME.

THERE ARE MANY WAYS OF GIVING PLEAS-URE.

INDEED. MAYBE ONE DAY I'LL ADVERTISE IN THE LONELY-HEARTS COLUMNS: LITTLE OLD AQUARIUS, SINGLE MALE, NON-SMOKER, SENSE OF HUMOUR, LIKES MUSIC, ART, LIT-ERATURE, CAN'T GET IT UP BUT WOULD LIKE TO GO DOWN ON LIKE-MINDED FEMALE. EXPERIENCE UNNECESSARY.

HOW OLD WOULD YOU LIKE THE FEMALE TO BE?

ANYWHERE BETWEEN TWENTY AND FIFTY.
DEFINITELY NOT AS DRIED-UP AS I AM. IF I
RING UP THE NUMBER ON YOUR HOMEPAGE,
WILL YOURS BE THE VOICE I HEAR?

YES, BUT WE CAN TALK ABOUT THAT LATER.
NOW COMES THE BIG QUESTION: WOULD YOU
SAY, RUGGIERO, THAT YOU LIKE WOMEN?

ARE YOU ASKING THIS BECAUSE I ENJOYED
THE ANAL RAPE STORY?

I'M ASKING, THAT'S ALL.

I'VE ALWAYS THOUGHT I LIKED WOMEN.
I'VE ALWAYS NEEDED A WOMAN; I'VE AL-
WAYS WANTED WOMEN. AFTER MY WIFE
DIED THERE WERE WOMEN I LOVED. BUT
NOTHING BETWEEN MEN AND WOMEN IS
SIMPLE. IT'S POSSIBLE TO LOVE WITHOUT
LIKING. DO YOU LIKE MEN?

I'M NOT SAYING.

IS THAT YOU IN THE PHOTO GALLERIES?

YES.

HOW CAN YOU DO ALL THOSE THINGS?

I WORK OUT.

YOU KNOW WHAT I MEAN – CAN YOU
POSSIBLY LIKE DOING WHAT YOU DO IN
THOSE PICTURES?

I DON'T DO ANYTHING I DON'T LIKE TO
DO.

IT SEEMS TO ME YOU MUST BE CHAINED
TO SOME KIND OF ROCK.

LIKE EVERYONE ELSE I'M CHAINED TO THE
ROCK OF REALITY.

I CAN'T BELIEVE THE WOMAN I'M TALK-
ING TO IS THE ONE IN THE PHOTOS.

BELIEVE WHAT YOU LIKE.

BY THE WAY, WHO WROTE THE MONICA STORY?

I DID. WHY DO YOU ASK?

THE POINT OF VIEW SEEMS MASCULINE.

WHAT YOU CALL THE MASCULINE POINT OF VIEW IS NOT A DIFFICULT THING TO IMITATE. MEN DO IT ALL THE TIME.

I NEED TO KNOW MORE ABOUT YOU.

I DON'T NEED YOU TO KNOW MORE. NOT YET.

WHEN? THIS YEAR, NEXT YEAR, SOME-TIME, NEVER?

MAYBE SOMETIME. THE PHONE NUMBER ON THE HOMEPAGE IS USUALLY ENGAGED. USE THIS ONE IF YOU WANT TO TALK TO ME. GOODBYE FOR NOW. X

IS THAT A KISS I SEE BEFORE ME?

FROM MY LABIA MINORA. TILL NEXT TIME, RUGGI.

Klein wrote down the telephone number, disconnected from the Internet, and switched off the modem, visualising her kiss as he did so. His fantasy partner that evening was the imagined Angelica in the horn-rimmed glasses. When he went to sleep he dreamt that he was hurrying down a rainy street at three o'clock in the morning, seeing her ahead of him and hearing her heels on the pavement. He walked faster and faster, then began to run, but he never caught up with her.

14

DOE NOT CALL UPP

HOP-ON HOP-OFF AT 100 STOPS ON 7 ROUTES, said the London Pride Sightseeing Bus parked in Southampton Row by Russell Square. Its redness was of a piece with the hard sunshine of the end-of-October day. The driver sat at the wheel; there was no one else on the bus.

'They've all hopped off,' said Klein to himself, 'speaking French, German, Spanish, Greek, Russian, Polish, Urdu, Hindi, Arabic and goodness knows what else. They're speaking those languages out loud and they're speaking them to themselves in their heads, even the children.'

He was meeting his friend Seamus Flannery for lunch at Il Fornello, an Italian restaurant with Spanish waiters. Seamus wrote radio, screen, and stage plays and taught History of Film at the National Film School. The waiters Paco and Juliano called the two of them 'Dottore' or 'Professore' interchangeably. Flannery was already there in their usual booth.

'Professore!' said Juliano. 'Nice to see you. Are you having something to drink?'

'Half lager, please. Same for you?' he said to Seamus. Over their half-pints they brought each other up to date.

'That's really awful,' said Seamus when Klein told him about the loss of his inner voice. 'Some of my best conversations happen inside my head.' He was as bald as an observatory dome; Klein imagined echoes.

'Different voices?' he said.

'No, just mine. Did you have an inner voice that was different from yours?'

'No, but I suppose one might.'

'Where would it be coming from?'

'From a different part of oneself, I should think.'

'How different?'

'Well, mostly I'm Harold, right? But maybe I've got a Jim part as well.'

'Chelsea supporter, hangs out with the lads at the pub, owns a Rottweiler, has a tattoo?'

'Maybe not that different.'

'Jekyll and Hyde spring to mind, or maybe *The Case of Charles Dexter Ward*. "Doe not call upp Any that you cannot put downe." Flannery and Klein were both well-grounded in H. P. Lovecraft.

'Nothing like that,' said Klein.

'Has Jim said anything interesting lately?'

'Not yet.'

They talked of Klimt, Kieslovski, and Egberto Gismonti over their tortellini and lasagne. 'Do you use the Internet?' said Klein.

'I haven't got round to that yet, I'm afraid I'd become addicted to it. You?'

'From time to time; it's useful for research.'

After lunch they walked down to Great Russell Street, then over to Tottenham Court Road and Oxford Street and the Virgin Megastore, where they headed for the video department. Klein bought, among others, *Bring*

72

Me the Head of Alfredo Garcia. Flannery included *Point Blank* in his purchases. They both possessed recordings from TV of these all-time favourites but they liked the pretty boxes.

15

SECOND SESSION

Klein ignored holidays and celebrations as much as possible. On Hallowe'en, his neighbourhood being ever more gentrified, little groups of middle-class trick-or-treaters rang his bell but he didn't answer the door. On Guy Fawkes night the gunpowder-smelling streets were hung with smoke as fireworks near and far lit up the sky but he stayed indoors.

On the appointed day at the appointed time he presented himself at Dr DeVere's office. DeVere looked him up and down, saw no slings or casts, and said, 'Well done! You've kept out of Casualty for two weeks. How's it going?'

'Variously. I think too much Internet can make you go blind.'

'A new development?'

'I'm not sure development is the word for it.'

'Go on.'

Klein told Dr DeVere about the various websites he'd visited; he told him about Angelica's Grotto, the homepage with the Ingres painting and the pictures in the galleries.

'Interesting,' said Dr DeVere.

'She asked me onscreen if I wanted to take a walk on the night side. I clicked on YES and got a picture story called

'*Monica's Monday Night*' in which a young woman on her way home from a late meeting at King's College is pulled into a van by a black man and forced to perform oral sex, after which she's anally raped. She has to do other things as well. Afterwards this person who calls herself Angelica and I had an onscreen one-to-one dialogue and she asked me if I'd enjoyed it.'

'Had you?'

'Yes.'

'How do you feel about the fact that you enjoyed it?'

'Troubled. I've always thought I liked women but now I'm wondering if that's really so. Maybe I've never liked them; certainly I've always been afraid of them.'

'Did that contribute to your enjoyment?'

'Well, if you see someone you're afraid of being forced to submit to a more powerful person you can take pleasure in it, right? Or maybe, as they say, the enemy of the enemy is a friend.'

'You think of women as the enemy?'

'I've never thought I did. But I believe it's generally accepted that men who sleep with as many women as they can don't really like women.'

'Have you slept with many?'

'My opportunities were limited but I did what I could.'

'Did your wife know about it?'

'I tried to be discreet but I think women always know one way or another – you sound funny on the telephone or you come home smelling different or things fall out of your pockets.'

'Were these one-night stands or something more?'

'They were affairs that went on for a while.'

'How did you feel about them?'

'Guilty.'

'Anything else?'

'Successful.'

'I think it might be useful if you tried to understand where you are with women in general.'

'Where I *was*, you mean.'

'Well, you've got something going with this Angelica woman. Can you say what it is?'

'I can't say because I don't know. I'm pretty confused right now.'

'Confusion is OK; confusion is generally the first step in the process of change.'

'Confusion is nothing new to me; I'm like those people who divide their time between a house in London and a villa in Tuscany except that I do it between confusion and panic.'

'Can you describe the panic?'

'Well, I used to wake up in the morning like a man trapped in a car going over a cliff.'

'And now?'

'Like a man lost in a cave.'

'That's when you first wake up. What about later?'

'At breakfast I settle into the day, read the papers, plan what I'm going to do. After breakfast I go to my desk and then it's just the normal work panic.'

'What's the normal work panic?'

'It's a state of not knowing each time whether you can make it happen. For a writer that's an OK state to be in – it's respectful of the unknowable thing-in-itself of whatever you're writing about. If that goes I'm in big trouble. Winter is coming; in November there's always a big rain that leaves the trees black and bare. This is the November of me – there's no getting away from that. Sometimes I go to a bookshelf and stand there

76

with my hand outstretched, not knowing what I came there for.'

'What can I say? Everybody grows old except those who die young. Naturally that's part of your current problems but I'd like to get back to the sexual area.'

'Me too.'

'Please don't be offended by my next question: when your wife was with you, how would you have felt about seeing her in a picture-story like the Monica one?'

Klein blushed. 'That's a very uncomfortable question.'

'Don't answer unless you want to.'

Klein took a deep breath. 'Bear in mind that the Monica story was a fantasy – it wasn't presented as something that really happened. I mean, I've had fantasies about murdering one or two people but I haven't ever got those fantasies mixed up with reality.'

'Understood.'

'A *fantasy* like that with my wife in it – my response would have been pretty much what it was with the Monica story.'

'How do you feel about that?'

'Ashamed.'

'You didn't feel ashamed of your murder fantasies but you feel ashamed about the idea of enjoying a rape fantasy with your wife as the victim, yes?'

'Monica wasn't altogether a victim; at some level she almost wanted it to happen and when it happened she found herself sexually responsive to the man who was mastering her.'

'Are you saying that you'd enjoy a fantasy in which your wife wanted to be raped and was responsive to her rapist?'

'Yes.'

'But you'd feel . . . ?'

'Ashamed.'

'Can you say why?'

'I loved my wife and I've never gotten over her death. In her absence she's a constant presence. I see or read something I want to tell her about and she's not there. You don't really know what someone is to you until that person's gone.'

'Would you say that the mind is capable of holding contradictory thoughts?'

'I know that.'

'I've talked to a lot of people and it seems to be true for all of them that you can have two opposing thoughts or images in your mind – really weird ones. A friend of mine, driving away from his wedding to begin the honeymoon, had a mental picture of himself strangling his beautiful bride. Yet he was truly in love with her and still is; for the five years since the wedding it's been a good marriage with no signs of big trouble. Try to remember that kind of thing while you're dealing with the loss of your inner voice. I want to stop there because I don't want to put anything else on top of this. See you in a fortnight.'

16

ROCK OF AGED

'Angelica,' said Klein as he walked around her in his mind, 'is not what she first appeared to be; she's something else. I'm sure that her name isn't really Angelica and I very much doubt that she's the one in the photographs. She smells strongly of sweat plus her own funky odour. There is a mystery between us, however ridiculous. In her words on the screen there was someone trying to reach me while keeping her distance, someone talking hard while wanting to be soft, maybe wanting to be rescued from the rock of her hard self. Can I possibly be, in some way as yet unknown to me, her Ruggiero? I've not yet heard her voice. Shall I ring her up?'

Looking at Klimt's nudes he saw Angelica naked except for her horn-rimmed glasses, Angelica saying, as she offered herself, 'There are many ways of giving pleasure.' It was only a fantasy of course. 'Only a fantasy of course,' he said, 'but it's a good one. Maybe she's looking for father substitutes, wants to see Daddy's face between her legs.' Mentally he rubbed his face in her pubic hair, opened her, tasted her.

'No word from Oannes,' he said. 'I suppose he's just leaving me to it. I haven't all that much time left and

I'll die hungering for what I've never had enough of. What's the title of that Courbet painting, the one looking up between a woman's naked thighs? *L'origine du Monde*. In one of my books there's a picture of a knickerless virgin lifting her skirt and scaring off the devil with a flash of her naughty bits. And Sheela-na-Gigs on churches – the stone female spreading her vulva to avert evil or promote fertility. It's where the power is, it's where life comes out of. Maybe Angelica will rescue me.' He saw the imagined woman naked again and found her body beautiful, rich and well-fleshed like the one in the Courbet painting. He saw her nakedness close to his face, felt the heat coming from it. 'They gave Abishag the Shunamite to King David for his bed but he gat no heat from her. Still, he must have liked having her firm young body touching his old one. This woman whose name isn't really Angelica, what is her voice like? I think she speaks correctly but sensually, like some of those sexy female reporters on the TV news. They almost never show them below the waist but you can hear in their voices *L'origine du Monde* of them, the moist warmth between their thighs.

'This is Sunday; I wonder if she's answering at that number? She's a night person, I think. I'll wait till evening. He scanned the parts of the *Sunday Times* and the *Observer* he'd not read at breakfast, worked on Klimt a little, and watched Walerian Borowczyk's *Immoral Tales* on video, running the Lucrezia Borgia part twice. He napped a little, drank a little as the November dusk gathered in, and spoke to himself about the woman who called herself Angelica.

Finally he connected the telephone tape recorder, set it to start recording when he picked up the telephone, and dialled the number she'd given him. He heard it ring three times, four times. 'I wonder if I'm interrupting

80

anything?' he said. 'Maybe she has a live-in girlfriend.' He imagined the two of them in bed while the phone rang a fifth time.

'Hello,' she said. Her voice was not sensual, only clear and academic, the voice of someone correcting proofs for a scholarly journal. Or the voice of a reporter on the Six o'Clock News. The thought of her naked was maddening.

'Hello,' he said. 'This is Ruggiero.'

'Ruggiero, you're American!'

'Everybody has to be from somewhere.'

'You don't sound seventy-two – you sound much younger.'

'There's a young man in me but he can't get out.'

'Hasn't age given you anything to compensate for that?'

'I enjoyed my mind until my inner voice went.'

'You mentioned that before. When did it happen?'

'About a month ago.'

'What made it happen, do you know?'

He told her about the piece in the *Times*.

'Well,' she said, 'maybe your thoughts were too much for your inner voice, so it quit on you.'

'That could well be. Now you're in my thoughts. I know you're not the Angelica in the photographs. Can we meet?'

'Why?'

'I don't want you to be only a voice and a mental image, I want you to be all of you.'

'What's your mental image of me?'

'You know the Courbet painting, *L'origine du Monde*?'

'Very flattering. That painting stops just north of the tits. First I'm a naked blonde chained to a rock, then my hair goes dark, I lose the chains, put on a little weight, and get headless.'

'Not headless – I see you with a clever face and horn-rimmed glasses.'

'Horn-rims do it for you, do they?'

'They enhance the imagined nakedness of you.'

'And you want to meet me so you can have the whole actual me in your mind to look at. With my clothes off, I suppose.'

'If possible.' He watched the little red light on the recorder fluttering as he spoke.

'What kind of rock are you chained to, Ruggi?'

'Rock of Aged. Rock of impotent lust and madness.'

'Definitely my kind of guy but give me a better reason why we should meet. Convince me.'

'I feel as if it's Destiny: mine and yours.'

'Destiny's a funny thing – it could well be that we'll meet and you'll wish we hadn't.'

'Whatever. Can we make it soon?'

'Tomorrow night – is that soon enough?'

'Where?'

'Surrey Street off the Strand. Be at the Arthur Andersen entrance opposite the old Norfolk Hotel and Surrey Steps.'

'When?'

'Quarter past ten – 22.15 hours. Does that work for you?'

'I'll be there. How shall I know you?'

'You won't need to know me; I'll know you. There won't be that many old Ruggieros standing in that particular spot at that time on a Monday night. See you then.' She hung up.

'See you,' said Klein to a dead phone. 'Harold's Monday night. Destiny? *Something's* moving me; it's like being swept along by a fast-flowing river. Am I going to drown, be broken on rocks – what?'

He poured himself a large Glenfiddich, knowing that it would make him sleepy, and put on Astor Piazzolla's *Tango Sensations*. The music was sombre, dark, fateful. He saw Hannelore walking towards him, smiling with the sun behind her shining through her hair. 'I haven't seen much of you lately, Hannelore,' he said. 'Mostly what I get are memories from further back. Much further back. Well, whatever's happening now, things will be what they want to be.' And he fell asleep in his chair.

17

THE GOODBYE LOOK

Monday afternoon: Temple Underground Station. '"*Waltz me around again, Willy,*"' Klein sang softly to himself as he climbed the stairs to WAY OUT, '"*around, around, around. The music is dreamy, it's peaches-and-creamy — oh don't let my feet touch the ground . . .*"' His meeting with the pornographer known as Angelica was almost seven hours away but he wanted to reconnoitre Surrey Street before dark.

The station was full of motion as people came and went, their various destinies intersecting and diverging. '"Look thy last on all things lovely,"' said Klein, '"every hour."' Beyond the turnstiles he saw golden sunlight and the fruit and vegetable stall, brightly lit and festive, the gloss and colour of its offerings ticketed with white price cards. To the right of it was the flower stall, its blooms flaunting themselves under fluorescence and sunlight. To the left of it was the bright and cosy world of the newsstand, its wares ranked under the blazon of *The Economist*, the white title stentorian on a scarlet background.

Men and women waiting to meet someone stood by the station entrance. A *Big Issue* vendor, bearded and lonely, held up a magazine hopefully. Beyond him was the rush

84

of cars on the Victoria Embankment; beyond the cars the river with its boats and sunpoints in a golden haze. 'Sunpoints on the water,' said Klein, 'sunpoints dazzling on different waters, different times, other rivers watched by faces speaking and silent.'

Integral with the station entrance, the Temple Bar Restaurant was a haven for drinkers of coffee, perusers of newspapers, and those given to contemplation. 'They mostly look like regulars,' said Klein. 'They can come into the Temple Bar Restaurant and say, "The usual." Or maybe they just go in and sit down and it's brought to them. Probably the regulars were here before the restaurant; they brought their coffee in thermos flasks and they read their newspapers leaning against a wall until the tables and chairs, the coffee urn and the steamed-up windows happened around them. This may be a demonstration of the anthropic principle.'

He mounted the steps to the street as men and women young and old, fast and slow, singly and in couples and groups, came down past him towards the station entrance. 'Golden, golden,' he said, 'such a goldenness in the November afternoon sunlight!' He crossed Temple Place with the low sun on the left side of his face, looked briefly up the long perspective of Arundel Street with its vanishing point somewhere beyond the Strand, and turned left with the sun in his eyes, his gaze following an adorable pair of legs moving briskly towards the Howard Hotel. 'Don't reify,' he admonished himself, 'but how can one not?' The legs, diminishing rapidly, kept on straight ahead as he turned right into Surrey Street on the other side of which stood a King's College building.

He moved slowly uphill, keeping to the right-hand pavement. About halfway up he came to broad steps on which sat some young men smoking and chatting, wide glass doors behind them at the top of the steps. 'Excuse me,' he said to the nearest one, 'what building is this?'

'Arthur Andersen.' Being helpful to the little old tourist, he added, 'Over there across the street are the Roman baths.'

'Thank you,' said Klein. Opposite was a long tall cocoa-coloured Victorian edifice making its way up the street in reiterated gables, balconies, balusters, pilasters, Tudor-arched windows, cornices, and various ornamented out-crops and escarpments. Klein saw a sign, SURREY STEPS, and a dark archway beyond.

He continued up Surrey Street, the long cocoa-coloured succession continuing with him. On a portico he saw, in raised letters, Norfolk Hotel. Signs in three of the ground-floor windows said that the sometime hotel was now devoted to War Studies in London. He crossed to that side and walked back down to Surrey Steps and the dark archway where a sign guided him to the Roman baths. He went down the steps and found himself in a little alley facing a wall that said WARNING! HAZCHEM.

'HAZCHEM,' he said, putting a Hebraic spin on it. He went back to the other side of Surrey Street and up to the Strand where he watched a 91 doubledecker, magisterial in its redness, westering with the lesser traffic. He looked eastward to the spire of St Clement Danes sharp against the autumnal afternoon, westward to the church of St Mary-le-Strand in the valedictory gold of the declining sun. '*De Schimmel*,' he said as a remembered image surfaced. '*The Grey*.' It was a picture he'd seen at the Rijksmuseum in Amsterdam, by the seventeenth-century Dutch painter Philips Wouverman. In the foreground was a path ascending a hill with a background of cloudy sky. A rider had dismounted and was holding the reins of his horse while he peered past a gnarled tree-trunk that ended eight or nine feet from the ground. Bare shoots grew out of this tall stump that stood at the left-hand edge of the picture; what the rider was looking at could not be seen. On the right-hand side were visible the head and shoulders of a second man coming up the curving path behind the rider. 'That second man,' said Klein, 'is he mounted or on foot? Has the man with the horse seen him? What's that one looking at beyond the edge of the picture? I'm not sure he should have got off his horse.'

'What horse?' said a man who now stood facing him and breathing alcoholic fumes on him. He was tall and shabby with a peaked cap at the top of him; he was dirty and long unshaven, looked as if he'd been sleeping rough.

'Sorry,' said Klein, 'I was just talking to myself.'

'What's the name of that horse?'

'De Schimmel.'

'Pah! No good.' He wagged a dirty finger. 'Don't put your money on De Schimmel.'

'Why not?'

'Never bet on a Jewish horse.'

'Why not?'

'They think too much.'

'How do you know De Schimmel's Jewish?'

'Because he thinks too much. At the off he'll be thinking how to invest his winnings while the other horses are already out of the gate and halfway round the track. You Jewish?'

'What's it to you?'

'You are — I can tell. So was Jesus, and look what happened to him. Can you spare ten quid or so? I need to get drunk.'

'No.'

'Give me the money you were going to put on De Schimmel.'

'I wasn't going to put any money on him.'

'Won't even back one of your own! Pah! Bad cess to you.' He lurched away.

'"Bad cess"!' said Klein. 'I've only ever read that – I didn't think anyone said it any more.'

It was a little after four when he turned and went back down Surrey Street towards Temple Place and the river, towards the glittering sunpoints and the boats moving and still. He was walking on the Norfolk Hotel side, and when he reached Temple Place he saw, in the middle distance to his right, Waterloo Bridge between him and the setting sun. 'There was a time,' he said, 'when there was no bridge. There was a time when there was nothing except the river.'

On his way along Temple Place to the tube station he paused at the Victoria Embankment Gardens sign and went up the steps to the paved and balustraded area overlooking the river. He'd never been there before. To the right and left below him were the trees that had not been visible from Temple Place. There was a man sitting on one of the benches, no one else. 'They're going to refurbish this and make it a tourist attraction,' he told Klein, 'with a fountain in the centre, I believe.'

'Tables and chairs and umbrellas?' said Klein.

'Probably.'

'That's too bad, really.'

'It is. This is a quiet place – the way it is now it's nice to come here and sit for a while.'

'Most changes are for the worse.'

'I think you're right.'

Klein went to the balustrade and looked out over the Embankment where the early rush-hour traffic east and west made a continuous blur of noise in which the white eyes of headlamps and the red eyes of taillamps came and went. Still gold and silver under the darkening sky, the river was garlanded with lights on both sides. On the water bright pleasure boats with their music and working craft without moved up and downriver, the beat of their engines calling to the shorebound. 'So elegiac,' said Klein, 'so full of departure and farewell. Shining waters hung with lamps; gold and silver on the river and a goodbye look.'

At the station he went into the Temple Bar Restaurant for coffee and a bun. He sat there for a while, whispering his thoughts with his hand over his mouth. Then he went out, walked past those waiting to meet someone, past the *Big Issue* man to the edge of the traffic on the Embankment. Across the river the word OXO, spelled vertically on the side of a building, glowed palindromically in red neon. 'Yes,' he said, 'I know.'

In the station a black cleaning woman wearing an orange London Transport hi-vi vest was singing to herself. It sounded like a Bach cantata. 'There you have it,' said Klein, and went home.

18

HALCYON DAYS

'It was a two-masted schooner being built in a back yard,'
said Klein to himself, 'close by the railroad station at
Ambler. Not all that big – I think it was only thirty-six feet.
I passed it every day when I was commuting to art school in
Philadelphia. I kept wondering about it until one day on the
way home I got off the train and introduced myself to the
man who was building it: Harley Davidson, his name was
– no relation to the motorbike. He seemed old to me at the
time; I suppose he might have been between fifty and sixty,
a freelance inventor who used safety pins where he lacked
buttons and kept his trousers up with a piece of string.
The name of the boat was *Halcyon Days* and Davidson and
his son were building it from the William Hand *Tornado*
design. They intended to sail around the world. That was
back in '41 or '42. When I was drafted in 1943 the *Halcyon
Days* was still up on stocks in the Davidson back yard.
When I got out of the army in 1945 I went to New York
and never saw the boat again. I wonder if they ever made
the trip. Davidson showed Jim and me the moon through
his telescope one evening; it looked like a mouldy orange.'

For his meeting with Angelica Klein put some neces-
saries in a shoulder bag: M.R. James to re-read on the

Underground; reading glasses; hearing glasses (a microphone in each ear-piece); notebook and spare pen; sugar cubes in case of a hypoglycaemic reaction; glyceryl trinitrate for angina; tissues; Sony microcassette with spare batteries and cassette; Olympus point-and-shoot loaded with Fuji 1600; Swiss Army knife; Mini-Mag torch. 'Why the torch?' Klein asked himself.

Monday evening, 21.00: on the platform at Fulham Broadway the yellow light was sickly. Five or six people murmured or shouted into their mobile phones; others embraced what silence remained. The wincing of the rails announced the arrival of a Tower Hill train and when the doors opened the platform emptied into the carriages. When he sat down Klein wrote in his notebook, 'This seems a very tired train, worn out after a hard rush hour. The aisles are choked with crumpled newspapers; there's barely enough open space for the beer and soft-drink empties to roll around in. Twenty-three people in this carriage: twenty-three Its or just one It for the lot. No, there has to be one for each person, otherwise there'd be Itlock. Twenty-two inner voices, all of them presumably saying different things. Twenty-three destinies, coiled like intestines in each of us? Or not. Twenty-three continua to where?'

He opened *The Collected Ghost Stories of M.R. James* and began 'Casting the Runes', covering his mouth as he murmured, unavoidably, the words. He'd reached the part where Mr Dunning saw, on the tram-car window, the message: 'In memory of John Harrington, F.S.A., of The Laurels, Ashbrooke. Died Sept. 18th, 1889. Three months were allowed' when, TEMPLE! said the sign in a Dalek voice as that station appeared.

'All right,' said Klein. 'No need to shout. I'm coming.'

The woman next to him looked up, then returned to her *Evening Standard* as he left the carriage and went slowly up the stairs.

The turnstiles were deserted, the station desolate. Beyond the exit the newsstand, the fruit and veg, and the flowers were gone into empty darkness. The warmth and light of the Temple Bar Restaurant had withdrawn from that venue like a soul from the body. On the Embankment the cars hissed and hummed east and west without pause. Across the river the OXO sign repeated its neon mantra upwards and downwards. The silence that hid under the voices, the footsteps, and the sounds of the day's activity now showed itself alert and waiting, listening between the boats on the river and the cars on the Embankment.

Klein went up the steps to Temple Place, crossed to the other side, turned left, walked past the beckoning lamps of the Howard Hotel to Surrey Street, turned right, and went to the steps of the Arthur Andersen building where people were still going in and out of the brightly lit glass doors.

He looked at his watch: ten past ten. 'Harold's Monday Night,' he said, 'and no rain.' He looked at the SURREY STEPS sign and the dark archway that led to the Roman baths. 'HAZCHEM,' he said.

Business types came down the Arthur Andersen steps and went their various ways. Klein waited. 'Is this wise?' he asked himself quietly. Again he saw *De Schimmel*, worried about the dismounted rider. 'Why did he get off his horse?' he said. 'What does he see out there beyond the edge of the picture?'

At quarter past ten a white van came down from the Strand and stopped beside him. The rear doors opened and a male voice said, 'Hey, Ruggiero.'

Klein couldn't see the driver, saw only the black man

standing in the open doors. He looked athletic, was wearing a Nike shell suit and trainers.

Klein took the microcassette recorder out of the shoulder bag, started it, and put it in an upper pocket of his jacket. 'Where's Angelica?' he said.

'She's in a meeting but I'll be looking after you. I'm Leslie.' Klein recognised him as the male lead in 'Monica's Monday Night'. Leslie took his arm and helped him into the van. As he closed the doors the interior was suddenly brilliantly lit. Klein saw the mattress on which Monica had done her stint. The lights looked professional and there was a videocamera on a tripod.

'Your mobile studio,' he said as the van moved out.

'That's it,' said Leslie. 'There's been some great footage shot in here.'

'You take pride in your work, do you?'

'Well, the Good Lord gave me something to be proud of and there's no point in hiding it under a bushel.'

'Especially when there are so many more interesting hiding places, right?'

'Right, Grandad. Would you say that somewhere in you there's an old lady trying to get out?'

Klein had a mental picture of what the Good Lord had given Leslie and Leslie had given Monica. His left arm was feeling somewhat leaden and his heart seemed to be clutched by a heavy fist. 'I'd say that somewhere in me there's a dead man trying to get out.' He reached for the glyceryl trinitrate and gave himself a double spray under the tongue.

'Freshening your breath for the love scenes?' said Leslie.

'What love scenes?'

Leslie took off the bottom of the shell suit to reveal his bulging Y-fronts. 'One thing kind of leads to another,

93

Grandad. We can do this in easy stages. Take out your dentures and let's get started.'

'You're going to do to me what you did to Monica?'

'You got it.'

'I have to say that I'm curious: how can you find me attractive enough to get it up?'

'It's all in the mind. I don't want to talk about it.'

'Why not?'

'Once you start talking about it you could lose it.'

'Have you ever lost it?'

'Nobody's perfect.' His Y-fronts looked eager.

'Be still, my beating heart,' said Klein, and did the glyceryl trinitrate again.

'How many times you going to do that, Grandad?'

'Leslie, this is not a breath-freshener – it's glyceryl trinitrate.'

'What are you going to do, open safes with your tongue?'

'Very funny. It's for heart trouble, and if you don't want to end up with a snuff movie I think you'd better let me out.'

'What's the matter, don't you fancy me?'

'I'm telling you the truth; I've already had one myocardial infarction and a triple bypass and right now I'm getting heavy angina. What do you want, a note from my mother?'

'OK, Grandad, I'm convinced. Actually, no offence but I wasn't looking forward to it all that much.' Leslie switched off the lights and put his talent back into the shell suit. 'I told her that sex with OAPs was too kinky for me but no, she's against ageism. You want me to call an ambulance?'

'Thanks, but I think I'll be all right if I just sit quietly for a few minutes.'

'Al, pull over and park by the tube station,' said Leslie. To Klein, 'You mind if I smoke?'

'Perhaps you could open the doors and let some air in while you do it.'

The cold air felt good to Klein, like a breath of sanity. Leslie lit up, took a deep drag, and blew smoke out into the night. 'Now I'm curious,' he said. 'What did you think was going to happen when you turned up tonight?'

'I thought I was going to meet this woman who calls herself Angelica and we'd go somewhere and talk.'

'Maybe a little more than talk, right? Maybe get some geriatric jollies, eh?'

Klein shrugged.

'You want to be careful surfing the Internet, Grandad – it's a jungle out here in cyberspace. Best not believe everything you're told.'

'There's no fool like an old fool,' said Klein. 'You do this sort of thing often?'

'Depends on what she's into with her research.'

'Research for what – a book?'

'She doesn't want me to talk about it.'

'What's her name?'

'I'm not meant to give that out.'

'How much is she paying you for tonight?'

'Two hundred.'

'I'll pay you two hundred for her name.'

'You must want it pretty bad.'

'I'd like a level playing-field, that's all. Will you tell me what her full name is?'

'Have you got two hundred quid on you?'

'All I've got is a tenner and some change. Will you take a cheque?'

'If I take a cheque I want to know where you live. We

can drop you off at your place and I want to see you unlock the door and go inside.'

'I don't think it would be a good idea for me to show you where I live.'

'You think I'm going to come and rob you?'

'No.'

'Sneak in when you're out and bug the place? What?'

'It's not you I'm worried about – it's the one who calls herself Angelica; you'll tell her where I live and I won't feel easy about that until I know where *she* lives.'

'So how are you going to pay me for her name?'

'I'll get out here and go home by tube and I'll meet you here at the Temple Bar Restaurant tomorrow with two hundred cash. Afternoon all right for you, say four o'clock?'

'Now *I'm* wondering how good an idea that is for *me*.'

'What could be bad? All I want to do is give you two hundred quid for a name.'

'Maybe you won't show up alone. Maybe I could come out of this with grievous bodily harm.'

'I give you my word that I'll be alone.'

'You might change your mind between now and tomorrow; you might think back to what I was going to do to you and get really pissed off. That kind of thing happens.'

'Well, what do you suggest then?'

'OK, I'll take a chance on you. Tomorrow night at ten be standing in the same place where we picked you up tonight. You hand me the money, I'll give you her name.'

'Good. See you tomorrow then.'

'See you tomorrow.'

They shook hands and Klein got out. As the van pulled away he noted the number and wrote it down, then he switched off the microcassette.

19

THE QUARRY

'It's a jungle out here in cyberspace,' said Klein to himself. He was looking across the river at the building that said OXO. 'I'm remembering the quarry in Wendell's Woods. So deep and green and cold that water was.' He saw it closing over his head as he went down, down into the chill and the darkness. 'I can't remember the name of the dog. I was with Bill Muller and Freddie Schulz. Freddie's dog was with us. I must have been nine or so. We went to the old quarry – I don't know what they'd quarried there but it was deep and full of water. The side where we were was a sort of clifftop twenty feet above the water but you could climb down if you were careful. There was no cliff on the other side, just flat rocks. The dog went down to a little ledge just above the water and he wouldn't come back up when Freddie called him. 'I'll get him,' I said. I don't know why I didn't leave it to Freddie. I climbed down but I slipped and fell into the water with all my clothes on.

'I could dog-paddle a little, and I swam back to the steep side where I'd fallen in. I could have swum across to the flat side but I was too panicked to think of that. I clung to the cliffside while Bill and Freddie went for help. There

97

were two tramps living in a shack made of corrugated iron and signs that said PURINA CHOWS and RED MAN CHEWING TOBACCO. They came with a tow chain and let it down to me and pulled me back up. Why didn't I swim across to the flat place? The dog got back up by itself. The next day my father brought the two tramps a hamper of food. I wonder if Wendell's Woods and the quarry are still there. Maybe the quarry's been filled in, the woods cleared and developed. How strange it is that places where I was young still exist! Can this time really be a continuation of that time?'

OXO, said the building across the river, backwards and forwards the same. 'E621VGD,' he'd written in his notebook as the van pulled away. 'Ford Transit.' He stood looking at the lights on the river, the boats coming and going. 'Why did I get off my horse?'

20

EVERYBODY'S SOMEBODY'S FOOL

When Klein got home he phoned Angelica. After three rings she picked up the phone. 'Hello,' said Klein.

'What?'

'It's me, Ruggiero.'

'Hang on, Ruggi.' There were sighs and moans of pleasure from Angelica. 'Oh yes!' she breathed to an unknown partner. 'Like that, keep doing it like that! So good, so . . . !' Her orgasm followed with appropriate crescendos and diminuendos, duly noted by the little red light on the telephone recorder, then there were murmurs of satisfaction and endearment from her voice and that of another female. Next he heard glasses being filled, heard the two of them drinking with pauses for kisses and fondling and laughter.

'Hello, Ruggi. Are you there?' said Angelica.

'Yes, I'm here.'

'I must say, Ruggi, that I feel more than a little disappointed in you tonight. I was looking forward to a really interesting videotape and now Leslie tells me that you weren't up to it.'

'It wasn't very nice of you to say you'd meet me and then set me up to be Monicaed.'

'I never said I was very nice. I'm not even sure you'd like me if I were very nice. You do like me, don't you?'

'I don't know that liking comes into it. Was the other voice your regular partner?'

'Lydia? No, she just dropped in for some popcorn and a video and one thing led to another. I haven't got a regular partner. "Every day is a winding road . . ." yes? Ahhh, Lydia! I have to go, Ruggi – she's at me again. I'm sorry this isn't a videophone but you can listen to us until I can give you my undivided attention. Or better still, I'll give you a running commentary on what we're up to, and all for the price of a local call. Happy Hour for you, Ruggi.'

'Why not?' said Klein. He listened and enjoyed.

'Now, then, Ruggi,' said Angelica when she and Lydia had reached an interval. 'What shall we talk about?'

'Perhaps we could start with why you wanted to do that to me.'

'Do what to you?'

'Leslie and the van: Harold's Monday Night.'

'Aha! Your real name! Not all that heroic, is it.'

'Are you going to answer my question?'

'Are you going to tell me you wouldn't have enjoyed it?'

'*Enjoy* it! I don't think I'd have *survived* it.'

'It might have been a good way to go, though, mightn't it?'

'So you were hoping for a snuff movie, were you?'

'*Please*, Ruggi – I'm not a monster! I just wanted to see how you'd like what you found so entertaining when it was done to a woman. And really, that's what you were expecting, wasn't it? You wimped out at the last minute but you knew it was on the cards, right?'

'No, I didn't; I was expecting to meet you as arranged.'

'I don't believe you, Harold. When we arranged this rendezvous I gave you plenty of clues: same place, same time of a Monday night – everything but the rain, which was forecast but didn't happen.'

'I don't think the way you do; you said you'd be there and it was you I expected to see when the van pulled up.'

'Poor you! Can you really be that simple?'

'Yes, I really can. Are you always devious, never simple?'

'I'm devious in a simple way, Ruggi: you just can't count on me for anything but trouble. Got to say goodbye now. Bye-bye.'

21

NOAH'S ARK

'This is not a good time in my life,' said Klein. 'When was a good time?' He saw the Hungerford Bridge over the shining evening river, the lights of boats coming and going, the Royal Festival Hall brilliant with expectation across the water, and Hannelore at his side. '*Die Schöpfung,*' he said, 'that was a good time.' He put on the Berlin Philharmonic recording with von Karajan conducting, and the first bars of the orchestral prelude opened *The Representation of Chaos.* 'What a beautiful chaos,' he said: 'so warm and dark and full of good things. 1970 that was, or 1971. Was that the same chaos that Oannes arose from? A different part of it maybe, not so black.'

The music lifted him out of the present, cradled him in the safety of that good time long gone. When the chorus reached '*Und es ward Licht*' he wept as always, then hummed along with Fritz Wunderlich on the first day. When Gundula Janovitz made her entrance as Gabriel on the second day he wept some more, marvelling at the perfection of Haydn's world that never grew old, never filled up with rubbish and defeat. 'How beautiful London was at night, with its illuminated domes and spires and clocks,' he said, 'how shining the river!'

Gone, said his inner voice.

'You spoke!' said Klein. 'That *was* you, wasn't it, Oannes? You said, "Gone." I'm sure it wasn't me. Or was it?'

No answer.

'If it was you, why did you speak then? What does it mean that you chose this moment to break your silence? I know very well that the good time is gone, so why do you need to belabour the obvious with that one word like the voice of doom? Are you trying to tell me something, like my life is no longer worth bothering with and I should pack it in? What?'

There came to Klein, dim and shadowy, lit by one bare light bulb, the cellar of the house he had lived in as a child. In it were a coal furnace, a coalbin, and a large black boiler lying down against a wall. Elsewhere in it were sledges, rolls of tar paper, various lumber, rakes, shovels, and mouldering bits of carpet. 'My Noah's ark,' he said. 'It had a red roof and Mr and Mrs Noah and the animals were printed on glossy paper glued to plywood shapes. I used to think it was lost behind the boiler. Why would it have been down there? I can't remember. I still think that's where it ended up. I looked under the boiler with a torch and I poked behind it with a stick but I always imagined huge spiders there and I never felt around for it with my hand. Even now, in dark corners of this country where I was never a child, I think of looking for my lost Noah's ark. Are you with me, Oannes?'

No answer.

22

THIRD SESSION

'My inner voice,' said Klein, 'it spoke. Oannes said a word.'

'What was the word?' said Dr DeVere.

'"Gone". I'd been talking to myself about how this was a bad time and I was remembering a good time when Hannelore and I went to the Royal Festival Hall for *Die Schöpfung*. That's when he said, "Gone," which of course they are – Hannelore and the good time both.'

'Try to remember as precisely as you can: where was this voice coming from?'

'From me, the same as it used to. I could feel the word in my throat.'

'From inside your head, not from outside?'

'Look, Doc, I'm not crazy. When I say that Oannes spoke I mean that that part of me spoke, OK?'

'What did you think when you heard that word?'

'I was wondering if he, if I was telling myself that I had nothing good to look forward to.'

'And after that thought?'

'After that I saw in my mind the Noah's ark I lost as a child.'

'Can you remember how you lost it?'

'No.'

'Did you ever find it?'

'No. All I can remember is the smell of the cellar and the darkness and that big black boiler I thought the Noah's ark had fallen behind. I kept looking for it and it was never there.'

'Gone.'

'Gone. Life is full of gonenesses; I'm used to it. I keep on doing what I do; I'll finish the book on Klimt and then if I'm still around I'll do another one. The main action right now is with Angelica. Have a look at these.' Klein had printed out 'Monica's Monday Night' and he laid the pages on Dr DeVere's desk.

DeVere scanned them quickly. 'This is the picture-story we talked about in our last session?'

'That's right. The man in the photos is called Leslie; he's an associate of Angelica's. She and I had arranged to meet last night but it was Leslie who showed up, with a van. He was about to do a Monica job on me in front of a videocamera but I started to get angina and he let me go.'

'You were surprised when it was Leslie instead of Angelica?'

'Yes, I was.'

'What about the angina? What brought it on?'

'I was afraid of what was going to happen.'

'You mean anal rape?'

'That's right.'

'You didn't want that?'

'You don't take anything for granted, do you?'

'I can't afford to in my line of work. Did you or didn't you want him to do to you what he did to Monica?'

'I didn't want him to do that, OK?'

DeVere was looking at the first page of 'Monica's Monday Night'. 'Where and when had you arranged to meet Angelica?'

'In Surrey Street at a quarter past ten.'

'That's where and when Monica was pulled into the van on *her* Monday night.'

'I know.'

'Didn't that set any alarm bells ringing in your head?'

'OK, when we made the date to meet in Surrey Street on a Monday night my first thought was that I might be getting into a Monica situation.'

'So you weren't all that surprised to see Leslie, were you?'

'All right, at some level I might've been half-expecting it.'

'And how were you feeling about the possibility?'

'Scared, but curious.'

'Curious about . . . ?'

'About how it would be.'

Dr DeVere was looking at 'Monica's Monday Night' again. 'Here Monica's recalling newspaper stories of rape,' he said, 'then "She sees her thighs being forced apart; she makes an O with her lips, imagines the taste of semen on her tongue and the sweat of brutal men on filthy mattresses in evil-smelling rooms." Were your thoughts running along those lines?'

'Look, I'm not homosexual.'

'I never said you were. People have all kinds of thoughts and that's what we're talking about.'

'All right – my thoughts were running along those lines, the same as Monica's, OK? Tell me, do you enjoy rubbing people's noses in what they don't want to have their noses rubbed in?'

'I'm not rubbing your nose in anything; if that's how you experience this it might have to do with the judgements you pronounce on yourself. All I'm trying to do is clear away the bullshit. Do you think we can do that?'

'I'll make an effort.'

'People have all kinds of wants and needs and they have different ones at different times. Sometimes I want to listen to Beethoven quartets; sometimes all I want to hear is Argentinian tangos.'

'I know you're trying to make me feel more comfortable, Dr DeVere, but sometimes I'm afraid of what's in my mind.'

'Mr Klein, you have got to learn that you're not on trial for anything. Everybody has a public life and a private one; the private one is full of things that are not public business. This double life is part of the human condition. Nobody needs to know where you flick your bogies and I don't need to know all your private thoughts but we've got to establish some points of reference. Can you say exactly what it is that you want from Angelica and/or Leslie?'

'I'm not sure yet. Right now what I want is her real name and I'm meeting Leslie tonight to get it.'

'Why does that require a meeting?'

'Because I have to give him money for it.'

'Ah! The question, "Do you know what you're doing?" springs to mind.'

'Yes, I do. Oannes hasn't been very forthcoming but I've talked it over with myself out loud. I really need to know who this woman is and why she's doing what she's doing.'

'But Oannes *has* been forthcoming – he said, "Gone." It might be useful to consider the implications of that word.'

'I have, but I'd rather this Angelica person didn't get away with being inexplicable. Have you seen the Antonioni film, *Beyond the Clouds*?'

'No.'

'In it there's a filmmaker who travels around looking for characters and stories he can use. He has an encounter with a young woman who says to him, "It's better if I speak to you plainly. Whatever you have in mind, I'd rather tell you who I am: I killed my father – I stabbed him twelve times." We learn that she was acquitted but we never find out why she did it. This young woman is played by Sophie Marceau. Have you ever seen her?'

'No.'

'It wouldn't matter what she'd done – she's irresistible. She and the filmmaker sleep together, after which we see him through the window waving goodbye and that's it. We never find out why she stabbed her father twelve times.'

'Maybe we don't need to know.'

'I think Antonioni left it that way so it would stay in our minds, unexplained and unforgettable. That's OK in a film but this is real life and I need to know more about this woman who calls herself Angelica.'

'Just remember that if a scene in a film doesn't work they can take it out . . .'

'But real life is full of scenes that don't work and we're stuck with them. I know what you're saying.'

'Be careful.'

'I will.'

Oannes – deep-sea habitat – K getting in over his head? wrote Dr DeVere in Harold Klein's folder. Then he slowly and carefully perused 'Monica's Monday Night'.

23

DEATH AND LIFE

'In Klimt's painting *Tod und Leben*,' wrote Klein, 'we see the very essence of his mature art; he has emerged from the decorative excesses of his gold period and is now coming to grips with unadorned elementals; the grinning skeleton, *ein Knochenmann* (bone-man), in his cross-bedecked robe, wielding the red sceptre of his authority, feasts his empty eye-sockets on the living naked bodies (all but one with closed eyes) intertwined in love and procreation. In successive revisions of this painting from 1911 to 1916 Klimt changed the background to a non-space and removed the aura once worn by Death. This same Death, naked and lascivious, looks out, unseen, from the ardent and indolent bodies of the half-dressed and undressed women in his ghostly sketches: every one of these drawings is a matter of life and death; the snaky lines barely contain the transience of the flesh that cries out against the death that waits within, lusting for consummation.' Klein sighed. 'And in me too a death is growing; it's getting bigger as I get smaller, and when we're both the same size we'll change places – I'll be my death and my death will be me.'

He quit the word processor, went to the Internet, and put Angelica's Grotto up on the screen. 'Why can't I be dignified in my old age?' he said, and patiently trawled through the galleries in which Angelica did every possible thing in every possible position with partners of both sexes, singly and in groups. With his face close to the screen he lusted after the firm flesh in the photographs, flesh that could be touched and tasted, flesh in which Death nestled, cosy and warm and smiling. 'What good is this?' he said. 'Why am I wearing out my eyes on it? Why am I insulting my intelligence with it? I'm pathetic.'

Do something, said Oannes, speaking for the first time in a voice that seemed not to be Klein's own. Was it a deeper voice? Were the words somewhat slurred?

'I *am* doing something – I'm meeting Leslie at ten o'clock and he's going to tell me Angelica's real name. OK?'

No answer.

'If that's not enough, just tell me what else you want me to do.'

No answer.

'All right, have it your way: maybe I'll go out and do something really crazy and it'll be on your head. Is that what you want?'

Klein dug around in a box where he kept tools and other ironmongery and came up with a hunting knife bought for a long-ago camping trip. He went down to the kitchen and sharpened it. Then he put it in a pocket of a shoulder bag, got his jacket, and went out.

24

HOKA HEY

At ten o'clock the van with Leslie at the wheel pulled up in front of where Harold Klein was standing in Surrey Street. Klein walked around to the driver's side. 'I've got the two hundred,' he said. 'Have you got a name for me?'

'Melissa Bottomley,' said Leslie as he took the money and pulled away.

'Melissa Bottomley,' said Klein. 'Honey Bottom.' He visualised her wearing nothing but her name. His hand closed on the knife in his pocket. 'Stupid,' he said. 'I'm not going to stab anybody.' He moved a little way up Surrey Street towards the Strand, muttering to himself, 'For the first time I think of time as a sphere, as a globe on which, at various intersections of latitude and longitude, all things past and present are located, some near, some far from where I am. I'm thinking of Crazy Horse. On that great globe of Time, in western plains across the ocean, herds of long-gone buffalo make the ground shake and shadow hoofbeats sound down endless trails of sleep. Who am I that I should think of that strange one, the mystic, the great warrior who painted himself with lightning and hail and wore a little stone behind his ear? Riding into battle he shouted, "Hoka hey! It is a good day to die!" Now in

111

the long yesterday of the place that once was his the visions flicker but there is no one to see them. In Paris at the Crazy Horse Saloon the naked dancers shake and wiggle for the tourists.

'Melissa Bottomley,' he said as he continued up Surrey Street, 'could well be an academic; Monica was a lecturer at King's.' At the Strand he turned left and headed for King's College. As always, the traffic seemed full of urgency and purpose, pressing westward between dark buildings that loomed speechless and strange in their nighttime mode.

'DANGER, SLOW DOWN,' said the sign at the barrier. '5 MPH. ALL DRIVERS HALT AT THIS POINT AND REPORT TO PORTER.' There was no porter visible as Klein walked around the red-and-white barrier and went into the quadrangle beyond it. There were cars parked in almost all the spaces, and at the far end he saw the white Ford Transit, E621VGD. 'Probably it's locked,' he said.

He tried the rear doors: not locked. He opened them. Inside were the mattress, a folded blanket, and the tripod and lights for the videocamera. 'Is this a sign that I should do something?' said Klein.

Hoka hey, said Oannes.

'Oannes,' said Klein, 'you're a hell of a guy; you're a wild thing, you don't care about consequences. If I get inside I can't make myself invisible – they'll get in and they'll see me. Then what?' His bowels indicated that they were on standby. 'Forget it,' he said, 'I can't go looking for a toilet now.' Windows stared down at him from both sides of the quadrangle. 'What am I going to say – that I'm a homeless person looking for a place to sleep? Any suggestions?'

No answer.

'On the other hand,' said Klein, 'how much difference

does it make what happens to me? I'm old, my health isn't good; whether I ever finish the Klimt book isn't really going to matter all that much to anyone. I could go at any time – heart attack, stroke, whatever.' He heard hoofbeats on the plains, saw a blue sky in which a hawk circled. 'Hoka hey,' he said. 'Maybe it's a good day to die.' He got into the back of the van, covered himself with the blanket, and tried not to look like a little old man covered with a blanket.

'Who will it be?' he wondered. 'Leslie and Al? Leslie and Melissa? Maybe the van belongs to somebody else altogether. Maybe they leave it here overnight.' He listened to his tinnitus and looked at the pictures in his head until he heard voices and footsteps approaching, then the sound of the driver's and passenger's doors being opened and closed as the van shook a little.

'I don't know,' said the voice of Melissa. 'The money from Leeuwenhoek's almost used up.'

'There's bound to be more out there,' said the voice of Leslie. 'Have you tried Penthesilea International?' He started the van, backed out of the parking space, turned around, drove to the barrier, waited while the porter raised it, then turned left into the Strand.

'They don't want to know unless you're a big name like Candida Stark or Gnostia Mundy,' said Melissa.

'There must be big-money guys hitting your website all the time.'

'I know what you're thinking.'

'I bet you do: if you could arrange a meeting with a bit of action on camera they might find it in their hearts to offer a little financial support for your project.'

'That kind of thing could backfire – big-money guys mostly have high-priced help for making trouble go away.'

'What were you going to do with the tape if Harold's Monday night had gone as planned?'

'Hadn't decided yet.' She turned in her seat and slung a heavy shoulder bag on top of Klein. 'What's under the blanket – a body?'

'What're you talking about?'

'This.' She prodded Klein.

'It's me – Harold Klein.' He threw the blanket aside.

'What the hell are you doing here?' said Melissa.

'What can I tell you? If you play games with little old men they're likely to come looking for you.'

'How do you know I'm the one you're looking for?'

'It's your voice I've heard on the telephone, speaking as Angelica.' Her face was alternately lit and unlit as the van passed under street lamps. It was not the Waterhouse-nymph face of the website Angelica but a delicate oval art-deco face, neatly stylised features, precisely red mouth, dark hair in a short bob and fringe – most of all it was a serious face, a face that meant business.

'That doesn't prove anything,' she said. 'What do you want?'

'Where are we going?' said Leslie. They were on Waterloo Bridge.

'Turn around when you get to the other side,' said Melissa. To Klein, 'Well, what is it you want?'

'I want to talk to you, just the two of us, and not in this van.'

'All you want is conversation?'

'For starters.'

'Tell me why I should accommodate you, Mr ex-Ruggiero.'

'Do you want me to tell the police that I was forcibly abducted for a sexual assault but my angina scared you off?'

'Why would they believe that?'

'I've recorded my brief encounter with Leslie on Monday night; I've printed out "Monica's Monday Night", featuring Leslie and this van, and my doctor has a copy of it; and I've recorded my telephone conversation with you. You might consider your website and other activities a legitimate form of research but various academic and municipal authorities could well take a different view. Howzat?'

'I'd no idea you were such a cold and calculating little old non-hero, Harold. Evidently you're determined to get what you want. If I called your bluff you might well come out of it worse than I but in a spirit of academic research I'm half-inclined to help you act out your fantasy.'

'As any proper academic would,' said Klein.

'OK, old cock, we'll have our little assignation at your place, not mine. Where do you live?'

'Fulham.'

'Fulham, Leslie. You can drop me off at Harold's place and I'll find my own way home.'

'Are you sure this is a good idea?' said Leslie.

'We'll find out, won't we. He's weird but I don't think he's dangerous. Let's cross the water and get on with it.'

'That's the way to do it,' said Klein. 'It's a good day to die.'

'Why did you say that?' said Melissa.

'It's a quote – something some guy used to say before going into battle.'

'Did he die in battle?'

'No, he was stabbed in the back after the battles were over.'

'What was his name?'

'I don't remember. It was a long time ago.'

Melissa's face, into the light and out of it, was attentive, interested, calculating? The traffic sounds were like those in a dream and the geography of London inflected itself in unfamiliar ways, looming here, passing unnoticed there, strange music to the eye. 'Like a sixteenth-century map,' said Klein, 'full of odd shapes and terrors: the winds have faces and there are anthropophagi in unknown corners.'

'What are you on, Harold?' said Leslie.

'Mortality,' said Klein. He tasted, like fruit gums, the intensely red, green, and amber of traffic lights. Cars on both sides, ahead and behind, were silent worlds of otherness with bright reflections sliding rearward on their tops. Again there appeared the Embankment and the river garlanded with lamps, jewelled with boats, shining with lost years.

'What's happening?' Klein murmured to Oannes. Marlene Dietrich appeared in his mind as Lola Lola with naked thighs, black stockings, suspender belt, top hat. Emil Jannings, at the end of his tether, crowed like a rooster. 'Are we getting into a *Blue Angel*-situation here?'

'There are worse ways to ruin yourself,' said Melissa.

'Like Russian roulette?'

'Think about it: the professor's canary was dead at the very begining of the film but when he moved in with Lola Lola, up jumped a new canary singing like a steam whistle. How's your canary, Harold?'

'The last time I looked it was on its back with its feet in the air. Are you wearing black stockings?'

'Of course, with a suspender belt. I like to be correctly attired for mental undressing. Sorry about no top hat.'

'No wanking while we're on the road,' said Leslie to Harold as the Tate Gallery and the Vauxhall Bridge came and went. 'How do we get to your place?'

'Carry on down the Embankment past the Battersea Bridge and around into the New King's Road where you turn left.' To himself, 'Before that there's the Albert Bridge and Daphne.'

'Who's Daphne?' said Leslie.

'A bronze nude. When I lived in Beaufort Street I used to go jogging on the Embankment and I always slapped her bottom when I passed. I think she was vandalised and now she's fibreglass.'

'That's life,' said Melissa.

'Who vandalised you?' said Klein.

'Would you believe me if I told you I stabbed my father twelve times?'

'I'd believe you saw *Beyond the Clouds*.'

'You're so five minutes ago in a sort of twenty-five-years-ago way, Harold. You're a hippy replacement.'

'"By brooks too broad for leaping the lightfoot lads are laid,"' said Klein, 'but a lot of us old retreads are still around.'

The Albert Bridge wedding-caked and diamonded its way over the river. 'Albert Bridge, my delight,' sang Klein, 'let your lights all shine tonight.'

'You just make that up?' said Leslie.

'Something from a long time ago,' said Klein. It was a rhyme he'd composed for Hannelore back in the good time. For the rest of the trip he whispered into his hand except when he had to give directions. Arrived at his house, he looked out across the common towards the District Line. 'The place hasn't changed since I left it earlier this evening.'

'Did you think it would?' said Melissa.

'These days time goes in and out like an accordion,' said Klein.

117

'Listen,' said Leslie, 'I'd love to stay and talk about relativity with you, but the boss wants me gone.' To Melissa, 'Watch your ass, sweetheart.'

'I'll do that,' said Klein, as he left the van with the object of his desire.

25

A TASTE OF HONEY

For a moment they stood by the steps of Klein's house. On the far side of the common a Wimbledon train dopplered its way to Parson's Green. The night was warm for December; there was a nightingale singing; there was an almost-full moon.

'Waxing or waning?' said Klein. 'I'm never sure.'

'Three-quarters full or three-quarters empty,' said Melissa. 'Maybe there's not all that much difference.'

'Are you so world-weary?'

Unbelievably, she moved closer to him and laid her head on his shoulder; he was just tall enough for that to be comfortable. He put his arm around her, feeling through her jacket the heat of her body. 'Sometimes,' she said, 'I'm not sure what I am; sometimes I'm not sure *if* I am.'

'You? The formidable Lola Lola?'

'Nobody is the same all the way through like a stick of seaside rock. Or from moment to moment, for that matter – you must know that, living as long as you have. Put your other arm around me. You're older than my father.'

'The one you stabbed twelve times?'

'Whatever.'

'Is this happening?' said Klein, recalling her legs as she

stepped out of the van in her very short skirt. 'I'm an old man, close to the end of my life, and I feel like a sixteen year old on a first date. This isn't real, of course, but can we say that reality is whatever is the case?'

'You think too much, Harold.'

'Like a Jewish horse.'

'Are we going inside or are we putting on a show for the neighbours?'

'Sorry, you felt so good that I didn't want to move.' He went up the steps ahead of her, unlocked the door, and held it open for her. Once inside, before he turned on the hall light, he leant towards her, said to himself, 'What are you doing, Harold?' and drew back.

'What *were* you doing, Harold?' The moon shining through the fanlight glazed the oval of her face, made her like porcelain, fragile and collectable.

'It's that sixteen-year-old feeling – I was going to kiss you.'

She moved into his arms. 'Do it, Harold, this is your fantasy and my scientific enquiry.'

Madness is good, said Oannes.

Klein kissed her, feeling faint as she opened her mouth to him. They stood that way for a while before anyone spoke. 'That was quite acceptable, Harold,' she said. 'I was wondering if you'd smell and taste old but you don't; your tongue certainly carries its years well.'

'You weren't disgusted?'

'In my line of work I can't afford to be. Any response below the belt?' Her hand asked the question as well.

'Vestigial there but ten out of ten in my head.'

'That's where it counts. Are we going to move out of the hall?'

He hung up their jackets and they went into what used

to be a living-room but had long since been taken over by his work. There were bookshelves on all the walls except the one where the bay window fronted the street and the chimney breast where *Pegase Noir* hung alone. There were boxes and stacks of videotapes, piles of newspapers and unanswered correspondence. The desk was occupied by a PC, modem, and printer of recent manufacture, a very old Apple II computer for running unconverted floppy discs, a mini-hi-fi, and a variety of owls in glass, brass, china, bronze, spelter, stone, and plastic. On the printer a little naked china female presented her rear view as she reclined on one elbow and made eye contact with a tiny mermaid who leant against the groin of a large violently green-and-gold ceramic frog of almost abstract design. Two other little china females in the bookshelves danced in different periods while a third charmed a snake. Various sargassos of old and current yellow A4 pages drifted in the stillness of the desk.

Red file cabinets stood where possible, and in the odd shelfless corner there were posters: the 1933 King Kong atop the Empire State Building with a crushed aeroplane in one hand and Fay Wray in the other; Vermeer's *Portrait of a Young Girl*; Caspar David Friedrich's *The Stages of Life*; and a brightly coloured toucan advertising *der bunte Vogel BIERKAFFEE RESTAURANT* in Munster. Bric-à-brac, beach pebbles, seashells, a model of a Portuguese fishing boat and the Meissen girl kept station on the mantelpiece of the bookshelf-blocked fireplace. In deserts of desuetude on floor and tables tottering babels of defunct workroom cultures and buried civilisations awaited the archaeological spade.

On a well-worn Kelim stood a TV with two video-recorders; facing those a soft chair, a footstool, and a little

121

Indian table inlaid with ivory on which was a bowl of banana skins and tangerine rinds, beside which stood an unwashed glass that smelt of Glenfiddich. Under the rear window squatted a downtrodden couch in a geometric pattern of browns and reds, its seating space occupied by archive boxes and *National Geographics*. A variety of lamps, mostly articulated, arranged light and shadow to Klein's liking. 'This room is my exobrain,' he said.

'It looks about ready for a moult, but well-organised in an overwhelmed sort of way.'

'I don't know where everything is but I know where a lot of things are. Can I get you something to drink?'

'Like a real date, eh, Harold?'

'It's my party and I'll buy if I want to.'

'Whisky for me, please.'

'Water?'

'No, just as it comes.'

He was able now to see her with more objectivity than before. She was actually pretty but her art-deco style of face and hair formalised the prettiness with a sophistication that hardened it somewhat. Her hair was hennaed, her eyes blue, her features very like those of some of his china ladies. She was wearing a short-sleeved, low-necked black jersey top, a red skirt, the shortness of which he had already noted, the *de rigueur* black stockings, and medium black heels. When she sat down in the TV chair and crossed her legs he took in her white thighs and the black suspenders. Scarcely able to believe this windfall of goodies, Klein remained, as always, critical: she was not beautiful like the lithe and supple Angelica and her legs were 'definitely not in a class with Dietrich's', he heard himself say.

'If you can do better, feel free, Professor.'

'Sorry. It's just as well that I can't hear your thoughts

122

about me – I'm sure they're a lot more critical than mine about you.'

'That's where you're wrong – when I'm into something and going with it I suspend all disbelief.' She was still looking around the room. 'I don't see a stuffed owl; the place seems somehow incomplete without one.'

'I know. I'm waiting for the right one to turn up.' He went down to the kitchen, came back with the Glenfiddich and two clean glasses, and poured. Melissa was standing in front of the Meissen Girl. She touched the nipple of the bare right breast.

'That's Meissen,' said Klein nervously.

'Christ, what a simper. This was obviously done by a man, probably an old man. Do you think she's pretty?'

'I think she's beautiful.'

'That's what I mean – it's the sort of gymslip prettiness dirty old men go for: virgin pussy in porcelain. Figures like this are somehow crying out to be smashed.'

'O God, please don't!'

Her eyes moved up to *Pegase Noir*. 'Is this an original?'

'Yes. Odilon Redon.'

'Harold! Are you a closet millionaire?'

'No. There was a time when I made a few bob in art deals for collectors. Now I write books and make a whole lot less.' He showed her *Darkness and Light: the inner eye of Odilon Redon*. 'This is my latest.'

She opened it to the copyright page. 'Published four years ago. What've you done since?'

'This and that: articles, TV. I've just started research and notes for the next book.'

'Which is?'

'*Naked Mysteries: The Nudes of Gustav Klimt*.'

'Haven't you had enough naked women on the Internet?'

'Naked women by Klimt aren't the same as naked women on pornographic websites.'

'Why not?'

'The women on the Internet have become product. That's what the bad guys call drugs in the movies. "How much product can you move?" the suppliers say to the dealers. Pornography dehumanises women; Klimt explores their humanity.'

'Very smooth, Harold. Maybe we'll come back to that later. You've got some very deep thoughts in this Redon text.' She read aloud, '"It is evident that Redon was not so much the master of his material as its servant; his images and ideas forced him to give them form and substance, compelled him to find the shapes and spaces they required. Always his forms are hypermorphic – the gesture configures the shape and the shape becomes itself to a greater degree than ordinary vision allows. In *Roger and Angelica*, the tiny distant Angelica is the pearly flaunt of her nudity; the hippogriff is the quivering thrust of its haunches; and these, like all of Redon's figures, are celebrants of a mystery in which they themselves are the sacrifice. The colour, dream-haunted and strange, bursts from the seed-pods of his *noirs*. 'Black,' he said, 'is the most essential of all colours.' In the black is where his creatures live, the black from which Oannes, half-fish and half-human, emerges, saying, 'I, the first consciousness of chaos, arose from the abyss to harden matter, to regulate forms.' And in this same black, Venus, all rosy and golden, becomes visible in the nacreous genitalia of her birthing." Does anybody buy your books?' she said.

'Academic libraries, mostly.'

'And this is all you do?'

'That's it.'

'What do you live on?'

'I invested the money from my picture deals. Do you require a financial statement?'

'Sorry, I always want to know the facts of people's lives. So you live shut up in this room, devoting your life to the work of others.'

'Art raises the worldwide level of perception, it takes the mind to places beyond ordinary experience. Do you think the study of it is a waste of time? It beats running a porno site, wouldn't you say?'

'No, I wouldn't. I'm gathering information about sexual attitudes, studying emotional dysfunction in male/female transactions. Do you think that's a waste of time? Look at the state of the world, look at the sorts of things our law-makers and heads of state get up to when they're not creating gridlock, destroying the environment, and deciding the fates of nations: MPs dying in women's underwear with an orange in the mouth while trying for a better orgasm; every level of politician celebrating the virtues of the family while his willie votes the other way. Look at advertising – to sell ice-cream they have to show naked people eating it, and coffee's promoted as a sexual catalyst. Look at the fashions designed by queers for skeletons with tits. Look at the rape statistics. Look at you, a presumably intelligent man, spending hours on the Internet with your pleasure hand working overtime and your nose up the vaginas of women who'd call a cop if you got within sniffing distance of them. No wonder your inner voice packed up – it was embarrassed for you. There are millions of you out there and nobody's asking the right questions.' She picked up her drink. 'Cheers.'

'Here's looking at you. This is the first time you've told me what Angelica's Grotto is about. I heard you and Leslie talking about funding in the van. Where's the money going to come from next?'

She looked at him warily. 'Why do you want to know?'

'I'm interested, and I have some connections. Maybe I can help.'

'I'll think about it.'

'OK, Melissa. I'm still not sure whether you qualify as gamekeeper or poacher but we don't have to go into that just now.'

'How come you know my name?'

'Your filofax with your name on it is in your shoulder bag. Your name comes from the Greek word for honey.'

'I know.'

'Do you mind if I put on some music?'

'If that helps you get into the mood. You aren't subject to lingual impotence, are you?'

'Not so far. What would you like to hear?'

'You choose, it's your party.'

Klein put on Portishead's first album.

'Not too bad, Harold. I was expecting Bach or Haydn or Engelbert Humperdinck.' She pulled off the black jersey top; her arms were pleasingly round and her unshaven armpits delighted him; she slid the strap of her little black bra off her left shoulder and exposed one small girlish breast with its rosy areole. She undid the red skirt, dropped it, and leaned back in the chair. 'Would you like to remove my knickers, Professor?'

He sank to his knees and took hold of the black silk with shaking hands. She was wide-hipped, with shapely thighs and a belly like a Matisse odalisque. Her black pubic hair was as he had imagined it, coarse and springy to the touch of his lips. The heat of her body and the scent of her flesh made him giddy. He rubbed his cheek against her thigh, closed his eyes, breathed in the odour of her sex.

Yum yum, said Oannes.

'I read in this morning's *Times*,' said Melissa, 'about an eleven-year-old boy who's eaten nothing but Marmite sandwiches ever since he was weaned.'

'Mmmm,' said Klein.

'*Wandering star*,' sang Beth Gibbons, '*for whom it is reserved – the blackness, the darkness, the river.*'

26

LAST TANGO IN FULHAM

'You're a tiger from the neck up, Professor,' said Melissa, now fully dressed. 'How was it for you?'

'Terrific: there's nothing like getting back to basics. And you – were those sound effects real or faked?'

'Below the waist I never lie. You're a very cunning linguist and as I've told you, when I'm into anything I go with it all the way.'

'You're a strange one, Melissa.'

'Life is strange. Is there a table in this house with nothing piled up on it?'

'Down in the kitchen. There's nothing on it but this week's papers and a bowl of fruit. Why?'

'Let's go there and I'll tell you.'

In the kitchen Klein switched on the bead-fringed lamp over the table. 'Plenty of room,' said Melissa. 'I'll sit here and you sit opposite. We're going to arm-wrestle.'

'Do you always do that after sex?'

'No, but I want to see which of us is the stronger.'

'Why? By now everybody's stronger than I am.'

'Tell you later. First let's do this. Best out of three.'

Looking at her serious face in the lamplight Klein said, 'Every day is certainly a winding road, isn't it.'

'Definitely. Are you ready?'

They rested their elbows on the table, lined up their forearms vertically, and laced their fingers together. Her grip was like iron.

'Ready,' said Klein, and his arm was immediately pressed flat. They did it once more with the same result.

'OK,' said Klein. 'You're the stronger one. What next?'

'Back upstairs for the next event.'

When they were once again in the workroom Melissa arranged some cushions on the floor, then opened her shoulder bag. 'We might as well have some more music, Prof.'

Klein went to the CD player, put on the Diana Krall *All for You* album. When he turned back to Melissa he saw what she had taken from the bag. 'I don't believe this,' he said.

'You'd better believe it, ducky.' She took off her skirt and buckled on a male member of respectable dimensions. 'You owe me.'

'What do I owe you?'

'You owe me your bottom for that time you got out of your date with Leslie. We can do this the easy way or the hard way. As well as being stronger than you I'm a karate black belt, so get face-down on the floor and do what I say or I'll hurt you.'

'You're going to hurt me in any case.'

'Are you going to show fight?'

'That would be more dangerous for me than for you.'

'You know you want it, sweetheart. There's no gain without pain but lubrication is included. Trousers down, bitch, this is what your prostate has been waiting for.'

'After all our intellectual discussions you turn out to be rough trade.'

'I'm academic trade,' she said as she moved into position, 'which means it isn't over until you answer my questions on the website.'

'Multiple choice, I hope.'

'You have no choice, Professor – you need to talk about it as much as . . .'

'O God,' said Klein.

'. . . you need to . . . Yes! . . . do it.'

'*Love makes me treat you the way that I do,*' sang Diana Krall, her silky voice all blonde and sultry. '*Gee baby, ain't I good to you.*'

Gee baby, said Oannes.

27

30,000 FEET UP

Klein in the shower was thinking about Karl Wallenda. 'He was seventy-three when he came off the wire,' he said to himself, 'a year older than I am now. Ten storeys up between two hotels in Puerto Rico when a gust of wind blew him away. That was in 1978 and ever since then he's been dead and he'll keep being dead from now on, rain or shine, nothing else in his diary for ever and ever.

'I don't remember what year it was when I last saw the Wallendas at the circus. It was in my other life, back in the States. I was there alone because I'd seen them years before and I wanted to see them again, high up on the wire and maintaining their balance while doing impossible things. Francine was at a dance class and I had no child to take with me, no excuse for being there except my own fascination with what they did.

'High up on the wire they were, two of them on silvery bicycles and Karl sitting in a chair that was balanced on a pole between the one in front and the one behind. Was the band playing a tango? "Jalousie" maybe? Or was there silence while the Wallendas crossed from one side to the other. I don't think there was a net. The tent was blue, the lights were on the Wallendas, darkness below them.

Everything sparkled. If I slip getting out of the shower I could break my hip and that's the beginning of the end. Wrong – I've already had the beginning; this would be the middle or some way past the middle. I should have a cellular phone with me at all times but I don't want to be like the people I see talking on cellular phones. Of course this is different but I still don't like the idea of them. It's like drinks in the Underground; why are so many people in the trains carrying bottles of mineral water or cans of beer or soft drinks? Why this constant thirst?'

This was Wednesday. On weekdays he had grapefruit juice, bran flakes, and lemon tea at breakfast but this morning he felt the need of his Sunday breakfast: a soft-boiled egg and two slices of toast instead of the bran flakes. He injected his insulin, poured the grapefruit juice, put the kettle on, started the toast, shook a few drops of malt vinegar into the pot, put the egg in, opened the *Times*, and read that animals in some British zoos were on Prozac and Valium.

The phone rang; it was Melissa. 'Yes?' he said, immediately ready for whatever she might suggest.

'Prof dear, around ten this evening could you go to Gallery 7 at my site, scroll down to the bottom of the page, and click on YES for a one-to-one? Thanks. Must run. Kisses from you-know-where.'

When he was at his desk he worked on notes for the Klimt book. 'Pornography has always been part of the visual arts,' he wrote. 'I don't recall any pornographic cave drawings but their art was more elemental, more religious – Mother-Goddess figures, fertility symbols – procreation and survival – huge breasts and buttocks – Venus of Willendorf. And the Greeks! Raunchy Athenian red-figure vase-painters drew the line at nothing. Oral sex?

132

Can't recall. Everything else, certainly, one-on-one and in combinations. What would those vases fetch at Sotheby's now? The Romans weren't far behind, look at Pompeii: probably half of them were *in flagrante* when Vesuvius blew. X-rated petrified corpses. India – they couldn't get enough of it. They would have had to do Advanced-level yoga before they could even manage those positions. Krishna and the cowgirls. And the Europeans: Rembrandt did it – Vermeer? He did a brothel scene with a madame and some punters fully dressed but no hardcore. Vermeer painted moments in arrest. What would he have done with some of the ANGELICA'S GROTTO activities? The mind boggles. An authentic Vermeer of a woman in period underwear accommodating five men would set an all-time auction record. All the recent masters put their hands to pornography: Daumier, Millet, Lautrec, Picasso, Pascin. The B-List masters too: Felicien Rops and his giant willies; Bruno Schulz and the naked woman with the stallions and the little eunuch – no penetration except in the cerebral cortex. How am I going to get through the day?

'I have a craving that can only be satisfied by a disaster film – air, sea, or submarine, I don't care which; but preferably one where somebody survives through sheer pluck and resourcefulness plus maybe a little help.' He went to his current stack of air, sea, and submarine disasters, considered *Freefall: Flight 174*; *Mercy Mission – the Rescue of Flight 771*; *A Night to Remember*; *The Last Voyage*; and *Gray Lady Down*, which starred Charlton Heston and made Klein think of *Airport 1975* with Heston and Karen Black. 'Yes!' he said, 'That's the one: there she is with a great big hole in the front of the 747 and nobody to fly it but her. Were the pilot and co-pilot sucked out through the broken windows

133

after the other plane hit them? Have I recorded that one? Did I record something else over it? Can't remember.'

Klein owned more than a thousand videotapes in shelves, boxes, and various stashes. After about an hour of moving the ones in front away from the ones behind and the ones on top from those on the bottom, with pauses for rejoicing over long-lost treasures, he satisfied himself that *Airport 1975* was gone. By now Must Have had set in and he accepted it without demur. 'Never mind,' he said, as he went to the telephone, 'I can hire it from Blockbusters.'

Blockbusters didn't have it, nor HMV, nor Virgin, nor the National Film Theatre shop. 'It's no longer listed,' was the telephone consensus.

'A secondhand copy!' said Klein. He put on his jacket and went to the local music and video exchange. When he asked his question they looked at him the way bartenders in films look at detectives.

'We haven't even got *Airport* or *Airport '77*,' one of them said without moving his lips.

'Do you know of any place that does video searches?'

They both shrugged. 'No idea.'

'Of course,' said Klein. 'That's the way things are – I understand. You could at least move your lips.'

'You need help getting to the door, Grandad?'

'Thank you, I can manage. What happened to the old-fashioned specialised geek? Have a nice day.'

At home he dialled the NFT shop again, was given the number of a place that did video searches. They were closed for two weeks starting now, said their answering machine. 'No problem,' said Klein. 'It isn't personal, it's just business.'

By now he had attained the calm that comes when Must Have has exhausted its passion. The sun having sunk almost below the yardarm he poured himself the first Glenfiddich of the post-Must Have, went to his computer, and put *Cinemania '97* up on the screen. He didn't have to load the CD-ROM – it was always in the machine. When *Cinemania '97* showed its contents he went to FIND and typed in *Airport 1975* which caused five lines of text to appear in which Leonard Maltin said it wasn't worth Klein's time.

'Right,' he said, 'if I look at the other reviews and the cast list maybe I can reconstruct it in what's left of my mind.' He read the Ebert and Kael reviews and looked at the cast list. 'O Jesus – there's Helen Reddy, the singing nun, and Sid Caesar reactivated but they should have let him lie. Gloria Swanson, of course! As herself with a jewel box and dictating her memoirs. Myrna Loy! They never die, they just get sent to disaster films. Along with ex-stars the usual cross-section of young lovers, old diehards, businessmen regretting they haven't told their wives, children, dogs and cats they love them, and wives running off with tennis pros.

'But the star of the film is Karen Black at the controls with her eyes close together in concentration and the wind ruffling her hair – she's scared out of her knickers but dead game while they try to talk her through it on the radio and finally they put her lover, Charlton Heston, on the mike – he's a veteran pilot and he'll talk her down safely but no, this is no job for a stewardess however ballsy and they've got to put a man on the flight deck. Scramble a helicopter, hook a 747 pilot on to a line, match speeds and swing him in through the window. Oops! Didn't make it. The line was severed by the jagged hole or he unhooked before he was all the way in and he's gone. Well, he was the wrong guy, wasn't he – this is a job for Charlton Heston. Aha! It's an

135

Angelica-Ruggiero situation: she's naked in her ignorance of flying, she's virgin at the controls; the 747 is the monster that's going to devour her, but wait! Here comes Charlton Heston on his helicopter hippogriff. Will he make it? Yes! Through the broken hymen of the window he squirms. Gotcha, baby!

'Where is *my* Ruggiero? Or have I said that before?'

28

PILLOW TALK

'I'll wait till quarter-past, maybe half-past ten,' said Klein. 'Why should she take me for granted? Waiting waiting waiting.' He waited till five past, logged on to the Internet, and moused his way to Angelica's Grotto. He clicked on a few of his favourite Gallery 7 thumbnails to kill five more minutes, then scrolled down to the YES or NO place and clicked YES.

IS THAT YOU, PROFESSOR?

IT'S ME, LOLA.

SO? HOW'S IT HANGING?

REARWISE?

WHATEVER.

I'VE BEEN AFRAID TO LOOK.

IT'S A JUNGLE OUT HERE IN ACADEME.

I'VE NOTICED.

ENOUGH OF THIS SMALL TALK. TELL ME ABOUT YOU AND YOUR TONGUE.

IT STILL HAS THE TASTE OF YOU.

YOU LIKE THAT TASTE?

YES.

DID YOU LIKE TO DO THAT WHEN YOU WERE YOUNGER AND STILL CAPABLE OF AN ERECTION?

YES, ALWAYS.

CAN YOU SAY MORE ABOUT IT?

I GUESS WE'RE BACK TO *L'ORIGINE DU MONDE*. IT HAS A STRONG ATTRACTION FOR ME. TO MAKE LOVE IN THAT WAY SEEMS TO ME THE HEIGHT OF PHYSICAL INTIMACY, A COMFORTABLE GIVING AND TAKING OF PLEASURE AND AFFECTION. FOR ME IT'S ALWAYS BEEN A TREASURING OF THE WOMAN.

SAY MORE.

THERE WAS A GREAT MOTHER GODDESS BEFORE THERE WERE MALE GODS. THERE STILL IS FOR ME. HERE'S A QUOTE I PREPARED EARLIER, IT'S FROM *THE LANGUAGE OF THE GODDESS* BY MARIJA GIMBUTAS:

> THE AMAZING REPETITION OF SYMBOLIC
> ASSOCIATIONS THROUGH TIME AND IN ALL
> OF EUROPE ON POTTERY, FIGURINES, AND
> OTHER CULT OBJECTS HAS CONVINCED ME
> THAT THEY ARE MORE THAN 'GEOMET-
> RIC MOTIFS'; THEY MUST BELONG TO AN
> ALPHABET OF THE METAPHYSICAL.

I'VE READ GIMBUTAS.

I LIKE THAT IDEA OF 'AN ALPHABET OF THE METAPHYSICAL'. FOR ME THE VULVA IS THE KEY TO THAT MATRIARCHAL ALPHABET AND IT HAS MYSTICAL POWER. I ALMOST DON'T WANT TO PUT THIS INTO WORDS.

WORDS ARE USEFUL. THEY HOLD THE SHAPES OF IDEAS.

WHEN WE TALK LIKE THIS YOU ALMOST SEEM A FRIEND.

I'M NOT A FRIEND, HAROLD. THE DATA I'M COLLECTING MATTER MORE TO ME THAN YOU DO. AND AT YOUR AGE YOU OUGHT TO BE WISER THAN TO PUT YOUR MOUTH ON STRANGERS. YOU DON'T KNOW WHAT YOU MIGHT PICK UP.

FROM YOU? I THINK YOU'RE PROBABLY A CAREFUL KIND OF LOLA.

DON'T BE TOO SURE. LET'S GET BACK TO THE VULVA. HOW DO YOU RECONCILE YOUR WORSHIPFUL ATTITUDE TOWARDS IT WITH YOUR PLEASURE IN VIEWING THE BUGGER-ING OF MONICA?

I THINK IT'S A POWER THING. FOR ME THE ESSENCE, THE ISNESS OF A WOMAN IS MORE POWERFUL THAN MY ISNESS. THAT MAKES ME ENJOY THE IDEA OF A WOMAN BEING FORCED TO SUBMIT TO ANTI-VULVA PEN-ETRATION. AND NOT JUST ME: MORE AND MORE IN FILMS I SEE WIVES, GIRLFRIENDS, MISTRESSES, AND STRANGERS BEING BUG-GERED BY CHAPS WHO DO THAT INSTEAD OF SMASHING CROCKERY AND FURNITURE WHEN THEY WANT TO SHOW WHO'S IN CHARGE.

ARE YOU SAYING THAT IT'S A CASE OF THE LESSER ISNESS REBELLING AGAINST THE GREATER?

YES.

SO IF IN FANTASY AND IN FILMS, WHICH ARE READY-MADE FANTASY, YOU LIKE TO

139

*SEE WOMEN ANALLY RAPED, ARE YOU NOT,
IN FANTASY, ALSO IN FAVOUR OF THE RAPE
OF WOMEN IN GENERAL?*

I GUESS I'D HAVE TO SAY YES – IN FAN-
TASY.

EVER FANTASISE DOING IT YOURSELF?

YOU'RE SOUNDING MORE AND MORE LIKE
MY SHRINK.

ANSWER THE QUESTION, PLEASE.

YES, I HAVE FANTASISED IT BUT NOT IN A
VIOLENT WAY. DON'T PRESS ME FOR DETAILS.

*NOT VIOLENT BUT AGAINST THE WOMAN'S
WILL, YES?*

YES.

*DO YOU THINK, IF YOU STILL HAD YOUR
VIRILITY, YOU'D EVER CROSS THE LINE FROM
FANTASY TO REALITY?*

NO.

WHY NOT?

IT ISN'T RIGHT TO FORCE A SEXUAL ACT
ON ANYONE AGAINST THAT PERSON'S WILL.

*WOULD YOU SAY THAT WHAT I DID TO YOU
LAST NIGHT WAS AGAINST YOUR WILL?*

YES.

*BUT YOU DIDN'T SEEM TOO TERRIBLY OUT-
RAGED. YOU DIDN'T SEEM TOO DISTRESSED
EITHER. YOU DIDN'T REACH FOR THE GLYC-
ERYL TRINITRATE AND YOU DIDN'T CRY
ANGINA. WHY WAS THAT?*

YOU MAKE ME FEEL LIKE A PRISONER
BEING INTERROGATED BY THE KGB.

DO YOU WANT ME TO STOP?

NO.

140

WHY NOT?

I DON'T KNOW.

I THINK YOU DO BUT YOU DON'T WANT TO SAY.

MAYBE.

YOU WANT ME TO SAY IT, DON'T YOU.

YES, I WANT YOU TO SAY IT.

YOU DON'T WANT ME TO STOP BECAUSE YOU LIKE SUBMITTING TO MY BIG ISNESS.

I LOVE IT WHEN YOU TALK DIRTY.

I KNOW YOU DO, PROF. AND YOU LOVED IT WHEN I DID YOU THE WAY I DID LAST NIGHT, DIDN'T YOU. EVEN THOUGH YOU DIDN'T WANT TO TALK ABOUT IT AFTERWARDS.

Go with it, said Oannes.

'With what?' said Klein.

Anything.

'You just don't give a damn, do you.'

No answer.

HAROLD, ARE YOU THERE?

YES.

ARE YOU GOING TO ANSWER ME?

WHAT WAS THE QUESTION?

I WAS SAYING THAT YOU LOVED WHAT I DID TO YOU LAST NIGHT EVEN THOUGH YOU DIDN'T WANT TO TALK ABOUT IT AFTER-WARDS. AM I RIGHT?

DATA-RAPE.

ALL RIGHT, IT WAS DATA-RAPE BUT IT WAS ALSO QUID PRO QUO. SO TALK TO ME, HAROLD.

I'M NOT COMFORTABLE WITH HOW I FEEL.

T.E. LAWRENCE HAD A LOT OF TROUBLE

WITH IT TOO, AFTER HE GOT BUGGERED BY THE TURKISH SOLDIERS. I'M NOT A NICE PERSON BUT THE INFORMATION I'M GATHERING IS IMPORTANT AND CONFIDENTIALITY WILL BE OBSERVED IN MY USE OF IT. ISN'T THERE AN AMERICAN EXPRESSION, 'TELL THE TRUTH AND SHAME THE DEVIL'?

OK. FOR ALL I KNOW, YOU'RE THE DEVIL. BUT HERE GOES. IT HURT BUT THE PAIN MADE ME FEEL THAT I WAS PAYING MY DUES IN SOME WAY. THEN I STOPPED NOTICING THE PAIN AND IT JUST FELT GOOD NOT TO HAVE TO BE A MAN FOR A WHILE.

DO YOU THINK THAT HAVING THAT DONE TO YOU WAS UNMANLY?

YES.

MEN DO ALL KINDS OF THINGS.

NOT MY KIND OF MAN.

WAS THERE A POINT WHEN YOU ENJOYED IT?

YES. THAT'S IT FOR TONIGHT, OK?

OK, HAROLD. THANKS.

WHAT'S NEXT?

WHO KNOWS? NIGHTY-BYE. X

29

THE GYBE

'It was a Beetle Cat,' said Klein to Oannes, 'only twelve and a half feet long, a wooden day-sailer that was patterned on a Cape Cod fishing boat – the mast up forward in the eyes of the boat, a single gaff-rigged sail, and what they called a barndoor rudder. This was back in my first marriage, in my other life back in the States.

'*Melisande*, I named her – the original owner hadn't bothered with a name. Francine never took to sailing and she didn't want to know the right words for the parts of the boat and rigging. Once in a while we went out to Ram Island for picnics, but most often I sailed alone, sometimes in fairly rough weather. The man I bought her from had told me how wonderfully safe and sturdy she was, and being wooden she couldn't sink. Francine wouldn't go with me unless the weather was mild. 'If you have to reef you shouldn't sail,' she said. She thought I drove too fast too.

'We'd been out in the boat one summer afternoon; it was a beautiful day with a good breeze. Coming back to the mooring we were running before the wind, the sail all the way out on the port side. About halfway in I wanted the sail on the other side. I'd learnt sailing from books and

I knew about bringing the wind across the stern. "Watch your head," I said to Francine. "The boom's going to swing around." I put the tiller up and WHAM! The boom came round and slammed into the starboard shroud and suddenly the boat was full of water.

'I was amazed – when you're running like that it's easy not to notice the strength of the wind because the boat is moving with it and if the water's calm it's very smooth sailing. I ought to have brought the boom midships and then eased it out on the starboard side instead of just letting it go as I did. There'd been such a stillness in the boat until I let the wind take the boom and the swamping was so sudden that it was a real shock to me and a bigger one to Francine. I'd been out in rough weather without a care in the world but here on this balmy day I was suddenly made aware of the power of that fair wind and the depth of my ignorance. We bailed the boat out and got back to the mooring with no further difficulty but I still remember how surprised I was that afternoon. When I think of van de Velde's seamen in rough weather and myself on that sunny Sunday I have to shake my head.'

Klein didn't want to look at the pictures in Angelica's Grotto. He wanted to hold in his mind Melissa's nakedness; he wanted to hold in his nostrils the scent of her skin, on his tongue the taste of her, in his hands the feel and the weight of her buttocks. 'No,' he said, shaking his head, 'I had no right to do what I did. All manner of things can be done that ought not to be done and this was one of them. Melissa is intelligent but she has no idea of correct behaviour, of what is appropriate for this old man. And of course neither have I. Why have I spent hours looking at the pictures in Angelica's Grotto? What hath it profited me? Where was the gratification? There is a never-enoughness in such looking. Why is that? Why is it never enough? What is this non-existent grail that millions are seeking on the Internet? What is hidden refuses to stay hidden; the collective mind, as in a delirium, vomits up treasures of knowledge and images of longing and madness into the Internet. The seekers after the grail of enoughness think to be secret in the dark but the synapses of that heaving brain lead back to them; they can be found, exposed, discovered, unhidden as I have been. There was no Internet when Klimt was alive.'

He went to the book of Klimt sketches, opened it at random to an elegant drawing of a woman in period underwear lying on her back with her knees up and her legs spread, masturbating. *Masturbierende mit gegratschten Beinen*, said the earnest caption. 'There you go,' said Klein. Then, recalling another book, 'It's a paperback with an orange cover. Yes,' he said when he found it, *Clay Gods: The Neolithic Period and Copper Age in Hungary*.' He turned to a photograph of an anthropomorphic urn, female, stylised almost to the point of abstraction – the eyes, nose, and breasts indicated by clay knobs, the shape primarily urn but numinously woman. 'Better than Klimt,' he said.

He got his video of *The Blue Angel*, watched the end of it again, with Professor Rath, broken and disgraced, stealing back at night to the school where he'd been a respected master, and resting his head on the desk of his onetime authority. 'And yet,' said Klein, 'for a while you had a singing canary.'

30

FOURTH SESSION

'Oannes has said quite a bit more since the last time I saw you,' said Klein to Dr DeVere.

'Up to then, all he'd said since the shutdown was "Gone", right?'

'Right. He said that after I'd been talking about the past, when Hannelore and I used to go to the South Bank for concerts. But since then he's spoken seven more times.'

'We need to be absolutely clear about this voice of Oannes. Are you hearing it the way you're hearing me, as a voice originating outside your head?'

No, said Oannes.

'No,' said Klein.

'How *are* you hearing it?'

The way you used to, said Oannes.

'The way I used to,' said Klein, 'in my head and with some tension in my vocal cords, as if they're almost forming the words. Oannes is nobody separate, it's just how I dress up mentally when I'm thinking Oannes thoughts.'

Dr DeVere was busily writing. His pen made a tiny sound as he put the dot under a question mark. 'And you dress up mentally because . . . ?'

'Because I feel like it, OK? Does that make me some kind of a textbook case?'

'Not that I know of. What was the next Oannes message after "Gone"?'

'The next thing he said was, "Do something."'

'When was that?'

'It was the evening of the day of our last session; I was going to meet Leslie because he'd promised to tell me Angelica's real name, remember?'

'Remind me, please – why did he make that promise? Why didn't he just tell you her name straight out?'

'Jesus, don't you take notes? He wanted two hundred quid for it. I didn't have the cash with me at the time so I said I'd meet him next evening.'

'Why was her name worth two hundred pounds to you?'

'Because she'd been jerking me around and I didn't want to be completely at her mercy. I wanted to track her down.'

'How had she been jerking you around?'

'I told you last time: the evening before this I'd arranged to meet her but Leslie turned up instead with a van and a videocamera and he was going to bugger me for posterity.'

'Why had you arranged to meet her?'

'Sometimes you ask stupid questions, you know that?'

'Indulge me. You could have wanted to meet her for a variety of reasons. It's important for both of us to know which it was.'

'How's this? I'm old but I'm not dead; I still become interested in women who interest me.'

'OK, but what were you hoping this meeting would lead to?'

'Do I have to tell you every goddamn thing? Sometimes you have to use your imagination.'

'You've got a pretty short fuse today.'

'I've got a pretty short fuse every day, and I'm getting tired of stamping it out.'

'Try to remember that I'm on your side.'

'That's a great comfort to me.'

'How did you feel when Leslie let you off?'

'I felt relieved. When the actual Leslie was in front of me my curiosity vanished.'

'Why was that?'

'You've looked at that printout of "*Monica's Monday Night*" and you must have noticed the size of his equipment – it's scary.'

'Are you saying that if it had been less scary you'd have been ...'

'Less scared but just as unwilling.'

'Because ... ?'

'Because I have all kinds of weird and wild thoughts but I don't really want to act out all of them. Do you use the Internet?'

'Are we changing the subject?'

'Yes. Is that allowed?'

'You'd rather not talk about Leslie?'

'I think we've pretty well covered all my Leslie material for the time being. *Do* you use the Internet?'

'Sometimes, mainly for research – libraries and so on.'

'Oh yes. Ever check out Angelica's Grotto?'

'I did after you told me about it.'

'What do you think of it?'

'It's very time-consuming.'

'I know; sometimes it takes for ever for those thumbnails to load. But did you enjoy it?'

'Not really; I've never been much interested in pornography.'

'You haven't gone back for another look?'

'No.'

'I guess I believe you although it isn't easy. Are you married, Dr DeVere?'

'Yes. Could we get back to Leslie for a moment? Why had he planned a video session in the van with you?'

'Because Melissa told him to. That's the name I paid for; she's the one who runs the Angelica's Grotto website.'

'And Melissa – what was her reason for wanting it done?'

'Research, evidently. Have you heard of an organisation called Leeuwenhoek?'

'Yes, the Leeuwenhoek Institute.'

'What's their field of interest?'

'Their prospectus says they're "dedicated to the ongoing exploration of the human microcosm".'

'And the examination of animalcules like me, I bet. "Subject K, seventy-two-year-old art historian, presented with loss of 'inner voice' . . .".'

'Let's not lose the thread of your story, Mr Klein.'

'By this time I should think you'd call me Harold.'

'All right, Harold. We've got up to the matter of Melissa's research. Is she on a grant from Leeuwenhoek?'

'Yes. What's your first name?'

'Leon.'

'OK, Leon, she's on a Leeuwenhoek grant and I gather that she's doing a study of emotional dysfunction in male/female transactions. But I want to get back to what Oannes has been saying.'

'It's just that you seem to be leaving out so much that I'm having difficulty in putting it all together.'

'Fear not, I'll fill you in later. I was guessing from the Monica story and the place where Leslie met me that Melissa was either a student or on the staff at King's College, so I decided to go looking for her. That's when Oannes said, "Hoka hey."'

'"Hoka hey?"'

'"Hoka hey. It is a good day to die." That's what Crazy Horse used to say when riding into battle.'

'Like, "Here we go, here we go, here we go."'

'Right. I went to King's College and there was the van parked but not locked, so I got into the back and covered myself with a blanket. After a while Melissa and Leslie turned up and off we went. It didn't take long for them to find me and they were going to dump me but I'd recorded our conversations and we did some negotiating and Leslie agreed to drop Melissa and me off at my place for some one-to-one.'

'I assume you'll go into that van trip in more detail in due course.'

'Sure. I was wanting to kiss Melissa and she said OK and then Oannes said, "Madness is good."' So we went on from there and a little later he said, "Yum yum." The next thing he said was, "Gee baby."'

'Apropos of what?'

'She was raping me.'

'*Melissa* was.'

'With a dildo.'

'And you said . . .'

'*Oannes* said . . .'

'"Gee baby."' Dr DeVere was copying down all the quotes from Oannes. 'Next?'

'Next evening we were talking onscreen about what happened. Melissa was asking tough questions and I was having a hard time answering and Oannes said, "Go with it." With what? I asked him, and he said, "Anything." He was about to include the Oannes remarks at the beginning of the session but decided not to. 'That's it from Oannes so far.'

Madness is the natural state, said Oannes.

'He just said, "Madness is the natural state,"' said Klein.

Dr DeVere wrote down the last quotes, massaged his face a little, and said, 'I remember, in our first session, telling you to meet Oannes halfway. But now I'm wondering whether you haven't gone more than halfway. The old inner voice functioned as a useful censor but with Oannes it seems that anything goes. Jekyll and Hyde come to mind just a teentsy bit.'

'The Spencer Tracy one or the Frederic March?'

'Does it matter? Actually I was thinking of the book.'

'In the later film version Spencer Tracy had scarier teeth and Ingrid Bergman. Frederic March's Hyde was more refined and the fiancée was very appealing although I can't remember her name. Stevenson pre-dated Freud, didn't he?'

'I guess so, but can we stick to the point which was the growing influence of your Oannes aspect.'

'Look, Leon – I'm not some kind of split personality; Oannes has the same relation to me that your opponent does if you play chess against yourself. The voice of Oannes comes from the part of me that assumes that persona in order to speak my Oannes thoughts. I'm trying not to sound crazy but on the other hand, madness *is* the natural state, wouldn't you say? Sanity is a trick we learn somewhere along the way, like how to use knives and forks. Although it hasn't said very much so far I'm hearing an inner voice again and it's telling me new things. Shouldn't we be pleased about that?'

'Mmmm.'

'Mmmm what?'

'It's a question of what *kind* of new things it's telling you. In our first session when I said that Oannes was the Babylonian god of wisdom you said that you saw him as something else – I think I have the exact words.' He went through his notes. '"Deeper and darker than wisdom – he's nothing safe, nothing explicable."'

'Yes, I remember that.'

'And you've just said only a moment ago that you recognise your Oannes as coming from the part of you that speaks the Oannes thoughts. So what we're talking about are new thoughts, a new outlook that's *you*. Makes no difference whether you call this outlook Oannes or Popeye the Sailor – what we have here is a new you who's dumped the old censor and is listening to the voice of "Do what thou wilt shall be the whole of the law."'

'Alesteir Crowley – I've thought of that too. I've even written that thought down.'

'So a little caution might be in order.'

'Yes, Dad, I'll keep that in mind.'

'Do. Would you now like to fill in the bits you left out in your Oannes update?'

Klein filled him in. Dr DeVere nodded, shook his head, rubbed his face, made notes when necessary, and looked at *Roger and Angelica* from time to time. When Klein had joined up all the dots and coloured in the whole picture, DeVere sighed and said, 'What's going to happen now?'

'I don't know. Clearly I'm an old fool but maybe folly is the reward for having lived long enough to be old.'

152

'Please, don't dazzle me with footwork.'

'I'm not. I can't get her out my mind, can't get the feel of her out of my hands, the taste of her out of my mouth. I want that canary to sing even if it can't carry a tune.'

'Down, Oannes!'

'Up yours, Doc.'

'You intend to see her again? Foolish question, I suppose. I keep thinking I'm here to help you and wondering if I can.'

'Do you remember the end of *Dr Strangelove*, with Slim Pickens whooping and hollering as he rides the bomb all the way down? Jumping off wouldn't have done much good, would it?'

'You and your movies!' DeVere looked at his watch like a boxer listening for the bell. Finally, after trying several facial expressions, he found one that felt workable, cleared his throat, and said, 'Oannes might well be right when he says that madness is the natural state but you must admit that the knife-and-forkery of daily life is a useful survival trick.'

'The question is: survival for what?'

'For the life you had before Angelica's Grotto and Melissa. For the work you do.'

'Really. I've shut myself up in a room and devoted my days and nights to other people's work. Would you call that a good life?'

'Time's up. We can go into that in the next session.'

'Saved by the bell, eh Doc? Righty-oh. I'll send you a postcard.'

'From where?'

'I don't know – maybe the Canary Islands.'

Dr DeVere shook his head, made a final note: *Madness – the natural state?*

31

UNKNOWN TONGUES

'Oannes, old thing,' said Klein. 'Why are you so sparing with your speech? What would it cost you to let me have a few more words now and then? On the other hand, forget that I said that; I live in fear of what you'll make me do next.' For a moment he saw Oannes hovering in the darkness, his long length undulating slowly, his dim face impassive. 'Are your eyes closed? Oh God, what if they should suddenly open and look straight at me? Don't tell me anything right now, OK? Why was I so aggressive with Dr DeVere? Hoka hey but I really must watch my mouth. Never mind. Be bold, Klein. *Toujours audace*. Let's go find Melissa.'

Ordinarily he had a nap after lunch but today he stayed awake, sharp and alert as he stepped out into the world. The day was sunny and cold, a day for travel and adventure. At Fulham Broadway cars and motorcycles snarled as the lights changed from red to amber. An eastbound 14 Bus loomed, gigantically red. Another 14 followed closely behind as if intent on coupling with the first. 'Even the buses!' said Klein. Crossing to the Underground station he felt wild and free and crazy.

VIRGIN STATUE WEEPS, said the headline at the newsstand outside the station. 'As well it might,' said Klein.

The entrance beckoned with its promise of darkness, its world of neither-here-nor-there. '*Big Issue!*' shouted a vendor to those coming and going.

'I know,' said Klein. 'It's the biggest.' He showed his pass and made his way down the stairs to the platform, holding on to the banister because of his vertigo. The sun stormed through the skylights like the eye of God. The board showed a Tower Hill train arriving in three minutes. Moving away from the others on the platform, Klein whispered into his hand.

'Crazy Horse,' he said, 'I'm talking to you. In yesterday's *Times* there was a photograph of the model for the Crazy Horse memorial they're carving out of a mountain in the Black Hills of South Dakota. The caption says they're using supersonic torches, whatever they are. Probably pneumatic drills and dynamite as well. It's going to be the world's largest sculpture, bigger than Mount Rushmore. They've been working on it for fifty years and it might take another hundred to finish. The model looks like the kind of thing you'd see in brightly coloured china on the bric-à-brac shelf of a caravan.'

'Wheats-yew!' cried the rails as the train approached.

'Over and out,' said Klein as the doors opened and he found a seat. He looked at the faces opposite, put his hand over his mouth, and whispered, 'Every one of them is thinking something. I don't want to be surrounded by all those thoughts.'

The silence rumbled, shook, and rattled until the train arrived at Temple. He got out at the now-familiar station with its Temple Bar Restaurant, *Economist* newsstand, fruit and veg, flowers, and *Big Issue* vendor. The day was holding steady at sunny and cold, travel and adventure. He checked the river, found it auspicious.

155

He walked once more past the Howard Hotel, its top-hatted doorman stern and dashing with his white gloves on his left shoulder. 'How's it going?' said Klein.

'Slow,' said the doorman.

Klein turned into Surrey Street, passed HAZCHEM and the Roman baths, and climbed slowly towards the Strand. After the Norfolk Hotel building he paused at the one that said PICCADILLY RLY, ENTRANCE and EXIT. 'RLY,' he said. 'Royal London what? Yoghurt? Youth? Yearning? Yurts? If I don't find out I might fall through the lattice.'

Outside the glass front of what was clearly King's College Reception he paused and swiftly muttered two or three rehearsals under his breath, then walked in, went up to the counter, and said to the young woman who sat at a computer screen, 'What room would Melissa Bottomley be in at this time of day?'

'Is she staff or student? I'm new here.'

'She's a lecturer but I can't remember the name of the course.'

'I'll have a look.' She did some keyboard work, then said, 'The Politics of Language, Room 231, second floor. I don't know if she's lecturing now or not.'

'Thank you. I'll go up and have a look.' As he turned towards the lift he whispered into his hand, 'So suave!'

On the second floor he found buff-coloured bricks, pigeonholes, a notice board, NO SMOKING, and a perspective of square illuminations in the ceiling. There was a smell of an unknown disinfectant or cleaning agent. Workmen came and went into and out of a taped-off area at one end of the hall. A pretty brown-haired girl in jeans was sitting in a chair and writing in a notebook. 'Is it that all the plain ones have gone away?' Klein whispered into his hand. The girl looked up with a dazzling smile. 'Room 231?' he said.

'Just down there.' She pointed.

'Thank you,' he said, and went as directed.

'I think of Melissa's voice,' he whispered, 'and I think of her nakedness in my hands.'

The door of Room 231 had two narrow vertical windows one above the other. He looked in, saw Melissa lecturing, and opened the door a tiny crack.

'. . . on the tongue, to produce Mr Punch's voice,' she was saying, 'is now called a swazzle but in Mayhew's day the Punchmen referred to it as an "unknown tongue" which is interesting I think. Listen to this, from *London Labour and the London Poor*, published in 1861. Here a Punchman is telling Mayhew about the Punch and Judy show as performed by an earlier showman, Porsini:

'"At first, the performance was quite different then to what it is now. It was all sentimental then, and very touching to the feelings, and full of good morals. The first part was only made up of the killing of his wife and babby, and the second with the execution of the hangman and killing of the devil – that was the original idea of Punch, handed down to prosperity for eight hundred years. The killing of the devil makes it one of the most moral plays as is, for it stops Satan's career of life, and then we can all do as we likes afterwards." Anyone have any thoughts on that?' A hand was raised by a young woman with a baggy jumper and black hair in one long plait down her back. 'Sarah?'

'Well,' said Sarah, 'that reminds me of Alesteir Crowley; he was a Satanist and said to be quite a wicked man, and his credo was "Do what thou wilt shall be the whole of the law." But the Punch showman says that the *killing* of

Satan allows us all to do as we like, so his Satan seems to have been a more Calvinist sort.'

'Satan was originally the guy who punished sinners,' said a man with large ears and a prominent Adam's apple, 'which is why Punch was happy about getting rid of him.'

'Very odd,' said a woman with a black pullover and a nose ring. 'The Punchman said that the killing of Satan made it a highly moral play! And it was highly moral for Punch to murder his wife and child, right?'

'Punch has no morals,' said the man who had just spoken. 'Punch is the id.'

'There's a lot of id about these days,' said the first woman.

'I like it that Punch speaks in an unknown tongue,' said Melissa, 'an unknown tongue that's at the same time a secret utterance but one easily understood by all.' She looked towards the door, saw Klein, and gave him a look that turned him to stone. Recovering quickly he closed the door and waited for the class to end. '"Do what thou wilt,"' he muttered.

The door opened and a freshet of good-looking women poured out with some males bobbing among them. 'Gnnggh,' whispered Klein into his hand as he pretended to cough politely. He looked inside and saw Melissa putting things into her shoulder bag. She was wearing a sweatshirt and jeans this time, with trainers. She gave him the Medusa look again as she slung the bag from her shoulder and came towards him.

Keeping her voice low she said, 'You're not welcome here, Prof, and I don't like being stalked. You've had your treat, OK? Any further traffic between us will be onscreen or on the phone. Now please disappear or I'll have you thrown out.'

'Perfectly understandable,' said Klein, 'but as it happens the reason for my being here is that I want to talk to you about funding your project.' He watched the words march out of his mouth in perfect order. 'Life is full of surprises,' he said to himself.

Her eyes widened, then became beady. 'You want to give me money?'

Two professorial-looking men approached. 'See you Wednesday,' said one.

'Right,' said Melissa, recomposing her face.

'Can we talk about this over coffee somewhere?' said Klein.

'You're not fooling me, Harold – you just want to worm your way into my life any way you can. You think your money is going to buy you more treats.'

'After all, what's money for?'

'Aren't you ashamed of yourself? A respected art historian, and look at what you've sunk to!'

'Melissa, don't come the shocked academic with me – I'm sure that my moral decline is in complete accordance with your findings on male inadequacy. Let's not piss about, all right? I heard you say you were almost out of money and didn't know where the next lot was coming from. Did I hear wrong?'

'Of course I need money; a study like the one I'm doing needs a whole lot more than the funding I've had. I just don't like your approach to this situation.'

'Would you believe me if I told you that all I had in mind was the good of humanity? Actually I *do* think that a study of sexual attitudes and emotional dysfunction in male/female transactions is a worthwhile thing. And if funding this study is a way of buying more time with you so much the better.'

'Have you no pride, Harold?'

'I'm long past such luxuries; have you never heard of obsession? Goethe fell in love with a seventeen-year-old girl when he was seventy-five or so.'

'Probably all he did was write letters – I can't imagine Goethe at seventy-five doing what you got down to the other night. Besides, you said he fell in love; you're not seriously going to tell me you're in love with me. That I refuse to believe.'

'Why? Don't you think you're lovable?'

'I know damn well I'm not and you certainly aren't.'

'"This can't be love because I feel so well,"' sang Klein, '"no sobs, no sorrow, no sighs . . ."' Several passing students turned to look.

'Please, go have your Alzheimer's somewhere else,' said Melissa. 'I work here.'

'I've already suggested somewhere else,' said Klein – 'any place where we can sit down and talk like civilised people. If you want to get rid of me that's the quickest way.'

Melissa shrugged. 'I'm sorry I ever started with you.'

'I don't think you are, really. I think you're enjoying your power and the action resulting from it which is all grist for your mill, isn't it?'

'This kind of grist I can do without. Let's go.'

They left King's College and went into the winter-evening Strand all bright and lively, its buses gleaming juicily in the nightshine, the traffic hurrying to make way for the silence of the small hours. Left high and dry in the rush, St Mary le Strand tuned its steeple to transmissions from the Almighty and waited for the Day of Judgement.

'Here we are walking together like friends,' said Klein.

Melissa shook her head and walked faster to put some

160

distance between them. They passed the Courtauld Institute, passed Indian, Thai, and Italian food. 'Here,' she said, indicating the Classic Crumb Cafeteria. 'We can have coffee here.'

'It sounds so nice when you say "we",' said Klein, turning aside to whisper into his hand, 'I've held her nakedness in my hands, I've tasted her secret places.'

'That is really creepy, that hand business.'

'What can I say? Open a website and strange types with strange problems are bound to fall into it.'

Between the window and a glass display case were two tiny tables, one of them unoccupied. Melissa sat down while Klein went to the counter. She wanted nothing but coffee; he allowed himself a jelly doughnut as well, just to show his diabetes who was boss.

As they sat facing each other he looked out at the passersby, the cars and vans and buses. He'd never seen so many different doubledeckers as those now thronging the Strand. There were 15s, 76s, 23s, 13s, 9s, 71s, 26s, 68s, 77As, a 4, and a 1. He'd never known there was a 1! 'The redness of them!' he said. 'The doubledeckerness of them! The white-on-black of their route displays! They're some kind of metaphor, they mean something, they have significance. Ultra Nate! Is there a rock group composed of one buttock?'

'What?' said Melissa.

'Ultra Nate – that's what it said on the side of a 15 bus.'

'It has an accent: Ultra Na*te*. That's the name of the artist. She's a singer. Are you going to tell me what's on your mind or did we come here for busspotting?'

'Right. As I've said, what's on my mind is this study you're doing. When you were at my place you got all

161

worked up about the state of the world but you didn't go into detail about your project. All I know at this point is that you run a pornographic website and maintain a phone line for further dialogue with the punters. You also seem to be in the hardcore video business with Leslie and the van. What's the extent of your operation and what's it going to result in – a dissertation, a book, what?'

'And you want to know all this because you seriously intend to fund the study?'

'That's what I said.'

'Can I trust you?'

'Absolutely. You can always trust an infatuated old fool.'

'But have you got the money for it?'

'That I don't know until you tell me what's involved in your study and how much it costs to run it.'

Melissa took a deep breath and blew it out like a locomotive letting off steam. 'OK, there's the website and the monitoring of it to see how many hits it's getting from anyone.'

'How can you trace who's hitting the site?'

'Every time you visit a website your computer leaves an electronic calling-card, what's known as a cookie.txt. So we can see who's hitting the site and which pictures they're going for – Anal, Oral, Facial, whatever. That goes into the database, and on the basis of their preferences I choose which hitters to do one-to-ones with.'

'These are the ones who get to see "Monica's Monday Night?"'

'That or "House of Correction" or "Sisterly Love" or "Night Games" – I'm only running four picture-stories because I don't want to get tangled up in too many parameters. The one-to-ones that follow go into the database

in the appropriate category. I give selected one-to-ones
a phone number so they can talk to me. The phone
conversations get recorded and filed the same as the rest
of the material.'

'That sounds pretty time-consuming.'

'Tell me about it! It's also a good way to lose interest in sex.'

'Have you?'

'I don't know. When I'm with someone I'm not always
sure whether I'm having sex or statistics, orgasms or
exponentials.'

'"Every hour wounds; the last one kills."'

'Where's that from?'

'I saw it written on the face of a grandfather clock a
long time ago and it just now popped into my head.'

'Did you hear about George and the tinnitus drug trial?'
said a man at the table behind Klein to his companion as
they stood up to go.

'No,' said the other man. 'What happened?'

'It made him deaf for three days and it gave him an
erection that also lasted three days,' said the first man as
they put on their coats.

'How did he deal with that?'

'Well,' said the first man as they went to the door, 'just
at that time his wife was called away because her mother
was ill, so George . . .' The door closed behind them and
they were gone.

'Did you hear that?' said Klein.

'He was probably making it up,' said Melissa. 'There are
people who do that in lifts and tube trains, then they get
out and leave you hanging.'

'Speaking of unfinished stories, what about you and
your father?'

'The one I stabbed twelve times? Actually I never knew him.'

'Is that the truth?'

'It's anything you like. Whatever deal you have in mind, my history isn't part of it.'

'Why is there so much anger in you?'

'Give me a break, Harold. Do you want to hear about the study or not?'

'Sorry, please go on.'

'What I've told you so far has to do with gathering and sorting data. This being a study of emotional dysfunction in men in their transactions with women, the data . . .'

'Hang on – isn't that kind of one-sided?'

'That's the side I'm working; others can explore other sides – there's enough dysfunction for everybody. You as a frequent visitor to Angelica's Grotto must be well aware of how long overdue such a study is; male perception of the female is generally at an infantile level – masturbation comes naturally to men but relating to women is something that has to be learned and mostly isn't. I'm aiming for a sample of five hundred and each one has to be evaluated in accordance with the criteria of the study.'

'What about your video material?'

'Yours would have been the first; it would have provided useful data but the video thing is too risky to be practical and I'm not planning any more at the moment. What I've outlined for you is quite labour-intensive. So far I've been doing it alone with occasional help from Leslie but I could use a part-time assistant on a regular basis.'

'How long do you think it'll take to get your sample of five hundred?'

'I've been working on this for six months and I've only got seventy-three so far, sorted but incomplete and not yet ready for evaluation. To get the whole thing put together I reckon another five years or so.'

'Right. Tell me what it would cost annually to keep the whole thing going the way you like.'

'OK, there's the monthly payment to the Dutch server and there's the online time plus four telephone lines; there's the cost of Leslie and the part-timer and the outlay for another computer, maybe two. Plus there are always unforeseen one-off expenses that you have to be prepared for.' She took a pocket calculator out of her bag and was busy with it for a couple of minutes. 'Say twenty thousand a year. How does that grab you?'

Klein was looking into her eyes. 'Such a deep blue,' he said, 'and so serious.'

'You're not in a position to patronise me, Prof. You wanted to know what was involved and how much it costs and I've told you. Now what about this funding you were talking about?'

'I'm going to start working on it right away.'

'What does that mean exactly?'

'It means that I'll have more to tell you the next time I see you.'

'Ah, we're into control games now, are we, Harold?'

'Could you blame me if I were?'

'No, it's just that my time-wasting time is limited. So if you want anything more from me you'd better not muck me about.'

'I'd never do that, Lola. Trust me, I'm an infatuated old fool. Shall we go?'

On their way out they passed a young couple who were the new occupants of the other table by the window. As the door closed behind Klein and Melissa the woman said to her companion, 'I wonder what the story is with those two?'

He shrugged. 'I don't know but my money's on Lola.'

32

UNDERWORLDS

Klein walked Melissa back to King's College, then headed for the tube. As he passed the Arthur Andersen entrance on his way down Surrey Street he encountered a sixtyish man leaning against a white TNT Courier van and swinging his left leg back and forth. 'Trying to restore the circulation?' said Klein.

'Hip's giving me bother. It's worse in cold weather.'

'That building on the other side, up towards the Strand, the one that says PICCADILLY RLY – I've been trying to figure out what the RLY stands for. Would you happen to know?'

'I believe it's an old defunct railway station that was probably built between the two wars,' said the courier, 'around 1920, something like that.'

'*Railway*! I've never seen it abbreviated that way before. Was it a Main Line station?'

'No, it'd be one of the Underground stations; they've probably diverted the line since then – I don't think it's in use now.'

'Tunnels underneath where we're standing, and empty tracks going nowhere!'

'Could be, unless they've torn up the tracks. Who knows what's down there by now, eh?'

33

TAKEOFF

Klein went to the HMV in the North End Road, said to the assistant, 'Have you got a new Ultra Naté CD?'

'*Situation: Critical*?'

'No worse than usual. Do I look that bad?'

'That's the title of the album. Did you want it?'

'Yes.'

When Klein got home he played the first track, listening for a message. He was not disappointed. The beat was steady, the words simple and homiletic, offering such nuggets as '*Somehow things must change/and it's got to be for the better . . .*' The refrain was, '*Don't, don't, don't you give up.*'

'Songs for simple minds,' said Klein. He went to where *Pegase Noir* hung and stood before it. 'The strangeness of things,' he said to Redon – 'I know it was always in your mind and it's always with me too; I used to think of it as a question that had no answer but now it seems to me that it's an answer for which no one can imagine the question. The world is full of strange answers and missing questions; each of us is an answer to some unknown question that we have to guess at and get wrong as often as not. Right now I'm the answer to the question, "Who will play Old Fool in a geriatric-sex farce?"'

He looked up Christie's in the phone book, dialled the number, asked for the expert on nineteenth-century French art, was transferred to a Mr Duclos, and made an appointment to see him the next day. When he put down the telephone and looked across his desk at the painting the winged horse with its darkness and its ascendant colours seemed already to be moving away from him. 'Going, going, going . . .' he said, raising an imaginary hammer. 'Where am I? The galleries of Angelica's Grotto no longer interest me; those images seem fraudulent and empty now; what I want is more reality, and it's not the reality of simple gratification that I'm looking for. When I recall my evening with Melissa it's the intimacy more than the physical action that I crave more of – to hear her voice, to see her looking at me as if I actually exist, even if it wasn't real. But I don't intend to be the Professor-Rath kind of old fool, no indeed. To be a successful old fool you've got to play your cards right, you must keep your Lola in suspense sometimes; you must find other things to occupy your mind.'

He had Klimt to occupy him of course but he felt in need of some diversion. Scanning *The Times* and the *Guardian* he found an ad for Tango por Dos, a company performing at the Peacock Theatre. He'd seen a theatrical tango programme once before and liked it so he rang up First Call and booked a seat for two days later.

Next afternoon he took the Redon in its frame down from the wall. 'Like our marriage,' he said, recalling his dead wife's words: 'full of darkness but it flew. I've got no one to fly with now, Hannelore. It's a whole new ballgame, played in the dark.' He wrapped the painting in brown paper and rang up Dial-a-Cab.

In the taxi he steadied the painting with his left hand while his right hand covered his mouth. 'I wrapped the painting, I called the cab,' he whispered. 'I told the driver to take us to Christie's but I feel as if all this is being done *to* me, not *by* me.'

It goes, said Oannes.

'What?' said Klein. 'What goes?'

No answer.

Basking in the iron-hard December sunlight like a lizard on a rock, Piccadilly took no notice of Klein. St James's Street was similarly indifferent as was King Street. 'It may be nothing to you,' said Klein, 'but it's quite a big thing for me.'

Christie's with its curved and urned pediment, its crimson marquee and banner and its doorman with matching tie, though long familiar, presented itself to Klein as part of another world where everything was in good order and utterly incomprehensible.

The doorman opened the door, took the painting from him, Klein paid the driver, received the painting from the doorman, and went inside. At Reception he was met by Mr Duclos, a pleasant young man wearing a dark suit, a big smile, a look of lightning intelligence, and X-ray eyes.

Mr Duclos conducted him to a further Reception where two vigilant women watched the unwrapping of the painting and ascertained that it was undamaged. Thence to a little square crimson-walled conference room with two framed Christie's posters, a print of a Cezanne self-portrait and another of a Raphael drawing of the Holy Family. There was a little square table covered in green leather on which stood a gooseneck lamp; there were two chairs.

Mr Duclos leant the painting against the wall, noting from the dust on frame and canvas that it had not been

170

whoring around but had been honorably residential some-where. He examined the back of the canvas, saw that it had not been lined and bore some decently yellowed labels from reputable dealers. Then he stepped back, regarded the painting with the look of a fond father ready, subject to a DNA check, to embrace a long-lost son, and said, 'Ah! *Dans son jus.*'

'It's the real thing,' said Klein. To him it looked strangely diminished, its colours dim. Mr Duclos picked up the phone and called for a *catalogue raisonné*, meanwhile find-ing the signature in its proper lower lefthand corner, noting the rusty nails, the period frame, and other signs of authenticity.

When the *catalogue raisonné* arrived Mr Duclos traced the provenance of the painting through two French galleries to the private collection in Zurich, followed by 'Whereabouts unknown'. Klein produced the letter recording the transfer of ownership from the Swiss collector to him, which also showed the painting's date of entry into the UK.

'Since 1968, then, this painting has not been exhibited?' said Duclos.

'That's right.'

'Very good.' The measurements of *Pegase Noir* were listed in the catalogue and with a tape measure Duclos verified that the dimensions of the painting matched. He then switched off the lamp, and with an ultra-violet hand lamp he scanned the canvas for *pentimenti* or other overpainting and found none. 'So,' he said, 'the auguries are favourable and I believe we can do something with this horse; I think this horse is going to fly.'

'How high, would you say?'

'I think an estimate at five to seven hundred thousand pounds would be appropriate but I'd like to do further research and consult my colleagues on this if you can leave the painting with us.'

'Of course. When would the auction be?'

'Say ten weeks. Between now and then with your permission we'll tour the painting and arouse some interest. Naturally it will be fully insured.'

'Sounds a good idea.'

Mr Duclos explained the rate of commission and VAT, graciously waived the illustration fee, and a provisional contract was drawn up. They shook hands, smiled and nodded at each other, and Klein found himself in King Street walking away into the iron-hard sunlight. He felt, as an amputee might feel the tingling of a missing leg, the tingling of *Pegase Noir*.

34

'EL CHOCLO'

The Peacock Theatre was in Portugal Street, off Kingsway between Holborn tube station and the Aldwych. Walking down Kingsway Klein hummed 'El Choclo'. He owned more than twenty tango CDs and enjoyed them all, from the earliest onward through Gardel to Piazzolla. When working at his desk he was very careful to provide himself with a musical background that was supportive but not intrusive; lately he'd been listening to tangos more often than not.

He was surprised at how good he felt. 'Even now,' he whispered into his hand, 'burdened with infirmities as I am, I find myself experiencing *joie de vivre* every so often, especially when walking downhill.' The lights were bright, the Christmas decorations insistent as always but he ignored them. The evening was cold and clear, there was a sparkle in the air.

Klein was a half-hour early – he always was – but even so the pavement outside the theatre and the lobby were both crowded. The audience, many of whom, young and old, looked like dancegoers, would be a lively one. He bought a programme and a coffee and had another look at an item he'd noticed in the last *Observer*, reported by

Roger Tredre under the headline 'Grim Reaper is "kind and patient"':

> Mark Chorvinsky, publisher of *Strange Magazine*, told Unconvention 98, the fifth annual Fortean conference, yesterday: 'For centuries the Grim Reaper has been a cultural icon but it is not generally known that he exists.
>
> Chorvinsky told the London meeting that he had collected reports of more than a hundred sightings, mostly in the United States, and appealed for British eye-witnesses.
>
> Many of the reports were from nurses. 'In many cases, the Reaper is far from threatening. He seems to be waiting rather than actively seeking deaths. The Reaper in real life is kind and patient.'

'Death as a friend,' whispered Klein, remembering a drawing by Rethel, 'Death in pilgrim dress, with the scallop-shell badge of Santiago de Compostela, tugging on the bell-rope in a church tower high above the town, tolling the bell for the old sexton sitting dead in his chair. BONG! BONG! Probably the pigeons all scattering on the spreading sound-ripples, BONG! BONG!'

'Were you speaking to me?' said a woman who looked like Edna Everage.

'Sorry, I talk to myself sometimes.'

'I should get a cat if I were you. Or have you got one?'

Klein shook his head.

'Of course you couldn't bring a cat into a theatre. I suppose you must simply learn to think out loud more quietly.'

'Yes,' said Klein, 'and if you'd stop talking I could carry on thinking. Sorry!'

'Really! I suppose one mustn't expect good manners from Americans!'

'Or from women with harlequin glasses,' said Klein, and moved to another part of the room. 'Surely,' he continued to himself, 'he wouldn't have come for Hannelore wearing black and carrying a scythe, that would have been so tactless. A cardigan and old corduroys, maybe, like someone working in his allotment.' At this thought the tears started from his eyes and he didn't know what to do with his face except cover it with his hands.

'Are you all right?' said a young woman standing near him.

Klein wiped his eyes. Her voice was warm, her face open and interesting. 'Thanks,' he said, 'it's just a little memory attack. Where were you when I was young? Sorry, that just slipped out.'

'Not yet born, I should think,' she said, and turned away.

'We were talking about Death,' Klein whispered into his hand.

Death as a friend, said Oannes.

'Or as an editor,' whispered Klein, 'writing *Delete*? in the margin.'

Eventually he was able to go to his seat; the appointed time arrived, the house lights dimmed, the music began with '*Milonga de Mis Amores*', the murmur of the audience ceased; the curtain went up to reveal shadowy musicians and the gleams of instruments in purplish light and smoke, and the first couple appeared, dancing to '*La Cumparsita*'. Tango followed tango; the couples changed, sometimes the stage was full of dancers, sometimes there was only

175

a single figure obedient to the unremitting exactions of the music.

That music, breathed in and out by the bandoneon and augmented by double bass, violin, saxophone, flute, and piano, contained the dance, and the dance caught the dancers in a web of urgent and elegant evolutions: swivelling of hips and scissoring of legs, back kicks and caracoles and discontinuities of embrace. In their partnerships the heat of sexuality was refined into the negotiations of experience: sometimes the woman took charge; sometimes the man; the women like man-devourers ready to surrender utterly; the men as if they had been born with gold fillings and two-tone shoes.

In the second part of the programme, after Piazzolla's 'Libertango', Roxana Fontan, beautiful and Goyaesque in black and glittering silver, took the stage alone to sing the Villoldo classic, 'El Choclo'. Her silky mezzo was both delicate and powerful, her delivery now reflective, now assertive, always seductive. 'Con este tango nacio el tango,' she sang, 'y como un grito salio del sordido barrial buscando el cielo' (With this tango the tango was born, and like a cry it left the squalid slum, seeking the sky). Sometimes as the song went on she leant back into the words and caressed them, sometimes she sent them out like calls to battle. Klein had no Spanish, didn't know what the words meant, but they seemed vitally important to him, seemed the very flame of life in the darkness – he whispered this thought into his hand. 'Luna en los charcos,' she sang, 'Canyengue en las caderas . . .' (Moon in the puddles, canyengue [pronounced canjengay] in the hips . . .).'

'I can't actually put canyengue into English,' said the Argentinian translator Klein found in the phone book the next day. 'It's a lunfardo word,' she said. 'Lunfardo is a local vocabulary in Buenos Aires and it's used a lot in tango lyrics. *Canyengue* carries the idea of the suburbs and the common person of low social condition whose manner of dancing the tango is earthy and full-blooded with no added-on refinement; *canyengue* in the hips means dancing with the real feeling of the tango.'

'*Canyengue*,' said Klein to himself later. '*Canyengue* in the mind, from the outlying districts of the cerebral cortex and the limbic system. Either you have it or you don't. Right, Oannes?'

No answer.

35

DECK THE HALLS

Being a Jewish atheist, Klein always half-expected a brick through his window in the Christmas season. No one chalked CHRISTKILLER on his door but child carollers menaced him with 'We wish you a Merry Christmas' and public-school boys politely intimidated him with holly wreaths which he bought several of. Christmas trees bloomed in windows all around him, and some houses sported external twinkling lights.

He withdrew into his video collection, surfacing intermittently to watch Yuletide films in which Germans spoke broken English before being blown up by Lee Marvin and Telly Savalas. Even when the TV was turned off, Christmas carols, seasonal piety, and adverts for computer games leaked out of it and spread in a greasy puddle on the floor. Walt Disney manifested his undead self in various ways, sometimes sliding under the door as a mist, sometimes like a bat at the window or a wolf howling in Fulham Broadway. On Christmas Day a grey sky squeezed out a thin snowfall on which fresh dog turds stood out sharply.

Klein phoned Melissa several times and got her answering machine; he left messages but she never phoned him back. Sometimes he imagined her writhing naked in steamy orgies; sometimes he imagined her in the bosom of her family somewhere in the provinces, eating and drinking and sleeping with whoever was handy without a thought for him.

When the partridges had left the pear trees and the lords had ceased to leap, Klein emerged blinking and unshaven into the Christmas-New Year interval. The ghost of New Year's Past now came to visit with clanking chains of memory and action replays of champagne, soft words, and kisses. Sometimes it hunkered down beside his bed and improvised sad songs of happy times departed; sometimes it rocked back and forth and moaned.

36

GYNOCRACY

'How am I going to get through the time between now and the auction?' said Klein to himself. 'I don't want to call Melissa until I have something to tell her, some bargaining power.'

He went to his computer, put his last Klimt page up on the screen. 'Sorry,' he said, 'I'm no longer interested in Klimt.' He went to his shelves and got *The Drawings of Bruno Schulz*, edited and with an introduction by Jerzy Ficowski. The first drawing he turned to was the *cliché-verre* engraving, *Eunuch with Stallions*. There was the naked woman prone on the tousled bed, indolently looking back over her shoulder as a white stallion, rampantly crouching, licked her bottom. Rearing up beside the white stallion was a black one. Little pariah-men watched from behind the bed, and in front of it the dwarfish eunuch, face black with lust and impotence, grovelled on the floor.

'Is there anything new to be said about Schulz and sado-masochism?' said Klein. 'Is there in all men a secret desire to abase themselves at the feet of a woman who has contempt for them? Or is it simply that I'm naturally depraved and losing control of myself?'

Wild thing, said Oannes.

'Are you taking the piss or what? You think I should lose control more than I already have? Speak, Oannes.'

No answer.

'I'm getting tired of your one-liners,' said Klein. 'Why do you always chicken out of a real conversation?'

No answer.

Klein turned the pages, looking at drawing after drawing of the ghastly little wretch at the feet or under the feet of beauties naked and clothed who spurned him. He turned back to the introduction, in which Ficowski explained:

The mode of expression and the subject matter of this early cycle of engravings [*The Book of Idolatry*] are governed by the principal idea of 'idolatry' – veneration of a Woman-Idol by a totally submissive Man-Slave. That motif dominates all of Schulz's graphic works – the proclamation and celebration of *gynocracy*, the rule of a woman over a man who finds the highest satisfaction in pain and humiliation at the hands of his female Ruler. Suffering does not kill but nourishes and intensifies love.

'Of course,' said Klein, 'I'm not in love with Melissa: what I feel for her is nothing more than some kind of kinky impotent old-man thing that makes me replay that night with her over and over – what she did and what she said when I was face-down on the floor. The feel of her nakedness against my back! Her not-to-be-questioned authority, her physical strength, and her utter contempt!'

He put on a new CD, *Garbage*: '*I'm only happy when*

181

it rains,' sang Shirley Manson, sounding naked under her mac, '*I'm only happy when it's complicated.*'

'Me too,' said Klein.

37

A FIRM HAND

Days passed, each one with hundreds of hours in it, but Klein held to his resolution and did not phone Melissa. She phoned him one rainy evening, and at the sound of her clear academic voice all of his senses instantly replayed the unforgettable night. 'Hello,' he said, choking a little over the word.

'Hello, Harold,' she said, sliding a leg between his, tango-fashion. 'I haven't heard from you for a while.'

'I know. I've had nothing to tell you yet and I know you don't like me to waste your time.'

'Ah! I think I may have been a little unkind when I saw you last. I'm not really a very nice person but I was nice to you that time I came to your place, wasn't I?'

'Are you playing with me?'

'Yes, but you like it when I play with you, don't you?'

'Yes.'

'And you *were* serious about funding my study, right?'

'Absolutely. I told you I'd be working on it and I am.'

'How?' Her leg was around his waist, pressing him to her.

'I'm not ready to tell you.'

'But why make such a secret of it?'

'I'm superstitious – I don't want to jinx it by saying anything before it actually happens.'

She moved her leg so that her knee was in his crotch. 'Before *what* happens?'

'Can't say yet.'

'Harold,' a slight pressure from the knee, 'you're not getting beyond yourself, are you?'

'Oh dear, I hope not.'

With her thigh between his legs she lifted him a little. 'Because it seems to me you're being very naughty.'

'I don't mean to be but I can't help it.'

Supporting him with one hand, she bent him back and brought her face close to his. 'Some discipline might be in order at this point, eh?'

'I know I need a firm hand to keep me in line.'

'Yes, and the sooner we get you sorted, the better. When should I come over?'

'Whenever you like – your time is scarcer than mine.'

Her hand was clamping the back of his neck. 'How about right now?'

'Whatever you say,' said Klein.

When she rang off he felt giddy from the swiftness of the changes in the dance. It suddenly seemed terribly important to have the right music going when she arrived – tango wasn't right for the occasion nor were rock, pop, jazz, or blues. He rejected various modern albums, at length chose *Olympia's Lament* as sung by Emma Kirkby to the accompaniment of Anthony Rooley's chittarone.

There were two versions of it on the CD, one by Monteverdi and the other by Sigismondo d'India. '*Voglio, voglio morir, voglio morire*,' began the Monteverdi: '*I want, I want to die, I want to die*,' sang Olympia, abandoned by Bireno on a rocky and pitiless shore. 'Another one of Ariosto's hard-done-by women,' said Klein, listening briefly to the measured outpouring of her woe and deciding that it would go better with the evening's activities than the more overt emotion of the d'India. 'For our visiting feminist,' he said.

He scanned the room, moved *The Drawings of Bruno Schulz* from the littered couch to the little table by the TV chair and left it open at the spread with *Eunuch with Stallions* on the left; on the right was *The Feast of Idolaters*, in which a whole grovel-group queued up on hands and knees to kiss the foot of a seated woman who was showing a lot of leg.

He was busy adjusting lamps and rearranging clutter when the doorbell rang. Melissa was wearing a long and baggy black pullover, her usual black stockings, thigh-high shiny black boots, and nothing else that he could see. Klein moved back from the door to let her in but when he moved towards her again in the hall she stopped him with an outthrust arm. 'Don't try to approach me as an equal, little man – it's time for your spanking. Trousers down!'

Klein obeyed, first putting on the Monteverdi track. Melissa sat in the TV chair, exposing her thighs and suspenders, took him across her knees, and smacked his bare bottom hard, again and again while the golden voice of Emma Kirkby rose and fell on behalf of all hard-done-by women.

'What a miserable-looking bum you've got,' she said as she spanked him.

'I'm sorry,' said Klein. 'I wish it were nicer for you and I wish it were raining.'

'Little pervert!'

I'm only happy when it's complicated, said Oannes.

185

'Get me a drink,' she said when she'd finished: 'whisky, and don't get dressed – I'm not through with you yet.'

When Klein came back from the kitchen she had the Bruno Schulz book open on her lap. She accepted the drink without a thank-you and extended her booted left foot. 'Put your neck under my foot,' she said.

Klein obeyed and she rolled his neck back and forth for a few moments. 'You can imagine me being mounted by a stallion,' she said. 'You can imagine my screams and the neighing of the horse.'

Klein imagined. 'Who ever thought we'd get this far this fast?'

'You obviously did. I notice the wall's bare where the Redon used to hang. Tell me about that.'

'I'm still not ready, Lola.'

'I see. There's no rest for Lola, is there. Face-down on the floor with you, Prof.' She removed her pullover and her bra, took the necessary equipment from her shoulder bag.

'Please be gentle,' he said.

'No way, Prof.' She buckled it on and went to work.

'Right,' she said, fastening her bra and vanishing into the pullover, 'you can pop your things on now.'

'Have you ever trained as a nurse?'

'No. Why?'

'No reason, it just popped into my head.'

'Pour me another drink and have one yourself, why don't you.'

He poured. He drank. He admired her stockinged legs, her shiny black boots, her white thighs and black suspenders, *l'origine du monde* between her legs.

'Poor little Prof! Would you like a kiss now that your punishment's over?'

186

'Yes, please.'

She took him in her arms. Her whisky-flavoured mouth was delicious, her tongue inventive. When she released him he said, 'It's just business for you, though, isn't it?'

'Everything's business in one way or another, Harold. Now let's talk about the Redon. Where is it?'

'How can you be so cynical so young, Melissa?'

'I'm not cynical, I'm educated, that's all.'

'Do you really think you can be impartial in your study of emotional dysfunction in male/female transactions?'

'I don't have to be – my questions will be there with the answers they elicit, so I'm not hiding anything and my conclusions are admittedly subjective. Now, where's the Redon?'

'At Christie's.'

'You're going to auction it?'

'That's what they do.'

'Aha! And what's their estimate?'

'Give me another business kiss.'

She gave it. 'Now tell me,' she said.

'Five to seven hundred thousand pounds.'

'Nice one, Harold!' She kissed him again. 'How soon will it happen?'

'Ten weeks.'

'I'm so excited!' She hugged him.

'I'm glad you're pleased,' he said, clasping her bottom.

'Actually,' Hannelore had said two or three centuries ago, 'I don't like that painting all that much. I don't like pictures that are symbolic of something. If you're going to paint a horse, study horse anatomy and do it the George Stubbs way. The best thing about this painting is the money it'll be worth when we're old. We can sell it and do some travelling on the proceeds.'

187

'You'll never be old,' said Klein to Hannelore.

'Why not?' said Melissa. 'Do you think I'll die young?'

RRRRAAAAARRGH! said Oannes, and flashed a picture through Klein's brain.

'No!' said Klein.

'Or did you mean age cannot wither me, nor custom stale?'

'What?'

'Pull yourself together, Harold. We were talking about the Redon.'

'Five to seven hundred thousand pounds.'

'You said that already.'

'What was the question?'

'I haven't asked the next one yet. Are you all right?'

'Would you excuse me while I whisper into my hand a little?'

'Private thoughts, eh? Carry on – I'll do a little more drinking while you're thinking.'

Klein went to his desk, whispered, 'Stop it, Oannes,' and hurried to put another picture in his mind. He loaded his *National Gallery Complete Illustrated Catalogue* into the CD-ROM drive, put Ingres's *Ruggiero and Angelica* up on the screen, then slid over to *Oedipus and the Sphinx*. 'I'd forgotten how shadowy she is,' he whispered. He went to the shelves, took down *Meisterwerke der Erotischen Kunst*, turned to *Der Kuss der Sphinx* by Franz von Stuck, contemplated the powerful beast-woman crushing the naked traveller to her breasts as he yielded to her kiss. 'What happens next in this picture?' he wondered without whispering, 'Why am I thinking sphinx?'

'Why don't you give art history a rest, Harold?' said Melissa as she freshened her drink. 'There are practical matters for us to talk about.'

'Yes,' he said, 'in a moment.' There were various things leaning against a wall in the order of their last viewing; he moved a portfolio to reveal a framed black-and-white wet pastel: *Sphinx* by Quentin Blake. The artist had first brushed water on to the paper in the approximate shape of the figure which he then drew with black pastel; he pushed the drawing about with his finger, then further defined it with his fingernail.

The figure was that of a naked young woman, three-quarter front view, her knees on the floor and her hands on a bed. The drawing stopped at mid-thigh; the bed was only a darkness that she leant on. From the waist up she was in shadow, her head and shoulders and arms shaped of darkness, her face lost in obscurity. The curve of her back, the lithe roundness of hips and bottom drew the eye to the animality of her body; the darkness and thickening of the upper parts suggested a minotaur. The figure seemed as if it had been made to appear by the stripping away of its invisibility.

'Looks as if she's about to be buggered,' said Melissa.

'Thank you for that penetrating insight. Can you see anything else in it?'

'Well, she looks as if she might be wearing half of a crop-top gorilla suit.'

'Good job you're not running an art-appreciation website.'

'Why? What do you see that I don't?'

'Never mind – let's get back to whatever you were saying before I took time out for thinking.'

'Hey, listen, Prof – don't do me any favours. You sound a little bored now that you've had your geriatric jollies. Maybe I should leave.'

'I'm sorry, Melissa – my mind always jumps from

189

one thing to another, sorting images and looking for connections. Don't leave yet, please – I like having you around.'

'OK, I'll stay a bit longer. Have another drink and tell me about Christie's. If the painting fetches five hundred thou, how much do you walk away with?'

He took a card out of his pocket. 'Commission is on a sliding scale – the more money you bring in, the less commission they charge. If the hammer price is from £300,000 to £599,999 the commission would be six per cent.'

Melissa got her pocket calculator out. 'Six per cent is £30,000. Leaves us with . . .'

'Leaves *me* with . . .'

'Four hundred and seventy thousand, which is not too bad.'

'Don't forget seventeen and a half per cent VAT on their commission . . .'

'Five thousand, two hundred and fifty,' said Melissa, 'from £470,000 leaves £464,750 which is still a nice little bundle to walk away with. Or are there more deductions?'

'The insurance premium is one per cent of the hammer price.'

'Five thousand! That leaves £459,750. Anything else?'

'That's it; Mr Duclos said they're waiving the catalogue illustration fee, and according to my accountant the Inland Revenue doesn't get any of this because the Indexation Allowance comes to more than one hundred per cent of the market value in 1982.'

'That's a mercy. So we're talking about a final figure of £465,625.00. How much of that can you use to fund me?'

'Funny – *fund* is a four-letter word.'

'I love it when you talk dirty, Prof. Keep talking.'

'Where were we?'

'Funding me.'

'I think I need to refresh my memory as to what I'm funding.'

'How can I help you?' she said, leaning back in the chair.

He knelt in front of her and slid his hands under her bare bottom. 'I'll think of something,' he said with his face between her thighs.

38

NUMBERS

Still the same evening. 'Now, then,' said Melissa. 'We were going to talk numbers.'

'"Ye shall not eat of any thing that dieth of itself,"' said Klein.

'What the hell's that about?'

'That's from *Deuteronomy*, it comes after *Numbers*. It just popped into my head, I've no idea why.'

'What you've been eating is still very much alive, Prof. What is it with you, post-cunnilingual depression?'

'It's not exactly depression – it's just that every now and then I wonder how I came to be where I am.'

'You mean where you are with me?'

'With you, with everything.'

'I notice that it happens after your treat rather than before.'

Watching her mouth and her steady blue eyes as she spoke, Klein thought that mercy was not a big part of her makeup. 'Don't you ever wonder about that?' he said. 'Don't you ever wonder how you came to be where you are and doing what you're doing?'

'I *know* how I came to be where I am and doing what I'm doing. But for now I'm wondering if you intend to

192

put your money where your mouth is – which might not be the best choice of words. Is you is or is you ain't my sponsor? is what I'm trying to say.'

'Hannelore and I had in mind to travel on some of the money from the sale of that painting.'

'Who's Hannelore?'

'My wife. She's been dead for a long time.'

'Great. I'm deeply moved. I'm so moved that I think it's time for me to go. Let me know when you're ready to talk seriously about money. Otherwise stop rattling my cage.'

'*Are* you in a cage, Melissa?'

'I'm out of here, Prof.' There was a rush of air as she picked up her shoulder bag and made her exit, slamming the door behind her. Klein listened to the sound of her heels receding into the night.

He looked again at the *Sphinx* drawing, the picture and the figure both divided diagonally into light and dark. From the obscurity of her face her hidden eyes looked back at him.

39

BY THE SWELLS, BY THE STARS

'Dying sea skills cost islanders their lives,' said the headline over an Associated Press report in *The Times*:

> Suva, Fiji: Possibly hundreds of Pacific islanders die slow agonising deaths from sunstroke, thirst and starvation every year because they have lost the seamanship skills of their ancestors, it was claimed yesterday.
>
> 'Today, about ninety-five per cent of Pacific islanders who fish at sea do so in small dinghies powered by poorly maintained outboard motors . . . They chase fish over the horizon, lose sight of their island and can't find their way back,' said Michael Blanc, who teaches basic sea safety skills in the South Pacific Commission's fisheries programme.

Klein spent about an hour searching through his video collection until he found a documentary called *The Last Navigator* that he'd once taped from Channel 4. It had been filmed in Micronesia, which at the time had massage parlours and Burger Kings but no Disneyland. On the island of Satawal in the Carolines the navigator, Mau Piailug, was first seen with a circle of stones on a mat and a group of less-than-keen children whom he was attempting to teach the star-compass memorised by his ancestors. 'I'll continue to voyage,' he said, 'and if I'm not disabled, or too old or dead I will pass my knowledge to the next generation.'

As a demonstration of the traditional skills, Piailug had organised the building of a sailing canoe for a 500-mile voyage with an adult crew from Satawal to Saipan in the Marianas. Piailug was perhaps in his forties; his compact brown body was sea-tempered and ready, his face intense with the island-finding spirit. 'We men should think only of our strength,' he told his crew, 'we are not children. When we're on the canoe it is my role to tell you the talk of the sea. Remember the canoe is our mother and the navigator is our father.'

The vessel herself seemed as eager as Piailug; she was a creature of quickness and memory, a magic of wind and wood, winged with a landfall-hungry sail, rigged with ropes of nothing-forgotten, keeled with the shape of answer-the-sea. At the start of the voyage Piailug, at the helm of the outrigger canoe, sang to his crew:

> I sing of this canoe, our canoe,
> of the life of the spirits, the life of people.
> Be with me, spirit,
> on the small beach, on the wide beach,
> on the beach of my island –
> I sing of this canoe, our canoe.

Out of sight of land Piailug's eyes were attentive day after day to the colours and shapes of clouds, to the winds that shifted or were steady, and to the swells. At night he steered by the stars that successively rose over the horizon on the chosen course, each night bringing the mother canoe and her children closer to the loom in the sky, the reflected light of the island landfall, and the tiny speck of land in the wide, wide sea. He had no instruments, only himself, his thousandfold memory and the dead who sailed with him, chanting the names of winds and swells and stars.

The outrigger canoe seemed less a man-made thing than a natural part of sea life, the sail as inconspicuous against the sky as the wing of a tern. Watching that swift and urgent vessel hissing through the blue water Klein was riveted. Saipan safely reached, he shook his head, then sat for a while whispering into his hand. He didn't want to hear what he was saying.

40

FIFTH SESSION

'I'm lost,' said Klein.

'In what sense?' said Dr DeVere.

'In the sense of I don't know where I am.'

'Can you elaborate?'

'I am of a people who have always been fearless navigators of the mind. The dead sail with us as we make our way from idea to idea, steering by the stars and sea-marks named by those before us. Such a wide, wide ocean! But you always know where you are by the waves, by the swells, by the loomings and the stars. Then one dark night the waves change, and the swells; the winds blow from not the usual quarters. Black squalls come, and heavy seas, the stars are blotted out, the wind moans in the rigging. You suddenly realise that you might never make your landfall, you might drown. A great wave hits the boat and takes you with it, you feel yourself going down, down, down and then you don't know any more which way is up and you can't hold your breath a moment longer and the wild wide ocean fills your lungs and then you're gone: down among the dead men.'

Dr DeVere kept respectfully silent for a few moments. 'It's good that you could get that out,' he said.

'Is it? I almost don't know who I am. I try to think of how I came to this and it's hard to believe how it all began. I read this lousy piece in *The Times* and Boom! my world fell apart.'

'Ronnie Laing said some good things in his time: one of them was, "The breakdown can be the break*through*."'

'Depends on what you break through *to*, I should think.'

'What do you think you've broken through to?'

'Way back in our first session – it seems a hundred years ago – you brought up Georg Groddeck and his theory of the It. When I wasn't too impressed by that idea you asked me to visualise a speaker in my head other than myself and I named Oannes. It looks to me now as if he's the It that's been living me and I'm not too happy with it.'

'Why not?'

'My involvement with Melissa Bottomley became an obsession; I got to a point where I wanted whatever I could have with her at any cost. Her Leeuwenhoek money is almost gone and she needs funding to continue this study she's doing. I told her I'd help her with that.'

'Can you afford to?'

'I own an original Redon that's going to be auctioned at Christie's for quite a bit of money.'

'Maybe you could fund the NHS – they're always coming up short.'

'Very funny, Leon.'

'Sorry. You were saying?'

'Well, I got carried away and told her I might give her some money for her study. I didn't say how much.'

'So if you're going to be coming into some money, what's the problem?'

'I'm not sure I want to give her anything now. That

painting was going to be converted to money for Hannelore and me to enjoy. Now Hannelore's dead, and in exchange for sexual treats and a bit of conversation now and then I've promised money to this woman who has only contempt for me.'

'When you spoke about your obsession with Melissa Bottomley you used the past tense. Are you no longer obsessed with her?'

'No, I'm not. Long before this I could see her for the cold and calculating bitch she is but I was more or less under her spell. Now that spell is broken.'

'So you're not having anything to do with her from now on?'

'I didn't say that.'

'Why not?'

'She gets to me in all kinds of ways: that first time she came to my house, we were standing outside on the pavement and she laid her head on my shoulder and said, "I'm not sure what I am; sometimes I'm not sure *if* I am." When I expressed surprise she said, "Nobody is the same all the way through like a stick of seaside rock. Or from moment to moment." Then she asked me to hug her and she said, "You're older than my father."'

Dr DeVere waited for more but Klein folded his arms and was silent, as if he had just presented an irrefutable argument. 'She's not the same all the way through,' he whispered into his hand.

'What did you just whisper?' said Dr DeVere.

'"She's not the same all the way through."'

'I see. But you're no longer obsessed with her.'

'No.'

'Could it be that you're in love with her?'

'That would be ridiculous, wouldn't it.'

199

'"Ridiculous" is not a word I throw around very much. *Are* you in love with her?'

'"I'm only happy when it's complicated."'

'*Are* you happy?'

'That's a line from a song.'

'Which you quoted because . . . ?'

'It *is* complicated and I'm confused. I know I'm nothing to her. At first I was just data for her study but I couldn't leave it at that; I wasn't satisfied with a voice on the phone or words on the screen, I wanted to meet her face-to-face, wanted to talk to her as real people do. Then when she set me up to be raped by Leslie I wanted to get back at her somehow so I hid in the van and kind of blackmailed her into coming to my house, but after that bit of intimacy . . .'

'Are you talking about the intimacy on the pavement or the oral and anal intimacy in the house?'

'All of it. I'm nothing to her and yet I *am* something; I think there must be some unfinished business with her father that she's working out with me.'

'And of course you're working out various things with her, or just one big thing really.'

'Which is,'

'You tell me.'

'How I feel about women?'

'You said it.'

'Are you familiar with the work of Bruno Schulz?'

'Yes, and I've been wondering if gynocracy was going to come into this. Is that part of the action with her?'

'Yes, but even when we get into that there's something touching about her. She's obviously got all kinds of personal hangups — maybe as many as I do — and she's not very nice but with this study of hers she's trying to find real answers

200

to questions that don't always get asked; there's not enough of that in the world.'

'So you're going to give her the money you promised?'

'I don't see how I can welsh on that promise. Of course I still have to work out how much.'

'What about Oannes? Are you still getting one-liners? The last thing I have is "Madness is the natural state."'

Klein consulted his Oannes list. 'In the taxi on the way to Christie's with the painting he said, "It goes," meaning of course everything – everything goes until everything's gone and that's all she wrote. The next thing from him was in the Peacock Theatre where I went to see Tango por Dos. In the bar before the show started I was whispering to myself about an item I'd seen in the *Observer* – people reporting sightings of the Grim Reaper; I was recalling a drawing by Alfred Rethel, entitled 'Death as a friend', and thinking about Hannelore. I started to cry and a woman asked me if I was all right and I made a verbal pass at her and when I got back to Oannes he said, "Death as a friend."'

'As a friend to whom?'

'He probably meant me; he's given to innuendo.'

'Do you think about death much?'

'Well, I'm seventy-two and not in good health; I'm surprised that I've lived this long – I never expected to. I've spent a fair amount of time in hospital and I don't want to die with all kinds of tubes coming into and out of me. It's the final landfall and I'd like to fetch a good one, maybe die in the middle of a really classy paragraph or a wholly improper act. But not in hospital.'

'I can understand that. What else has Oannes said?'

'"Wild thing." We were talking about my Schulzian

tendencies. He was taking the piss of course; he doesn't let me get away with much.'

'You and I haven't talked about your Schulzian tendencies – today is the first time you've mentioned them.'

'Oannes made that remark after I asked myself or him whether there was in all men a secret desire to abase themselves at the feet of a woman who has contempt for them. I was wondering whether I was naturally depraved and losing control of myself. That's when he said, "Wild thing."'

'Had you abased yourself at Melissa's feet?'

'Here we go, spelling out every fucking thing. When did you first begin to do your living vicariously?'

'What makes you think self-abasement is my idea of living?'

'Sorry, Leon – I was forgetting my place. Yes, I abased myself at Melissa's feet. Do you want her shoe size?'

'No, my question is, do you think you're naturally depraved?'

'I was wondering about that at the time but not now. I don't think I'm depraved and I do think there are all kinds of urges in everybody but . . .'

'But?'

'It's not as good as navigating by the stars without instruments. It's not as good as being a real man.'

'Where's all this navigation coming from?'

Klein told him about *The Last Navigator*.

'You have to remember,' said Dr DeVere, 'that Piailug's life is simpler than yours. When was the film made?'

'About ten years ago, I think.'

'Who knows how things are with him now? Even back then the kids didn't want his teaching any more and there was a steamer going round the islands like a bus. Maybe

202

he doesn't feel much of a man now either. Feeling like a man depends on quite a complex system of inner and outer psyche-shapers. A society like Piailug's had reasonably foolproof systems for a long time but not any more. Our urban society puts the burden of psyche-shaping pretty much on the individual and everybody has to work out his own system which makes everything more difficult.'

'You're such a comfort to me, Leon.'

'Once in a while at least. What's your next Oannes quote?'

'"I'm only happy when it's complicated." That's the second line of the song. The first is, "I'm only happy when it rains." Shirley Manson sings it; the name of the group and the album is Garbage.'

'When did Oannes come up with that line?'

'Melissa was spanking me at the time.'

'I have to tell you, Harold, you're really good value as a patient. With you there's always something new to keep me on my toes.'

'I do my best, Doc.'

'Was the spanking her idea or yours?'

'She said on the phone that I was being very naughty and I said I couldn't help it. Discipline was mentioned, one thing led to another and she came round to my house again. She was eager to please because I'd promised her money.'

'And did she please?'

'Yes.'

'It wasn't as good as navigating by the stars but you made the best of it?'

'Yes, I guess it's different strokes for different folks, isn't it.'

'Anything more from Oannes?'

'He said, "RRRRAAAAARRGH!"'

DeVere, startled, said, 'When was that?'

'It was during that same visit when Melissa spanked me and did the other. I was talking to Hannelore but I forgot to whisper, so I said out loud, "You'll never grow old," and Melissa said, "Why not? Do you think I'll die young?" That's when Oannes made that noise and put a picture in my mind.'

'What was the picture?'

'Melissa dead.'

'How'd she die?'

'I killed her – bashed her head in with a large round beach stone from Paxos.'

'Does Paxos have any significance for you?'

'Hannelore and I went there one summer.'

'Why'd you kill her?'

'I suppose it fits into a natural-depravity sequence: first she spanks me, then she buggers me, then I kill her. Just a normal fantasy any naturally depraved person might have. Which I seem to be although I said I wasn't.'

'Everybody has fantasies, Harold. Lots of them are a lot worse than that. Did you have any difficulty in not acting that one out?'

'No.'

'What went on with you and Melissa that evening – was it you that made it happen or Oannes?'

'Wondering whether it's time to wheel out the Mental Health Act, Leon?'

'Just give me a straight answer, OK?'

'Oannes is how my mind dresses up in order for me to say and do what I want to say and do in the Oannes mode, I've told you that before. It's always me, with a little help from Melissa that evening. Do you think I'm a danger to myself and society at large?'

'I think everybody's potentially a danger to himself and society; everybody is like a grenade that's safe until you pull the pin but it isn't always easy to know when the pin's been pulled.'

'You think my pin's been pulled?'

'I don't know, Harold – I haven't got all the answers, I don't even have all the questions. Do you think you might have a self-destructive urge in you?'

'Did you work that out all by yourself, Leon, or did you read it on the back of a cereal box?'

'Right. I'm afraid that's it for today. Try to stay out of major trouble and I'll see you in a fortnight.'

'Minor trouble isn't really worth bothering with, Doc. See you.'

DeVere shook his head as the door closed behind Klein. At the bottom of the session notes he wrote: *Locus of control?*

41

REALLY PERKY

On the day of the viewing for the auction Klein took the Piccadilly Line to Green Park, walked up Piccadilly to St James's Street and down St James's Street to King Street and Christie's. The afternoon was hot, the sunlight lay on it like a lid of heavy glass, the buildings leant and loomed threateningly.

Christie's looked august, impassive, authoritarian; it was hard to imagine the artists, some of them undoubtedly less than respectable, who had produced by the labour of hand and eye the works that would be sold here. Melissa was waiting for him in the lobby where the carpet seemed to belong to a hotel in somebody else's life. 'If this is what this is,' Klein whispered into his hand, 'and she is who she is, who am I?'

'Hello, Harold,' she said. She was very smart in a black trouser suit. Klein was wearing jeans, a tired-looking blue shirt, and some sort of safari jacket. Muttering under his breath, he was at the same time proud to be seen with Melissa and resentful of her presence; he would have preferred to be alone among these strangers with the winged horse that had for so many years been the tutelary god of his workroom. Seeing the painting in the catalogue that Christie's had sent him had already made it no longer his. The catalogue cost £25 and weighed about a kilo; he gave it to Melissa to carry as they went up the stairs to the Main Room.

The daylight through the skylight was reflected in the parquet floor on which the viewers' footsteps echoed implacably, saying flatly that anything can be bought and sold. The prospective buyers, singly and in groups, catalogues in hand, made their slow circuit, bypassing a TV cameraman focusing on an expert-looking man who held a sheaf of documents. Klein was usually able to spot Americans by the hang of their faces and he saw quite a few, some of them patently heavy hitters and others probably tourists making a culture stop among the serious punters who spoke three or four languages and had eyes like basilisks.

The fifty-three lots on view included French, German, Dutch, and English Romanticists, Impressionists, Post-Impressionists, Symbolists, and Pre-Raphaelites. There were major Monets, minor Courbets, middle Corots, an early Renoir, a late Degas, a stray Ensor, a Moreau *Salome* watercolour sketch, and a *Don Quixote and Sancho Panza* charcoal drawing by Daumier with what Klein considered an insulting under-estimate of £40,000–60,000.

'What are you whispering about now?' said Melissa.

'Market forces and mental flab.'

Pegase Noir, Lot 37, was between a Puvis de Chavannes *Regret* and a *Despair* by Watts. *Look at me*, said the winged horse to Klein. *Is this what you wanted? Are you happy now?*

'Those two set him off quite well, I think,' said Melissa. 'He really looks perky next to them.'

Klein whispered something into his hand but she didn't ask what it was.

A tall heavyset big-money sort of American with a big-money-sort-of-American's-blonde paused in front of the Redon. 'Look out, Odilon,' whispered Klein, 'Las Vegas has arrived.'

The man consulted his catalogue. 'Four to six hundred thousand,' he said.

'You into Symbolists now?' said the woman.

'I'm getting a feeling.'

'The last time you had a feeling it was a horse too.'

'That one couldn't run but I think this one's going to fly. It's strange, it's mystical.'

'The question is, how much do you want to put on a mystical horse?'

'Well, it's that kind of a time – lots of interest in UFOs, alien abductions, X-files, that kind of thing.'

'Would you call a flying horse a UFO?'

'Mystics are in these days. Glenn Hoddle even hired a faith healer for the England team.'

'Did they win whatever they were playing?'

'That's beside the point.' They drifted away, the man's gestures indicating that the feeling was getting stronger.

'He's right,' said Klein. 'That horse is going to fly.' 'Here I am and Hannelore's dead,' he whispered into his hand.

'What do you think of Moreau?' said Melissa. She was standing in front of the *Salome* watercolour, over estimated, in Klein's opinion, at £300,000–350,000.

'Some of his sketches are pretty good,' he said, 'but his finishes tend to be a little obvious.'

'You don't think he's as good as Redon?'

'For me he's not in the same class.'

'Why not?'

'Even when he's at his very best, you can see how Moreau reasoned out his pictures, how he put the elements

208

together; with Redon you can't: his ideas and images came from unknown places far away – they came looking for him and they made him visualise strange worlds. His kind of genius is very rare.'

'You like strangeness, don't you, Harold.'

'Yes, I do. Reality is so strange that it can never be completely grasped; it takes a strange artist to get past the front of it and Redon is the strangest artist I know, miles ahead of the surrealists. He didn't try to be clever – he just did it the way it showed itself to him.'

'Harold, are you unhappy about selling the painting?'

'Do you care whether I am or not?'

'Of course I care. Maybe I'm not the kind of person you'd like me to be and maybe you're not getting all you want from me but we *have* got a relationship; I'm something to you and you're something to me.'

'The question is, what?'

'Surely you know by now, Harold, that you can't always define things clearly and if you try too hard you can make them go away altogether. It's like Heisenberg's Uncertainty Principle: you can determine the position of a moving particle or its momentum, but not both at the same time.'

'OK, so what's the position with us?'

She looked at him sidewise and laughed. 'We've tried one or two, haven't we. They contribute to the momentum, don't you think? We've got a good little mysterious something going between us, Prof, something strange – don't spoil it.'

'I'm not in love with her,' Klein whispered into his hand. 'That would be too pathetic.'

'What are you whispering?'

'I'm not in love with you, Melissa.'

'That's perfectly all right, Harold, but if you want to be in love with me, that's all right too. An experience can be life-enriching even when it's emotionally frustrating.' She said this tenderly, with her hand on his arm and her blue eyes full on him. Klein kissed her and she kissed him back.

'This is my life now,' he whispered into her hair. 'The past doesn't go away but the present steps in front of it.' There swam into his mind the fish in the Chelsea & Westminster Hospital lobby, observing with perpetually open eyes the ichthyocentric world on the other side of the glass. He sighed.

'What's the matter?' said Melissa.

'I'm being attacked by random metaphors.'

'Try to avoid eye contact, maybe they'll go away.'

They continued their viewing, with Klein lingering longest at nudes and marine paintings. As they stood in front of a deliciously seductive *Nu allongé dans le studio* by Paul-Cesar Helleu she said, 'Tell me, Prof, how is this different from pornography?'

'That's a tough one, and I have lain awake many nights pondering that very question.'

'So what's the answer?'

'You'll have to ask Boots.'

'Boots the Chemists?'

'That's right.'

'How's that?'

'If I were to photograph this painting and take my film to Boots, they would process it and give me prints of Mademoiselle Allongé with no questions asked. If it were pornography they wouldn't.'

'Thanks. It's good that I have you to explain these things to me.'

210

'That's the advantage of hanging out with an art historian – you get these professional insights for free.'

'And what is it with all these sailing vessels in calm and heavy weather?' They had by then moved on to *Shipping in Choppy Waters* by the Dutch painter Abraham Hulk.

'Well, first of all life is a sometimes calm, sometimes stormy sea, OK?'

'Right.'

'So you've got a good solid metaphor to begin with; then there's the rigging.'

'What about it?'

'Look at the vessel in the foreground, with this diagonal spar that goes from the lower left to the upper-right corner of the sail – do you know what it's called?'

'Can't say I do.'

'It's a sprit: not a boom, not a gaff, but a sprit. Every rope and spar has its proper name so that nothing gets mixed up with anything else, and these seventeenth, eighteenth, and nineteenth-century painters got their rigging right; they believed in it. Take a painter like Caspar David Friedrich – he was heavily into metaphysics but when he drew a boat it was a boat that worked, both physically and metaphysically. That kind of thing is life-affirming for me.'

'Jesus, Harold – how did I get along without you all these years!'

'With difficulty, I fear. Come look at the Daumier.'

A tall silver-haired patrician couple had got there first and were examining it thoughtfully. 'That's the sort of horse the picadors used to ride in Barcelona,' said the man. 'They were expendable.'

'Don Quixote was a tall thin man,' said his wife, 'so it was natural for Daumier to give him a tall thin horse.'

'I realise that. All the same, I prefer Munnings for horses.'

'I'm glad he didn't like it,' said Klein when the couple had moved on. 'I'd have felt bad if he had.'

'Maybe you just don't like tall people.'

'I like Don Quixote – he was tall.'

'I like this Daumier a lot,' said Melissa. 'Please don't explain it to me.'

'I won't; I'll say only that the last time I was in Paris I left a thank-you note on Daumier's tomb in Père Lachaise.'

Mr Duclos found them back at the Redon. Klein introduced Melissa and Duclos gave them news of *Pegase Noir's* tour. 'There was a great deal of interest in Paris and Zurich and New York,' he said. 'Quite a buzz, really – I expect a lot of excitement at the sale.'

When they'd had enough viewing Klein and Melissa went back to Piccadilly and the Royal Academy for coffee. The Summer Exhibition was on; the statue of Joshua Reynolds, garlanded with flowers, looked towards the entrance arch where a black iron cast of Anthony Gormley hung by its ankles from a rope. Forty-five other effigies of the sculptor, occupying the courtyard in a variety of positions, were being infiltrated by tourists young and old who photographed each other interacting with them.

The restaurant was dark and cool with cryptlike arches, its globe-lamps cosy, its murals comfortably dated; time seemed in no hurry. 'Why here?' said Melissa.

'I like to be overcharged in a good cause,' said Klein, 'and I like to be with you in a place where I've often been alone.'

Melissa put her hand on his. 'That's a really sweet thing to say, Harold.' She looked at her watch. 'I have to go now, I've got a class to prepare.'

212

The sky grew dark as they went down Piccadilly towards Green Park Station, Klein whispering, 'A winged horse can't do my flying for me, I have to do it on my own. We *are* something to each other. You don't always know what's happening when it's happening. "This can't be love because I feel so well . . ."' Suddenly there was rain beating down, urgent and shining and steaming on street and pavement. 'You go ahead,' he said, 'I can't run.'

'A little rain won't hurt me,' she said, and pressed his arm closer to her. Drenched and smiling, he felt almost middle-aged again.

42

LOT 37

Surrounded by crimson walls, Klein whispered to himself,

'He did not wear his scarlet coat,
For blood and wine are red,
And blood and wine were on his hands
When they found him with the dead,
The poor dead woman whom he loved,
And murdered in her bed.'

'Really,' said Melissa, 'aren't you over-reacting? All you're doing is selling a painting.'

'I wasn't talking to you,' said Klein.

There were breaks in the crimson: the auctioneer's podium was in front of an eight-foot-wide white panel that went up to the ceiling; the enclosures for the telephone staff were also white. Above the auctioneer's head on the white panel an electronic conversion board waited to show the current lot number and the accumulating sales total in sterling, US dollars, Deutschmarks, Swiss francs, French francs, and Japanese yen.

Mr Duclos had left passes for Klein and Melissa at Reception and Melissa had also registered and received a numbered paddle. 'Are you expecting to bid?' said Klein.

'Who knows? I like to be part of the action.' Klein wanted to see the whole room so they stood by the back wall. Mr Duclos came over to them as the room filled up.

'There's very strong interest,' he said. 'We have the curator of an American museum here who came especially for the Redon; we've got a private collector who saw it in New York and wants to buy it and we've got two or three Europeans. Now it's time for me to take up my phone station.' He left them to join the other staff at the telephones as the auctioneer stepped up to the podium.

'Good afternoon, ladies and gentlemen,' said the auctioneer. 'Welcome to this sale of French Impressionist and Nineteenth-Century paintings. Please note that Lots Seventeen, Twenty-one, and Forty-six have been withdrawn. Lot One is a river view by Boudin, 1889. Let's begin at £35,000.'

Someone bald raised his paddle. 'I have thirty-five thousand,' said the auctioneer. 'Thirty-five thousand . . .'

The auctioneer was young, well-groomed, inexorable. He went smoothly through his litany of lot numbers, titles, and attributions, appealing for ever larger numbers as the bidders variably responded and his hammer rose and fell. The sale moved swiftly from landscape to seascape, from summer to winter, calm to storm, exterior to interior, portrait to still life to floral to nude. Painting after painting leapt on to the viewing stand and back into the hands of the crimson-aproned, crimson-necktied porter as the conversion board flickered its digits and the room sloped like a slide towards the moment when the Redon's number would be called.

When *Pegase Noir* was put up in front of all those people Klein was shocked. There came to mind *The Slave Market*, the Gerome painting in which a naked girl is displayed by her vendor to a prospective buyer who puts two fingers into her mouth, examining her teeth.

'Lot Thirty-seven!' said the auctioneer. '*Pegase Noir, Black Pegasus* by Odilon Redon, 1910, unique. Shall we start the bidding at four hundred thousand pounds?'

Someone had evidently nodded or raised a finger. 'I have four hundred thousand,' said the auctioneer. '*It's like our marriage,*' said Hannelore as Klein whispered her words, '*full of darkness but it flies.*' He closed his eyes and tried to see her face but recalled only the gesture of her hand as she spoke.

'I have four twenty,' said the auctioneer in response to another unseen signal. Klein spotted Mr Las Vegas and his wife or consort; they seemed reluctant to show early foot. 'Four thirty,' said the apparently telepathic auctioneer. The air in the room was stretched taut, filling the available space precisely. Klein breathed in the scent of Melissa, heard the faint rustling of her skirt and stockings as she changed position. 'This is exciting,' she whispered, and squeezed his hand.

'Four fifty,' said the auctioneer. The winged horse in the painting seemed very far away, seemed to be moving ever more into the distance, soaring into the oranges, the reds, the crimson walls and the roses of time past and love long gone.

'What is it?' Klein whispered into his hand.

'What's what?' whispered Melissa, her lips brushing his ear, her breath warm.

'Everything. We come into the world, we do our little dance, then we're gone, and what did it all matter?'

'Six hundred thousand,' said Melissa, and raised her paddle.

'What are you doing?' said Klein as Mr Duclos, looking in their direction, raised his eyebrows.

'It's going to go a lot higher,' said Melissa, 'I can feel it – I'm just speeding things up a bit.' Her face was flushed, her eyes bright.

'Six hundred fifty,' said the auctioneer as Mr Las Vegas nodded. 'Seven hundred thousand on the telephone. And fifty, seven hundred and fifty,' as Las Vegas responded. 'Eight,' as a paddle went up from a Japanese not yet heard from.

Klein was paying such close attention that by now he felt that he alone was holding the reality of the whole thing together; if he relaxed his grip it might tear loose and blow away like a sail in a storm.

The telephones sprang to life as the distant bidders, sensing the end of the chase, moved in for the kill. 'Eight fifty,' said the auctioneer. The bidding was now between two telephones, Las Vegas, and the Japanese.

'This horse is really taking off,' said Melissa as one of the telephones bid £950,000. 'Nine hundred and fifty thousand,' said the auctioneer. 'Any advance on nine hundred and fifty thousand?'

Up went Melissa's paddle. 'One million!' she said as Mr Duclos frowned at his telephone.

'"*Où sont les neiges d'antan*?"' said Klein as his left arm went leaden and an ache declared itself at the back of his throat. 'Excuse me,' he said to Melissa, 'I'll just pop into Casualty and see you later.'

'I have one million,' said the auctioneer.

'Harold, what's the matter?' said Melissa.

'It's only the usual thing – I'll be fine. You stay with it.'

'One million,' said the auctioneer. 'Any advance on one million?'

'Casualty where?' said Melissa.

'Chelsea & Westminster, they're my local.' He made his way past the others standing between him and the doorway, reached the stairs, descended without collapsing, achieved the Reception desk, and said quietly to the handsome young woman there, smiling and attentive, 'Please call an ambulance.'

43

HAPPY HOUR

'If you have to reef you shouldn't sail,' said Francine as Klein reefed the sail of his hospital dream. They were far out at sea in his little boat, it was a night without stars, the wind was moaning, the waves were huge.

'If I could see a star,' he said, 'I'd know which way is up.' He opened his eyes. It was still the day of the auction; the Coronary Care Unit was full of visitors and that hospital-afternoon daylight that is not the same as free-range daylight. Tubes were feeding heparin and insulin into his left arm.

'Just pop this under your tongue for me,' said Staff Nurse Francesca as she gave him a disposable thermometer and put the blood-pressure sleeve on his right arm. Klein had mentally undressed her several times; her skeleton was the perkiest of the day staff. 'Whuzzu lasname, Fruzzhezza?' he said.

'Miller.' She brought her bosom and name badge closer. 'You're losing the thermometer.'

'Schubert wrote a song cycle about a beautiful miller girl,' he said when he was able. 'What's my blood pressure?'

'One-ten over fifty. My boyfriend gave me a recording of it with Dietrich Fischer-Dieskau.'

'That's a bit low for me,' said Klein. 'Does he know about wine?'

'Funny you should say that. He's just bought a book about it. Finger.'

He gave her a finger and she pricked it for a drop of blood which she caught on a B-M stick. 'We go to wine-tastings sometimes. Fourteen point five.'

'That's a little excessive,' said Klein.

'It's fun though,' said Francesca. She put the glucose monitor back in its box and breezed off in a zephyr of pheromones.

Klein was still shaking his head appreciatively at her going-away view when a queenly Yoruba woman with cheek tattoos put menu forms on his table. 'What's good?' he said.

She gave him a sphinx-like smile. 'Everything.'

Torn between cottage pie and lasagne, he was whispering his options into his hand when the phlebotomist appeared, a Chinese woman with a serious face. 'Harold Klein?' she said. 'Date of birth: four, two, twenty-five?'

'That's me.' He offered his arm and made a fist as she applied the tourniquet. 'The blood is the life,' he said.

'Please,' she said, 'if you knew how tired I am of Dracula jokes . . .'

'Sorry.' He read her name badge as the needle went in: Pearl Epstein. 'Ever use the *I Ching*?'   .

'No, and don't ask me what my star sign is, OK?' She filled both vials and put a wad of absorbent cotton on the site. 'Press on this.'

Klein pressed. She labelled the vials, then secured the cotton with a strip of tape. 'Taurus,' he said.

Epstein registered surprise. 'What made you say that?'

'My first wife was a Taurus.'

220

She gave him a hard look, gathered up her tray and was gone.

'These inscrutable Epsteins,' Klein whispered.

There were six beds in his bay, arranged in two rows of three. At four of them platoons of family and friends clustered with grapes, oranges, apples, bananas, pears, plums, chocolates, biscuits, Lucozade, orange squash, Coca-Cola, Ribena, and mineral water. Some went down to the shop for further supplies while others of them chatted, read, knitted, and gave comfort in cockney and one or two other languages.

Klein had the bed nearest the door in his row. His opposite was a man in his early sixties who, like Klein, was without visitors. He was sitting, fully dressed, in the chair by his bed. At his feet was a blue holdall from which he took a map. He unfolded the map and perused it hurriedly, tracing some route with his finger; then he refolded it, stuffed it back in the holdall, stood up, and hurried anxiously from bed to bed on his side of the room, murmuring, 'Where is it?' He then came back down the line on Klein's side, returned to his chair, looked at the holdall, said, 'Here it is,' sat down again, took out the map, and ran his finger over it once more.

'I know the feeling,' said Klein.

'Where's Ealing?' said the man. He had an Australian accent.

'That's west London – you can get to it on the Underground.'

'But I'm not,' said the man.

'Not what?'

'Going to Ealing.'

'I never said you were.'

'You said, "Why go to Ealing?"'

'No, I said, "I know the feeling."'

'Of what?'

'Not going to Ealing, if you like.'

'With or without a bike, I'm not going.'

'Righty-oh,' said Klein, giving him a smile and a thumbs-up sign as Melissa appeared, elegant in her little black frock. Beds Three and Five reached for their inhalers as she aimed herself at him.

'Here you are,' she said, and gave him a long and intimate kiss.

'What's this?' said Klein when he found his tongue. 'Has God suddenly declared a Happy Hour?'

'I was worried about you, Harold. When you left the auction you looked not long for this world. You're still very pale. How are you feeling?'

'Great. They had to tether me to this machine to make the ward safe for the nurses.'

'No, really, was it a full-scale heart attack? Have you got any pain now? What are they going to do with you?'

'It was a small-scale heart attack. I haven't any pain now. I'm waiting for an angiogram and when they've had a look at that they'll decide what to do next. What happened with the painting?'

'It went to a telephone bidder for £1,250,000.'

'A million and a quarter! Mr Las Vegas was right – UFOs, alien abductions, and big money for mystics.'

'Wasn't Redon a Symbolist?'

'That's the label they've stuck on him but a mystic is what he essentially was. Your last bid was a million, right?'

'Right.'

'You've got a lot of balls, Melissa.'

'Fortune favours the bold, Harold, and one of these

days you'll be getting a cheque for £1,164,062.50 which is better than a kick in the head from a dead horse.' She made a circuit of the bed, sliding the curtains along the rails until Klein was closed off in a private cubicle.

'What's happening?' he said as she came to his bedside.

'Physiotherapy.' She took his right hand, moved it up under her skirt and clamped it firmly between her legs. No knickers. 'I want you to get well soon; you've got a lot to live for.'

'You mean, I'm a successful old fool?'

'Success is certainly within your grasp. Keep doing that, you're looking better already.'

'Melissa, why are you being so nice to me?'

'You've got the quids, I've got the quos. I can be bought.'

'Ah, it's just business then, nothing personal.'

'Not entirely; I can't be bought by just anybody.'

'I'm honoured.' He removed his hand.

'Don't be hurt, Harold; I've told you before this that everything's business in one way or another: that's what makes the world go around.'

'It certainly seems to be going around faster than it used to.'

'You're keeping up with it pretty well. When you're back to full strength we can talk about the future, but for now you should get lots of rest. Can I bring you anything?'

'Could you get me some things from home?'

'No problem. Give me a list.'

She sat on the edge of the bed while he made the list, her bottom touching his leg. 'It's funny,' he said, 'here I am in hospital after a heart attack and I feel more alive and in the world than I've done in years, just because you're sitting on the edge of my bed.'

223

She touched his cheek. 'You mustn't get too fond of me, Prof – I don't want to break your heart.'

He kissed her hand. 'Don't worry, you won't.'

The curtains slid back as a male technician arrived with an ECG machine.

'I'm off,' said Melissa. 'I'll be around tomorrow with your things.' She slid her hand under his pillows, kissed him and left.

When the ECG was done and the technician gone Klein reached under the pillows and found Melissa's black silk knickers. 'Hard sell,' he said; he held them to his face for a moment, then put them in his locker.

44

OANNES SAYS

At three o'clock in the morning the ward was fully itself, a place of darkness behind the membrane of apparent reality, a realm where nothing was certain and everything in doubt, an enclave of enforced intimacy where strangers hawked, spat, snored, farted, and peed in bottles while nurses ministered to them in stealth and whispers. Klein, now on the third of Patrick o'Brian's Aubrey-Maturin novels, was in the foretopmast crosstrees of HMS *Surprise*, considering, with Stephen Maturin and Jack Aubrey, 'the ship thus seen as a figure of the present – the untouched sea before it as the future – the bow wave as the moment of perception, of immediate existence'. The frigate was before the wind, her motion long and easy; the swing of the topmast as she pitched was hypnotic.

Harold Klein, millionaire, said Oannes.

Belay that, said Klein. You needn't tell the whole world about it; anyhow, a fool and his money are soon parted. 'Sorry,' he said as Staff Nurse Judy Magee approached, 'I was thinking out loud.'

'I didn't hear anything,' said Judy, offering a thermometer. 'Pop this under your tongue.'

'In a moment.' Testing, said Klein to himself. Testing,

one, two, three, four. To Judy he said, 'Did you hear anything then?'

'Like what?' She put the blood-pressure cuff on his arm and pumped it up.

'Words from me.'

'When?'

'Just before I asked you if you heard anything.'

'You said you were thinking out loud.'

'And after that?'

'One twenty over sixty.'

'Did I say that?'

'*I* did – that's your blood pressure.'

'But after I said I was thinking out loud, what did I say next?'

'You asked me if I'd heard anything. Would you like a sleeping tablet? They've written you up for one.'

'No, thanks, I'll be all right.' He popped the thermometer under his tongue and tried to keep his mind blank while she wrote down his blood pressure. 'OK,' she said when she had noted his temperature, 'I'll look in on you in another hour.'

'Right. See you.' He was always pleased to see her in the night; hers was a sweet face, what he thought of as a Forties face, the loyal sweetheart in black-and-white war films, working as a riveter in an aircraft factory while her fiancé fought overseas. The shape of her face and her short hair reminded him of Melissa but the spirit that animated her face was altogether different. Oannes, he said, is that you?

Were you expecting someone else?

You're different now, we're having a conversation and it's all in my head – I'm not talking out loud or whispering.

So?

226

You've become a proper inner voice! It's been so long since I had one! To what do I owe this change?

We have more to talk about than we did before.

Like what?

Like how much money are you putting into this Melissa thing?

I still have to work that out. Why?

You're not by any chance stalling, are you?

Stalling? Not really – it's just that it's something that requires careful thought.

I'm glad to hear that, because you don't really know anything about her except that she tastes good.

Aren't you the one who said that madness is the natural state?

Yes, but I never told you to go completely natural; there are practical limits to this sort of thing.

You're starting to sound like the talking cricket in *Pinocchio.*

Maybe guys with wooden heads need talking crickets.

Look, I'm kind of tired now. We'll talk again soon, OK?

Whatever you say, Boss.

45

LAST SESSION

In matters of wardrobe Klein was not burdened by his professional aestheticism; he was ordinarily to be seen in jeans and T-shirts when it was warm, jeans and polo-necks and various outdoor-man jackets when it was cold. Large black medically-bespoke boots were what he walked around in and he always wore some kind of hat to shade his eyes, as often as not a sort of bush-ranger affair in green canvas. Today, however, he sported a black shirt, tan linen jacket, and his hat was a Death-in-Venice panama.

'You look different,' said Doctor DeVere.

Klein shrugged. 'Things change,' he said.

'What things?'

'I had a heart attack, I've been in hospital, and my inner voice has come back. All the way.'

'Sorry to hear about the heart attack. How are you now?'

'I'm fine; it wasn't a big one. They did a balloon job on the right coronary artery and put in a stent and now I can walk a lot better than I did before.'

'What brought it on?'

'The auction was a little too much excitement for me.'

'Ah, the Redon! You've sold it then?'

'Yes, it's gone.'

'Did it fetch a good price?'

'A million and a quarter.'

Dr DeVere whistled. 'Crikey! I'm not surprised that you had a heart attack. Unless, of course, you're accustomed to dealing with that kind of money.'

'I'm not.'

'Will you be going ahead with your plan to fund Melissa's study?'

'Oh yes. We still have to work out the details. She visited me in hospital after the auction.'

'Pleasant visit?'

'Very.' Klein couldn't help grinning.

'Cheered you up, did it?'

You don't have to tell him everything, said Oannes. 'We had a nice chat,' Klein said to DeVere. 'She said she could be bought.'

'Did she! Is that how you think of the funding?'

'I've told you before this that I think her project is worthwhile. She appreciates my support and I appreciate her appreciation. Everything is business in one way or another, Leon.'

'That's one way of looking at life, I guess. You said you've got your inner voice back. Is it the same inner voice you had before?'

'No, it's Oannes now. I've told you about the last time I heard my old inner voice: it was that day in the Fulham Road when I was trying to walk fast enough to get a better look at a woman who was walking much faster. I said to myself, "One day you'll drop dead while something like that walks away from you." Then I said to myself in a different voice, "Well, that's life, innit." And that was the voice of Oannes.'

229

'So that was the transition, and since then it's been only Oannes, right?'

'Right, but he limited himself to one-liners until we started having real conversations in hospital.'

'When did that happen?'

'It was in the middle of the night, the same day Melissa visited me in the afternoon. He said, "Harold Klein, millionaire," then we talked about money and Melissa and I was doing it in my head, not whispering: talking with an inner voice the way I used to before all this began.'

'Not quite the way you used to. Did the old inner voice say things like "Madness is the natural state?"'

'Certainly I've changed. People *do* change, you know.'

'Let's go back to the beginning of this whole thing. How would you describe the losing of your inner voice? What would you say was happening in you back then?'

'My self stopped talking to me. I lost contact with myself.'

'Why do you think you lost contact with yourself?'

'All of me wasn't going in the same direction; I was drifting apart.'

'What would you say the different directions were?'

'Partly I wanted to loosen up and partly I didn't.'

'When did you first visit Angelica's Grotto?'

'It was after our first session.'

'Afternoon? Evening?'

'Evening. I didn't feel like working; I was having a drink and listening to Connie Francis. She was singing "Everybody's Somebody's Fool". I went to Yahoo and told it to search for Sexuality.'

'Were you feeling like somebody's fool?'

'I was feeling like anybody's fool.'

230

'So you went to Yahoo. Your Oannes, is he perhaps a bit of a yahoo?'

'Perhaps.'

'And Oannes is . . . ?'

'An aspect of myself.'

'Can you say more?'

'He's an aspect of myself I'm quite comfortable with. When I talk to myself as Oannes there's a lot less bullshit than there used to be.'

'And a lot more sex.'

'Well, I'm putting my money where my mouth is, and vice versa.'

'And is all of you going in the same direction now?'

'Looks that way to me.'

Watching Klein, DeVere was reminded of cop movies in which a guilty man with a foolproof alibi sat in his chair the same way Klein was sitting in his. 'So,' he said, 'how would you assess your present situation?'

Klein thought about that for a while. 'You've seen in amusement arcades a brightly lit glass case full of little prizes, and you have to manoeuvre a pair of claws to pick up what you can?'

'Yes, I've seen those.'

'Well, I've done the best I could with my claws.'

'What exactly have you picked up?'

'Little treats, little bits of Melissa-time.'

'No more than that?'

'Treats and bits are all I can manage – the whole Melissa is beyond my grasp.'

'Would you want the whole Melissa?'

'Actually, I like it the way things are now.'

'You think that's the best you can do?'

'It's the best I *want* to do; it feels right.'

231

'Why do you think that is?'

'Let me ask you a question: what do you think your function as a psychologist is?'

'Helping people to work through their problems.'

'And who decides when they've done that?'

'Usually it's the patient and the psychologist together.'

'What if they don't have the same opinion?'

'Can you elaborate?'

'Take Bruno Schulz's little eunuch, grovelling at the bedside of the woman he can't have while a stallion licks her bottom – would you say he's worked through his problems?'

'I very much doubt it.'

'But maybe that's how he wants things to be; maybe he likes that arrangement.'

'And what about you? Is that an arrangement you'd like?'

'You're a lot younger than I am, Leon. Maybe how you are now isn't how you'll be when you're my age.'

'You're not answering my question.'

'Look, in these sessions you've had me putting all kinds of things into words and you've helped me get to where I don't have to put everything into words any more. I know the way I am now probably isn't your idea of a good way to be but it feels right for me, OK? And from here on out I think I can go it alone.'

'Are you saying that you want these sessions to stop?'

'That's what I'm saying.'

DeVere ran his thumbnail down the outside edge of the notes stacked in Klein's file. 'It's your choice of course, but I have to say that I think there's still work to be done.'

'There's always work to be done but it doesn't always take two people to do it.'

'Then all I can say is, good luck and I hope you won't be sorry.'

'I feel lucky already, Leon, and I've given up feeling sorry.'

46

RUBICON GROVE

Melissa drove skilfully and with assurance, taking the van smoothly up the Embankment, over the Vauxhall Bridge, thence by various turnings to Camberwell New Road and Camberwell Grove. The day was delicately grey with a light rain, Klein's favourite kind of weather; the auguries were good, he felt, and things were definitely moving forward. Camberwell was lively with shops and off-licences; the colours were intensified by the rain and all of his senses were heightened.

'Well,' said Melissa, 'there's no turning back now: once you know where I live you'll always be able to find me.'

'Does that bother you?'

'No. We've come a long way from your first visit to Angelica's Grotto and this is where we are now.'

'Every life is a winding road, Melissa.' She was wearing a short denim skirt and black stockings as always. He put his hand on her thigh and she let it stay there.

She was able to park close to the house, a Georgian one with three storeys and a front garden. 'The flat's in the basement,' she said as they went up the steps to the front door.

Knowing for the first time where Melissa lived and

actually being in her place overwhelmed Klein with its intimacy, made his heart beat faster. He thought of her dressing and undressing; he thought of her naked in the bath. He recalled their telephone conversation when she'd been with Lydia: he'd imagined a huge bed in a large room full of warm colours – orange, rose, crimson. There were silk sheets and oriental cushions and flowers, possibly a canary as well. Their bodies had been golden in the lamplight of his mind.

Melissa led him through the hallway, down a narrow staircase, and suddenly they were in the bedroom. A bit of the front garden was visible through a small window that allowed a little grey rainlight to reveal a threadbare green carpet, a double bed in cracked white enamel with a rumpled India-print bedspread, a night table, a chest of drawers, and a chair with a white T-shirt and a pair of jeans draped over the back of it.

Smells funky, said Oannes.

On the floor by the chair were a pair of trainers several sizes too large for Melissa. 'Whose are those?' said Klein.

'Leslie's.'

'He's your partner?'

'He's an employee. We work late hours and he spends a lot of time here.'

'Much of it in bed with you.'

'I never promised you a nunnery, Harold. I need regular servicing.'

'I see.'

'That's a very unfriendly "I see". Is one displeased?'

Klein was imagining the two of them in bed, Melissa with her legs wrapped around Leslie. He heard her orgasm, watched the kissing that followed, heard her sighs of satisfaction.

'Harold,' she said, '*are* you displeased?'

'I don't know – it's just that I hadn't realised that I'd be subsidising Leslie as well as you.'

'He's part of Angelica's Grotto. And it's not as if we're proper lovers, you know – he's not the only one I take to bed.'

'Yes, of course that makes a big difference.'

'Are you going to sulk now?' She put her arm around him and brought her face close to his. He affected indifference. 'Don't be that way, Harold – be nice.' She kissed him and it was impossible not to return the kiss. There was a pounding of feet overhead. 'Children,' she said. 'Three of them. I'd love to get out of here. Wouldn't you like to have me closer to you?' She kissed him again and put his hand on her breast. 'Wouldn't it be good if you and I and Leslie were all under one roof? We could all work in peace and you'd be able to keep an eye on things,' another kiss, 'night and day.' He looked into the middle distance. 'Come on, Harold, you know you've been longing to see me do it with a stallion.' He looked at the ceiling, noted the cracks. 'And of course,' another kiss, 'there's a lot to be said for three in a bed.'

'I wonder,' he said, 'whether the gratification of one's desires is really what life is all about?'

'You have to admit that it's not a bad way to pass the time while you're wondering, mmm?'

'Do you think my place would do? I doubt that I could survive the hassle of moving house.'

'Your place would be lovely; it's a great location and it'd be the best possible arrangement. What about the finances? Will you give me a lump sum or do you want to do a contract of some kind? I don't want to sound too heartlessly practical but if you were to hop the twig without putting something in writing I'd be left high and dry, wouldn't I.'

'I won't leave you high and dry, Melissa. That'll all be taken care of.'

She kissed him again and hugged him. 'Whatever you think of me, Harold, I really am very fond of you. Underneath all the surface crap there is something good between us, isn't there?'

'Yes, Melissa, there is.'

'And do I taste good?'

'Delicious.'

'Perhaps you should refresh your memory.'

He refreshed it. The room took on warm colours; almost his tinnitus was like a canary.

'Show me the website setup,' he said.

'Through here.'

Beyond the bedroom were a tiny kitchen and a small room in which were two computers with modems, a printer, a scanner/copier, a fax machine, and three telephones. These occupied a long table and there was also a drawing table with a lightbox on it. There were two chairs; the rest of the space was filled by filing cabinets. 'This is where it all happens,' said Melissa.

'Amazing. I was expecting a much bigger setup, more like the control room for the national grid.'

'This is all you need – it's mostly in the software. We can't use a British ISP so we've got a file-transfer-protocol access to a Dutch server. We put everything together here and shoot it over there and it ends up on the Net where professorial types like you can drop in for intellectual stimulation. As I've said, we could really use one more person for the filing and the housekeeping on the database; it's difficult doing this and my job at King's as well.'

'How long have you been running the website, Melissa?'

'It's only about six months although it seems longer.'

'And what got you started on Angelica's Grotto?'

'I told you, Harold, I stabbed my father twelve times.'

'In other words, you're not going to explain.'

She cocked her head, closed one eye, and made a little noise out of the side of her mouth. 'My history is not part of the deal. Mystery yes, history no.'

'Will you tell me, at least, why you chose the Ingres painting of Ruggiero and Angelica for your website?'

'Yes, I will. For centuries, Harold, women have been chained to the rock of male fantasies, so I thought I might as well use naked Angelica to attract the types I wanted to study.'

'Emotionally dysfunctional types like me.'

'Right. So far I've compiled data on the eighty-one men who've been answering my questions as you did. Their fear of women and their feelings of inferiority are shown in how they react to the website material and what they say when we talk one to one – all of them feel less than equal to the female.'

'Do you think men ever will feel equal to women?'

'Obviously they can't feel equal until they *are* equal, and whether or not that'll ever happen I can't say. But before any change can happen there has to be recognition of the present situation, and that's the object of this study.'

'I'm afraid I'm too old to change, Melissa.'

'Nobody's asking you to. I'm not exactly a role model either and I'm too perverse to change, so I guess the two of us will have to carry on being less than perfect.'

'Is it possible that perversity is natural, that everything generates its own variations?'

'That's something else I'd like to look into but it'll have to wait until I finish this project.'

'While we talk there's nobody minding the store.'

'At this time of day we just let the website run itself. Later we'll do one-to-ones and take phone calls.'

'Where's Leslie now?'

'He's working in a porno flick and won't be back till this evening.'

'Don't you worry about AIDS?'

'We both get tested regularly and we always take precautions.'

'I can understand the appeal of rough trade, but he's so, so . . .'

'He's so what, Prof? So black? So well-hung? So good at giving me satisfaction?'

'Is he producing or performing in this porno flick?'

'Performing, and he's a very reliable performer, believe me – much in demand.'

'The people who make these films, do you associate with them at all?'

'It's a company called Labyrinth. They put me on to Lydia. She's the female lead in '*Monica's Monday Night*'. She also appears under different wigs in the other picture stories. She's very good but she's not cheap.'

'Who's Angelica?'

'That's Shannon. I got her from Labyrinth too.'

'She looks like a Waterhouse nymph.'

'Who's Waterhouse?'

'A Victorian painter. You must have seen reproductions of *Hylas and the Nymphs* or *The Lady of Shalott* here and there?'

'I don't recall but the Tennyson poem is certainly a load of crap. If she wanted Lancelot she could have found better ways of getting his attention than dying. That poem is a kind of snuff movie but it's respectable because they never actually get down to business. Typical wanker chauvinist piggery. And I doubt that Waterhouse's nymphs ever got up to or down to what Shannon does in a day's work.'

'At Labyrinth, are there any women called Kimberly or Tiffany?'

'Several. Do you want their phone numbers?'

'Not yet.' Klein's mind, like a tongue going into a cavity, kept giving him pictures of Melissa and Leslie doing what the Lady of Shalott and Lancelot didn't. 'You said that Leslie was an employee. Does his pay cover sexual services?'

'Yes, it does. With men I take nothing that I don't pay for.'

'What about Lydia? Do you pay her for sex?'

'No.'

'Why not?'

'Some things I'll explain, Harold – others not.'

'And you're paying me with sex in advance for what you expect to get from me.'

'I've told you: you've got the quids and I've got the quos. We also have something more but don't try to define it and don't try to romanticise it, OK?'

'OK, Melissa, I promise not to. If you'll drive me to Oval Underground Station I can make my way home from there.'

'Leaving in a huff, are we?'

'In a train, if you'll drop me off at the station.'

'So where are we, Prof?'

240

'In Rubicon Grove, Lola. I'll let you know when I've made the crossing.'

Nobody said anything in the van on the way to the station. Melissa took Klein's hand and put it on her thigh and he let it stay there while he spoke to himself in silence.

47

DEEPLY MOVING

'"The sense of danger must not disappear: . . ."' said Klein to Melissa on the telephone.

'"The way is certainly both short and steep,"' she replied, '"However gradual it looks from here; . . ."'

'"Look if you like, . . ."'

'"But you will have to leap." Are you leaping?'

'It seems that way. When can you and Leslie move in?'

'Are you sure you want us to?'

'Yes, I'm sure, Melissa.'

'It's a strange situation.'

'That's what life is, isn't it?'

'I mean, I know I'm taking advantage of you but at the same time I know that you want me to.'

'That's exactly right – I have no illusions about you and me and this is how I want it.'

'Well, we can do it tomorrow evening if that's a good time for you. We've only got the website gear and some clothes – no furniture except the tables and file cabinets.'

'Fine, come ahead whenever you're ready.'

'You've got two phone lines, right?'

'Right.'

'We'll need four more. I think it usually takes about a week before they can install them.'

'I'll order them now.'

'Thanks. I'm really looking forward to this move, Harold.'

'So am I, Melissa. Being an old fool is the most fun I've had in a long time.'

'If you're having fun maybe you're not such a fool. See you tomorrow. Kiss, kiss, kiss.'

He kissed her back. 'See you tomorrow.'

That Melissa had been able to quote the Auden poem with him pleased Klein greatly, made him feel that whatever was between them was growing and continually opening up new territory. After he rang off he paced the house restlessly, considering the working and sleeping arrangements. The front bedroom where he and Hannelore had slept would be for Melissa and . . . ? Him? Or Leslie? A hot wave of irritation flooded over him; he resented having to consider Leslie, resented the idea of yielding place to him. On the other hand, the thought of claiming a regular place in Melissa's bed in payment for a roof over her head embarrassed him; also the thought of his old body beside her young one every night made him squirm. No, the front bedroom would be for Melissa and Leslie. He would take the back bedroom and the website equipment could be set up in the guest room.

The house now wore a look of surprise and expectancy; encountering him in odd places scratching his head and muttering to himself, it found his presence changed. Standing before the Meissen girl, Klein was argumentative. 'Why,' he said, 'is there such a contradiction in you? You're a porcelain oxymoron: you've got a body that's made for sin and a face like the Virgin Mary and you've never looked at

243

me once in all these years – you've always got your eye on those invisible balls on that invisible pitch that's behind me when I stand in front of you. What's your message? Are you trying to tell me that the game is elsewhere, that I'm missing the point?'

Her eyes entranced and dreamy as always, she looked past Klein at the unseen world behind him.

'All right,' he said. 'Maybe I'm mad. It's the natural state.'

Just don't get too natural, said Oannes.

What can happen that's bad?

You never know.

That night Klein dreamt that Hannelore was walking towards him in the Fulham Road, the sunlight behind her shining through her hair. They both stopped and she looked at him sadly. 'You left *me*,' he said. 'I didn't leave you.'

Early the next evening he was watching at the front window when the van appeared with Leslie driving. Klein went out to meet them. 'Here we are,' said Melissa. 'Hi,' said Leslie.

'Hi,' said Klein.

There was no parking space in front of the house so Leslie and Melissa unloaded the van in the street and put everything on the pavement. Melissa kissed Klein. 'Well, Harold,' she said, 'this is it.'

'Yes, it is. I'm not strong enough to carry you over the threshold and of course it's not really that kind of thing.'

'Just as well, since there are two of us and Leslie's a lot heavier than I am.'

While Leslie drove off to find a space Melissa and Klein

carried things up the steps and into the house. 'Don't take anything heavy, Harold,' she said.

'I won't. The computers go in the room all the way at the back.'

This one too, said Oannes when Leslie reappeared.

That's how it is, said Klein. The work was soon done. He looked away when Leslie took his things into the front bedroom. 'Shall we order a pizza?' he said. 'I thought we'd do the shopping tomorrow.'

'Sounds good,' said Melissa. 'Cheese and tomato pepperoni, mushrooms, green peppers, onions, and anchovies?'

'Whatever does it for you.'

'Got any beer?' said Leslie.

'There's an Oddbins just up the road,' said Klein. 'Why don't you get a couple of six-packs while I order the pizza?' He gave him a twenty-pound note.

Leslie's eyes met his for rather a long time as he took the money. 'Any particular kind?'

'I mostly drink wine, so get whatever you like.'

'What beer do you drink when you *do* drink beer, Prof?'

'Beck's, and I'd rather you didn't call me Prof, Leslie.'

'Sorry! Should I call you Mr Klein?'

'Harold will do nicely, OK?'

'OK, nicely is how I want to do it, Harold.' He moved away pantherishly, the primal waves of his maleness continuing their transmission after he was out of sight. Receiving the message, Klein shrank into non-existence, reached into it, hauled himself out by the scruff of the neck, and shook his head.

He could be trouble, said Oannes.

Tell me about it, said Klein.

'Leslie's a lot of fun when you get to know him,' said Melissa.

'I'll bet he is. I can see already that he's got a great sense of humour.'

Melissa was standing by the wall where *Pegase Noir* used to hang. She touched the blank space it had left behind. 'That winged horse flew away with some of the past, Harold. Now there's more space for the present, wouldn't you say?'

'I suppose so.' He wished she would move away from the mantelpiece and the Meissen girl. She was running her finger over the nipple of the figure's exposed right breast, exactly as she had done the first time she was in this room. Maybe this is a dream, he thought. Maybe I'll wake up and she won't be here and I've never met her.

'We've got the makings of a very pleasant arrangement here, Harold.' She smiled suggestively. 'Don't spoil it for yourself.'

'God forbid.' He put Egberto Gismonti's *Sol Do Meio Dia* on the CD player and the guitar filled the room with Amazonian jungle shadows. 'That's a nice sound,' said Melissa. She shook her hips and rolled her shoulders to the music while he stood there danceless.

The pizza arrived, Leslie and the beer shortly after. They ate at the kitchen table. Klein opened a bottle of red which he and Melissa shared. Leslie drank Special Brew from the can. 'They were out of Beck's,' he said.

'Could I have the change?' said Klein.

Leslie gave it to him. There was a beaded lamp over the kitchen table; Klein had always found its light cosy but now it seemed to fix the strangeness of this gathering like a surveillance photograph. He imagined the police examining it and asking questions. Really, he said to himself, what have I to feel guilty about?

Don't ask me, said Oannes.

While they ate and drank, Gismonti continued in the living-room and the bedroom waited upstairs for what would come later. Klein tried to stop the pictures in his mind but couldn't. 'What's the domestic routine going to be?' he said to Melissa. 'Will you be cooking?'

'Hello, hello, are you there, Harold? This is 1998; unisex cooking has been going on for quite a while. What did you do until now?'

Over the years Klein had become a reasonably good cook, even essaying such advanced dishes as beef Stroganoff and goulash. He rebelled, however, at becoming the housewife of the group. 'I mostly bought frozen dinners at Safeway or I ordered in various kinds of takeaway,' he said. 'What did *you* do until now?'

'Sometimes we ate out; sometimes Leslie cooked.'

'Leslie, you're a real all-rounder,' said Klein.

'Some of us have to be. If I'm going to do the cooking here you and Melissa can do the shopping – I'll write out a list for you tonight.' To Melissa he said, 'We still have to get everything hooked up.'

While Leslie and Melissa organised the website room Klein went to his desk and put the last unfinished Klimt page up on his computer screen. Then he made it go away and put up a blank new page. He sat with his arms folded across his chest, looking at the wordless screen. He remembered an old Jimmy Durante song and typed:

> Sometimes I think I wanna go,
> And then again I think I wanna stay.

He needed music but wasn't sure what kind. He put on *Piazzolla Classics*. The first track was 'Three Minutes with the Truth' which always sounded to him like something struggling to move forward while being pulled back. The second track was 'The Little House of My Ancestors' which made him see it on a hillside under a flat blue cloudless sky, children playing in the dusty road. He listened through the disc, going where the music took him while staring at the words of Jimmy Durante on the computer screen.

'Beddy byes,' said Melissa, and kissed him. To his questioning look she said, 'Soon,' and went upstairs, followed by Leslie who said, over his shoulder, 'Sleep well, Harold.'

'No doubt in *his* mind about where he sleeps,' Klein muttered to himself. He went to the window, looked out at the street where the parked cars were frosting up under the unblinking stare of the pinky-yellow lamps. The winter night, sensing his attention, came up to the window, pressed its bleakness against the glass, mouthed *You and me, sweetheart*.

You're a pathetic fallacy, said Klein, and turned away. He went through his video collection, chose *The Passenger*, fast forwarded to the scene near the end when Jack Nicholson, having stolen another man's name, his passport, and possibly his destiny, lies on a bed in the *Hotel de La Gloria* on the Spanish border. In the stillness of late afternoon the camera, like his departing spirit, moves slowly out through the window and the grille to look across a dusty space towards the Plaza de Toros where there is nothing happening today except a trumpeter sending a solitary *paso doble* into the ambient silence. Little distant figures by its wall speak in diminished voices. The faint passing wail of a far-off train is heard, then the labouring engine of the little Auto Escuela Andalucía car. Maria Schneider, the unnamed Girl, appears walking slowly towards the bullring. The car of the driving-school comes and goes; a small boy runs across the window's view, throws a stone, is shouted at by the little distant figures. A white Citroën drives up; two men in light suits get out. There are church bells, car doors slamming, the roar of a motorcycle starting up and fading into quietness. People come and go in the dusty space, some of them look up at the window, some don't. A siren announces the arrival of a black-and-white police car; the policemen order the driving-school car to leave. Somewhere a dog barks. Other uniformed men arrive in a patrol car, perhaps they are border guards. With them is the wife of the man on the bed. He is dead now.

'Did you recognise him?' the wife is asked.

'I never knew him,' she says. The man on the bed is left behind as his story moves on without him.

The last shot in the film is outside the hotel at that time of *media luz*, all delicate pink and violet, when the sky is still luminous but the lamps are lit, first outside the hotel, then inside. The little Auto Escuela Andalucía car drives off under the music of a thoughtful guitar playing something uncredited that Klein had heard elsewhere: Julian Bream? He put on *La Guitarra Romantica*, searched patiently until he found it on Track 15, '*Canco del lladre*', 'The Thief's Song'.

'"The Thief's Song",' said Klein. 'He stole the identity of another man. This one that I have now, where did it come from? And the learner in the driving-school car, did he or she ever pass the driving test?' Then he realised that he was speaking aloud. He sighed and went upstairs.

Lying wakeful in the back bedroom he listened for sounds on the other side of the wall. There was some murmuring and he opened his door to hear better. The door of the front bedroom, he noticed, was now slightly ajar. There was laughter, more murmuring, then he heard

Melissa say, 'No, Leslie, no power games tonight!' Leslie laughed, there were sounds of a scuffle, Melissa cried out twice, then there was only the creaking of the bed. Klein closed his door. *Welcome to the ménage à trois*, said Oannes.

What am I going to do? said Klein.

We'll think of something.

48

LOOMINGS

Klein was accustomed to the looming of buildings and buses and he could handle it up to a point; he was troubled, however, by what seemed to him the unknown messages encoded in the 14 buses, the old Routemasters like the one that towered over him now as he headed for Safeway with a rucksack slung from one shoulder and a shopping list in his pocket. The 14s were definitely redder some days than others. '"The poor dead woman whom he loved,/ And murdered in her bed,"' he muttered.

You didn't murder Hannelore, said Oannes. *She topped herself.*

Blood and wine and buses are red, said Klein as the 14 puttered past him. *Love me*, whispered its diesel pheromones.

Everyone except one old lady on two sticks was walking faster than Klein. The morning was hot, the Fulham Road was full of traffic, the little green men on the crossing lights grudgingly allowed pedestrians a tenth of a second to get from one side to the other while the cars crouched, ready to spring. The sun was bearing down on the pollution to keep it within easy reach of anyone who happened to be breathing in; an examiner of early entrails would have found little to say for today. Another 14 bus appeared, possibly a male responding to the one ahead.

OK, said Oannes, *let's get into this 14 bus thing, shall we?*

I don't like the way they loom, said Klein.

Naturally – that's your guilt looming. Everybody's guilt looms or climbs on their shoulders or crawls up their asses or whatever. The looming is normal so don't let it bother you.

There's more to it and I don't know what it is.

We'll get to that. First let's look at what we've got here.

A big red in-your-face 14 bus.

A doubledecker, right?

Right.

What's the essence of a doubledecker bus?

They have an upstairs and a downstairs.

Like your mind.

OK.

So if you don't like it downstairs, go up on top.

Congratulations – you've just cut the Freudian knot.

Sometimes it needs cutting. These Routemasters – they're open in the back, right? Why are they open?

So you can jump on and off.

Nice one, Harold. You jumped on – now what?

You think I should jump off?

You tell me.

I'm of two minds on that.

So when the time comes you'll get rid of one of them.

One of the minds?

Whatever.

You said you were going to tell me about the more.

The thing about more is that it comes after what comes before it. When it's ready it'll make itself known.

You're such a comfort to me, Oannes.

After all, we're in this together for the time being.

252

What do you mean, 'for the time being'?

Well, nothing's for ever, is it.

Right, then while we're still together let's get on with the shopping.

I thought Melissa was going to help with that.

She had to be at King's all day today. And Leslie's out doing his thing.

Oh yes, Leslie's thing.

It looms.

Nothing's for ever, Prof.

When Klein reached the zebra crossing just after the little roundabout at the North End Road he looked neither to the right nor left but stepped off the kerb ignoring the squeal of brakes and walked without hurrying to the other side.

You got the action, you got the motion, said Oannes.

There was a nondescript brown dog parked outside Safeway. I could do shopping, it said with its eyes.

'Cleverness is not enough,' said Klein as the doors opened automatically, 'you need money.' He read his list: 1 cabbage; 3 carrots; 1lb onions; mayo; yoghurt; bunch parsley; codfish cakes.

You're not just a pretty face, said Oannes. *You can shop too.*

I'm a regular Renaissance man, said Klein. Despite the mental irritant of Leslie, he found that he was feeling good. Beautiful young women were sometimes to be seen in the shadowless fluorescent daylight, pacing indolently among the apples, pears, oranges, bananas, strawberries and pomegranates. These fruits had in the past lost their excitement when he got them home. The illuminated bottles of golden juice, heavy with sunlight from Jaffa and Florida and the gardens of the Hesperides, had become

253

simply the ghosts of citrus past in his fridge; potatoes had been mute lumps of carbohydrate. Now, even with the front-bedroom situation, there were good things to look forward to; the potatoes were solid with the promise of earthly delights and the pomegranates would still be musky with the scent of passing Persephones.

Moving from aisle to aisle, Klein filled his basket. Everything began to seem significant now, and the signs above the aisles became a mantra as he scanned them: COOKED MEAT, BACON & SAUSAGES, FRESH CHICKEN, FRESH MEAT, CANNED VEGETABLES, SOUPS, RICE & PASTA, COOKING SAUCES, BUNS & TEA CAKES, BREAD & CAKES, PICKLES & SAUCES, COOKING OILS, TEA & COFFEE, CANNED FISH & MEAT, BABY FOODS, MEDICINES, SHAMPOOS, TOILET SOAPS, SOAP POWDER & BLEACH, DOG FOOD, CAT FOOD, TOILET TISSUES, KITCHEN TOWELS, FROZEN CHICKEN, FROZEN MEAT, FROZEN VEGETABLES, FROZEN READY MEALS, FROZEN FISH, ICE-CREAM, RED WINES, WHITE WINES, BEER & LAGER, SPIRITS & LIQUEURS, BISCUITS, JAM & MARMALADE, SWEETS & CHOCOLATE, HOME BAKING, CRISPS, SNACKS, NUTS, SOFT DRINKS AND MINERAL WATER, MEMENTO MORI & LAST JUDGEMENT, GATHER YE ROSEBUDS WHILE YE MAY, OLD TIME IS STILL A-FLYING.

'Rosebud,' said Klein as the flames licked round him. He was standing in front of a display of autistic ties that gabbled in crazy colours and he thought of buying one for Leslie. He moved on to a phalanx of batteries, found it difficult not to buy some just for the power of it. When he left Safeway the dog was still there.

Gissa job, it said with its eyes.

'Fully staffed,' said Klein.

'*Big Issue!*' growled a bearded vendor.

'There are no small ones,' said Klein. Bearing his frozen codfish cakes and the other supper ingredients, he continued along the North End Road for no valid reason past the Parish Church of St John with St James, Walham Green, offering its crucified wooden Christ and COFFEE HERE, past the green and leafy churchyard and four jovial drunks on a bench towards the Cock that swung its sign above the eponymous pub and further flaunted its virility with a rampant golden chanticleer in three dimensions on the roof.

There's always Viagra, said Oannes.

'I need Viagra like a barnacle needs a treadmill,' said Klein, not realising that he'd spoken aloud until three passing schoolgirl smokers turned to look at him. 'As if!' said one. 'What did he mean?' said another, and the third brayed with all-purpose laughter.

Outside the public toilets a tumescent red motorcycle was parked. 'They really know how to hurt a guy,' said Klein, and headed for home.

49

NIMFB

Klein had written his own shopping list of salad ingredients, and at the appropriate time, feeling housewifely but trusting no one else to get it right, he made the salad and waited for the others to come home. The kitchen was in the basement, and as he sliced tomatoes and cucumbers he looked up at the legs and bodies – his view went no further – of the passersby on the other side of the area railings. The purposeful footsteps of the rest of the world made him wonder whether the place he had arrived at was as good as the ones they were hastening to.

Melissa was the first to arrive. 'Honey, I'm home,' she said, and gave him a deep kiss.

Klein disengaged his tongue and wiped his mouth. 'Did you have a good day?'

'Nothing special. What's the matter with you?'

'Matter? What could be the matter?'

'That's what I'm asking. Did you have a bad day?'

'Nothing special. I had a bad night, though, and so did you by the sound of it. Did Leslie demand his non-conjugal rights in a way you didn't care for?'

'The walls are really thin in this house, aren't they.'

'Especially when the bedroom doors are open.'

'What is it with men, anyhow, that they have to let off steam by buggering the nearest woman?'

'I wouldn't know – it's been so long since I had any steam to let off. You must be used to it, though, with Leslie.'

'Sometimes I don't mind but last night I wasn't in the mood.'

'Neither was I.'

'Harold – ' she put her hand on his arm, 'I know you were looking forward to joining in and I'm sorry it didn't work out that way but we've only just moved in and . . .' She wound herself around him and nuzzled his cheek, 'We've got lots of great nights ahead of us. Leslie has this heavy macho thing but I can settle him down and we'll have a really good time together – you'll see.'

'I think not, Melissa.'

She unwound with the speed of a striking rattlesnake. 'What do you mean, Prof?'

'I mean, you can stay but Leslie's got to go. I didn't mind it so much when he was doing you in Camberwell but I'll be goddamned if I want him doing you in my front bedroom.'

'But I thought, you know, you *wanted* a ménage à trois.'

'So did I but the fact is that I just don't like Leslie. Maybe we could ménage better if we found a woman to be the third in this house. I imagine I could find one without too much trouble – you're not the only one that can be bought.'

Go for it, Champ, said Oannes.

Melissa's eyes were frightening. 'Jesus, Harold, you're turning out to be a right bastard.'

'I never promised you unlimited old foolery.'

'The hell you didn't! You said you were going to take care of me financially and you strung me along so Leslie and I would move in with you, and now that we've given up the Camberwell flat you suddenly cop out on me. That's really shitty, Prof. If dumping Leslie was part of the deal you should have said so before this.'

'I honestly didn't know his presence was going to affect me the way it does. And it's deliberate on his part – he knows he's the alpha male around here and he rubs my nose in it with the way he talks to me and the looks he gives me and his body language. I might be old but I realise now that I'm just as territorial as he is and you happen to be the territory. I'm sorry but that's just how it is.' What a lot of testosterone there is in my cerebral cortex, he thought.

Melissa's face became something pale and grim that was all angles and no curves. 'Look at you, you useless old fart – I could easily finish you off with my bare hands and you're feeling territorial about me? That's really a laugh.'

'So laugh, but get rid of Leslie or the deal's off.'

'But I *need* Leslie – he's so good with computers and he knows the drill for the project. How am I going to break in somebody new at this stage?'

'Easily, I should think. There must be a million Leslies out there ready to step into the breach as soon as you drop your knickers. But not in my front bedroom.'

'You want to play hardball? How about if I let the tabloids know about the secret life of a respected art historian?'

'Go ahead, sweetheart. Not only will it give my books a new lease of life but I can sell *my* side of the story for a lot more money than I usually get in advances.'

'Good God, he's greedy as well.'

'This doesn't have to be a long drawn-out discussion, Lola. I've grown accustomed to your base but if you're determined to carry on with Leslie you'll have to do it without my financial help and in some other venue.'

He could see her thinking through various scenarios and discarding them until she had none. The deadliness went out of her eyes and she leant her head on his shoulder like a tired child. The lamp over the kitchen table backlit her hair and one side of her face and she was adorable in her defeat.

'I don't believe this is happening,' she said softly. 'I thought we were good friends and fond of each other.'

'I *am* fond of you, Melissa, but now that I've loosened up a bit I think I could become fond of someone else rather easily. Leslie's going to be here soon, I expect. Do you want to break it to him or shall I?'

'Don't do anything right away, Harold – give me a little time to think.'

'Certainly, but it's got to be tonight. While you're thinking we can have a drink. What's your pleasure?'

'Whisky.'

He poured a large Glenfiddich for both of them and raised his glass to her. 'Happy days, Melissa.'

'Whatever you say, Prof.' She closed her eyes and retired into a reverie while the frost did its nightly sparkle on the parked cars under the pinky-yellow lamps. Both glasses became empty quickly and Klein refilled them.

After a while Leslie's feet were heard on the outside stairs and he came in by the basement door. 'Honey, I'm home,' he said, and unslung his sports bag from his shoulder.

'We've done that one,' said Melissa.

'But not this one,' said Leslie. He put his hand between her legs and kissed her wetly.

Are you just going to keep taking this shit? said Oannes.

259

I'm thinking about it, said Klein. To Leslie, 'How was your day at the office?'

'Hard, which is how they want it,' said Leslie. 'And how was yours? Did you write lots of exciting words?'

'Not really.'

Well? said Oannes. *Cowardice is OK but this is* your *turf.*

'Good-looking salad,' said Leslie. 'You do that all by yourself, Prof?'

'Don't call me Prof.'

'Oh yes, I forgot. I'll try not to let it happen again.' He poured a Glenfiddich for himself and raised his glass to Klein. 'Here's to the world of the arts,' he said. He downed the whisky, poured another, set the glass on the drainingboard, opened the fridge, took out the vegetables, got a large knife and a bowl, and began to make coleslaw. 'We wrapped up *Dickerydoo* today,' he said to Melissa, 'so I'll be able to give you more time.'

'Right,' she said to his back. Looking at Klein, she shrugged.

Leslie was graceful and efficient. As he laid out what he needed without apparent thought he made a tidy little still life, then he peeled off the outer leaves of the cabbage, quartered it with professional speed, picked up the slicer, and sliced the cabbage into a bowl. He cleaned and grated the carrots, peeled a large onion and chopped it up fine, peeled and chopped an apple in, added some chopped parsley, black pepper, a pinch of salt, a dash of vinegar, then stirred in yoghurt and mayonnaise and a pinch of sugar. Everything he did was pleasing to the eye; his touch was deft and sensitive and his hands performed as stylishly as those of a TV chef. Melissa noticed Klein watching him. 'He's good at what he does,' she said.

'You know it,' said Leslie.

While Leslie was occupied with the coleslaw Melissa caught Klein's eye and looked towards the stairs. 'Right,' he said, 'I'm going up to the word machine. Give me a shout when it's eating time.'

'You got it, Mr Harold, sir,' said Leslie.

Once at his desk, Klein put up on the screen the page he called NEXT, and sat looking at Jimmy Durante's words:

Sometimes I think I wanna go,
And then again I think I wanna stay.

'No Klimt today,' he said. 'The Klimt is off. We can recommend . . . What?' He'd always tried to have a new project in mind to follow whatever he was working on – something to look forward to, but now he could think of nothing but Melissa and the conversation she was having with Leslie at this moment. He heard no raised voices from the kitchen but he wanted to make a little space around himself with music, so he put on the Charlie Byrd Trio with Ken Peplowski, *The Bossa Nova Years*. The songs of Antonio Carlos Jobim, instead of being soothing, seemed to be getting between him and something he wanted to look at. Or was it something that wanted to look at him? The *Knochenmann* with the red sceptre, was it, offering the next project?

He went to the window, looked at the frost-sparkling cars, thought of the seasons revolving inexorably while metal rusted and flesh decayed, thought of the trees across the common, now bare, how in the summer dawns they swayed their leafy tops in the early breeze, indifferent to humans who slept and woke and slept again.

From the trees on the common his mind went to the olive tree on Paxos, the olive tree he had drawn when

261

Mrs Lichtheim tested him. He saw the flash of silver as the summer wind stirred its leaves; he stood under it in the green-lit shade of the olive grove and looked at the ancient wrinkled trunk that was not dead and the dark opening out of which the naked Persephone had stepped, her body pale as moonlight, her face shadowed by her hair.

He was holding the Paxos stone, round and heavy, in his right hand, feeling in it the lapping of the sea on the pebbled strand, the flat blue of the sky, the Ionian sunlight. He read the Greek words he'd written on it, KINESIS/ANAPAUSIS: MOTION/REST, and tried to recall the balance of the moment when he had written them, tried to hear Hannelore's voice, tried to feel her body under his hand, felt instead the warm and pitted stone. What was his motion, where was his rest?

Leslie was standing in front of the desk with his back to the Meissen girl and the wall where *Pegase Noir* had hung. He had his drink in his hand and a reckless smile on his face.

'What?' said Klein.

'You the cool one, ain't you, Prof,' said Leslie. 'You the man with the plan – get us both moved in here and then throw my black ass out in the street and gobble that Melissa pussy night and day. Oh yes, you the man.'

Klein was looking at Leslie but he saw beyond him, on the blank wall, Lucifer rising out of the inkblot, transcendent, pale green and high above him. 'I didn't have a plan,' he said, 'but I want you out.'

'You want, Prof? Lemme tell you something, old numb-nuts ...' He reached behind him to put his drink on the mantelpiece and knocked over the Meissen girl. The porcelain figure fell to the hearth and shattered, and in that same moment the Paxos stone appeared in the middle of Leslie's forehead with blood streaming from it.

Leslie disappeared from view. 'O God!' said Klein. 'What have I done?' He stood up, peered over the edge of the desk, and saw Leslie lying on the floor, his face and chest covered with blood. He looked down at his right hand that had held the stone and saw that it was empty. He was breathless, the usual leadenness was travelling down his left arm and he felt as if a heavy fist had punched him in the heart. He reached for the glyceryl trinitrate, squirted it under his tongue, and waited for things to settle down.

You got the action, said Oannes. *You got the motion.*

What about rest? said Klein. To Leslie, not visible from where he sat, he said, 'I'm really sorry! I had no idea . . .'

Melissa appeared. 'What happened?' she said.

'Up jumped Lucifer,' said Klein, watching the ink-blot soar high above the world into the infinity of the blank wall.

'What are you talking about? Where's Leslie?'

Klein pointed. Melissa came round the desk, knelt by Leslie, felt for a pulse. 'He's dead, Harold.'

'I can't believe that I killed him, it doesn't seem real.' His mind was singing:

> Pack up all my care and woe,
> Here I go, singing low,
> Bye-bye, blackbird.

Melissa was looking at the bloody stone and the fragments of porcelain. 'What happened?' she said again.

'He came up here and he was all worked up about whatever you said to him. He was ranting about his black ass being thrown out into the street and he knocked

263

over the Meissen girl and I killed him with the Paxos stone.'

'Jesus, Harold! You killed him for breaking a porcelain figure?'

'The stone was in my hand and when I heard the figure shatter my arm went back and suddenly there was the stone in the middle of his forehead. It was nothing I'd intended – it just happened.'

Leslie fucked with the wrong guy this time, said Oannes.

'I wouldn't have thought you were strong enough to throw that hard,' said Melissa, shaking her head.

'I wouldn't have thought so either but there it is.'

'Poor old Leslie,' said Melissa. 'What a way for him to go.' She was silent for a few moments, then, 'We've got to get him out of the house.'

'Why don't we just dial 999?'

'And say what? That you killed a man because he broke your dolly?'

'It was almost an accident, really.'

'Whatever it was, it's the kind of thing they lock you up for. Maybe that's how you'd like to spend the rest of your days but I really don't want police all over this house investigating us and the computers – I need to stay respectable.'

'What do you want to do?'

'He told me Labyrinth had been doing some location work around King's Cross, so it's plausible that he might have gone back there on his own – he'd sometimes talked of doing a documentary off his own bat. We'll put him in the van with his camcorder and his other gear and we'll drive to King's Cross and leave him and it there with the doors open. Somebody'll steal the video gear and that should keep the police busy for a while.'

'Whose name is the van registered under?'

'Leslie's. Shit.'

'That's right. They'll trace him back to the Camberwell address and from there to here so there'll still be police knocking on the door.'

'Right. But if we just leave him somewhere without any ID it could be quite a while before they find out who he is and by then I'll have cleaned up the computers and installed some dummy programmes for them to look at if they want to.'

'What about the extra phone lines I ordered?'

'I can say I'm just starting a study of the politics of language – that would need the same kind of technology as Angelica's Grotto and I can fake it up from material I already have from the course I teach. So I can make all of that look kosher.'

'What about the van?'

'That fucking van! I've had too much to drink but I need another drink and the bottle's empty.'

'There's another bottle in the larder under the front steps; I'll get it.'

When he returned with a fresh bottle of Glenfiddich Melissa was sitting in his TV chair with her black-stockinged legs stretched out and her feet up on another chair. Her eyes were closed.

All yours, said Oannes, *but first* . . .

I know, said Klein. The body – we'll think of something.

He refilled the glasses. Melissa opened her eyes and he put her drink in her hand. 'Here's to whatever,' he said.

'Whatever. Dirty old man. Now it's just the two of us in this house, so you got what you wanted.'

'There are still three of us here, remember? We were

265

talking about the disposal of the defunct member of the group.'

'Poor old Leslie! Here's to you, Les, hung like a horse and always ready! You had your limitations but none below the waist. In the mist of, midst of Death we are in life. Or vice versa, whichever. To Les, Harold!'

'He was Les but he was more,' said Klein, and the glasses seemed to be empty again so he refilled them. 'I'm sorry for your horse, Melissa, but his next erection will be *rigor mortis* and we want him out of here by then. Try to focus on the matter at hand.' There was a pause of several minutes while they shook their heads and drank.

'The matter at hand,' said Melissa, 'is all bloody. We'll have to put him in a couple of dustbin liners so we don't get it all over ourselves. Got to clean the floor as well, pick up all your broken dolly bits. With her Virgin Mary face all smashed. This is more whisky than I usually drink, or have I said that?'

'Me too but it's an emergency, it has emerged. The Staxos pone, Paxos stone – that's bloody too. Did I ever tell you about the olive tree?'

'Smother time, Harold – trying to concentrate on the defunct member. Rest of him as well, all of him's defunct. Excuse me while I abseil from felicity awhile. Just close my eyes for a moment.'

'No prob, Melissa, we're all in this together. Maybe if we both close our eyes the world will go away.' He sat down on the floor by her chair, leant his head against her thigh, and fell asleep.

50

CATCHING THE BUS

Klein woke up with a headache, a dry mouth, and a crick in his neck. At first he didn't know who he was nor where he was. Melissa was snoring in the TV chair, and seeing her he recognised the room and himself. It was dark outside, the street lamps were lit, and it was raining. He looked at his watch: twenty past eight. Morning? Evening? 'Haven't we already done evening?' he said. He felt his face but learned nothing – the unbearded part of it was overdue for a shave most of the time. He went to the front door and saw the papers lying on the mat. 'Morning,' he said. 'Oh shit.'

You can say that again, said Oannes, *Action Man*.

Along with the headache Klein felt lightheaded and wobbly, hypoglycaemic. He went to his desk, got out the test kit, pricked his finger, and got a reading of 3.3. He ate lumps of sugar until he felt steadier, then he said, 'OK, I'm going to do it now.' He stood up, looked over the far edge of the desk, and saw Leslie lying among the fragments of the Meissen girl. His eyes were shut; he must have done that at the moment of impact. The blood by now looked sticky. 'You wouldn't figure Leslie for a thin skull,' said Klein, still speaking aloud from force of habit. 'Maybe his fontanelle never closed up properly.' The bloodstained Paxos stone lay on the floor like an egg from which something bad would shortly hatch.

'What do I do now?' he said.

Time, unless you come up with something clever, said Oannes.

Melissa, open-mouthed, continued to snore. Klein wanted to solve the problem alone if possible. 'Bruno Schulz's little guy never took out the stallion; this is a whole new ballgame. Cop films – think. *Internal Affairs*: Richard Gere's partner shoots an unarmed man. "I thought he was going for a weapon," he says. "It's OK," says Richard Gere, "it happens." He takes a knife out of his sock, wipes it carefully, and puts it in the dead man's hand. "It's cool," he says. "Don't worry." Knives and guns never fall out of people's socks when they're running in those films. Do they do it with Velcro or what? Matter at hand, must take care of.'

Klein found a pair of gloves, put them on, went down to the kitchen and got the knife Leslie had used when he made the coleslaw. He took hold of Leslie's right hand and found it stiff. 'He dropped the knife when the stone hit him,' he said, and laid it on the floor where it might have fallen.

'Yes,' he said to the police inspector in his mind, 'I was at my desk when he came up from the kitchen and began to shout at me. We'd all been drinking but he seemed out of control. He smashed the Meissen figure that was on the mantelpiece and then I saw there was a knife in his hand. He lurched towards me and I had this stone in my hand that I use as a paperweight. I threw it without even thinking and he went down. I'd no idea at first that he was dead, I expected him to get up and come after me again, the way the bad guy does in the movies.'

'Mr Klein, you say this happened between eight and

nine o'clock last evening. When you saw that this man was dead, why didn't you contact us immediately?'

'I was in shock, the balance of my mind was disturbed. I was temporarily insane. I had post-traumatic stress. I was drunk and fell asleep.'

'You fell asleep after killing a man?'

'Well, I passed out, actually. Listen, can I get back to you on this? I'm really knackered and I've just had a hypo and I've got an awful headache. What I need right now is a little lie-down, so if you'll excuse me . . .'

'Oh shit,' said Klein, 'this is really boring.' Melissa was still snoring. He watched her for a while until Hannelore entered his mind and looked at him sadly. 'Where have you been all this time?' he said. 'Look at what's happened to me. Did it have to be like this? I know I wasn't as good a husband as you were a wife and I know you wanted children but you oughtn't to have killed yourself. Surely the life we had was better than being dead.' He thought of their early years when he was middle-aged and she was young, how they had kissed shamelessly in public and held hands when they walked. He saw her face by candlelight in Le Bistingo in the King's Road. He looked at her coming towards him, he looked at her walking away. 'If you were still with me all this would never have happened,' he said; 'you would have rescued me from the rock of my aloneness and the monster of my impotent lust.'

Steady on, said Oannes. *Be a man, for Christ's sake, and stop embarrassing me.*

You're embarrassed! I'm kind of tired right now, Oannes, and I need to be alone for a while, OK?

Do what thou wilt, old chum. Catch you later.

The room was full of winter rainlight. Across the common the District Line trains rumbled eastward to Tower

269

Hill, Upminster, and Barking; westward to Wimbledon. Klein's headache wasn't too bad; it was as if all the nuts and bolts in his head had been tightened a little so that he was able to think more clearly. With this new clarity he picked up the kitchen knife from the floor and took it back to the kitchen. He discarded the gloves, put on his outdoor-man waterproof jacket and his bush-ranger hat, and went out into the rain. The trees on the common were black and bare. The sky was dark but he heard the whisper of the light behind the darkness.

'Yes,' he said, 'people grow old and die but every morning is a whole new thing, every morning never happened before.' He walked down Moore Park Road to Harwood Road, up Harwood Road to Fulham Broadway, where he turned left into the Fulham Road. Footsteps and umbrellas hurried past him. 'I'd really like to excuse myself from the sexual scene,' he said. 'Maybe if I bring a note from my mother.' He thought he heard laughter. 'Yes, the whole thing's pretty funny, really.' He was silent as he passed the Blue Elephant restaurant and Oza Chemist, contemplating the lights reflected in the shining street and listening to the hissing of tyres.

'Things are always much simpler than they appear at first,' he said. 'You do something and that's what you've done. If it's a police matter you tell the police about it.' He was standing at the pedestrian crossing waiting for the green man when he saw a woman waiting at the central divider. She was wearing a yellow mac and a short skirt.

'Great legs,' he said. She turned and it was Hannelore. 'Hannelore!' he shouted. 'Wait!' The little man on the pedestrian light was not yet green but Klein saw a clear space in the traffic and started across the road just in time to catch the full impact of the 14 bus that loomed above him, its redness heightened by the rain.

Fuck with me, will you, said the bus.

'He stepped right in front of me,' said the driver to the crowd that gathered around the body. 'I'd no time to stop.'

'I saw it,' said a man. 'It wasn't your fault.'

'What could he have been thinking of?' said a woman.

Shit happens, said Oannes, and moved on.

A NOTE ON THE AUTHOR

Russell Hoban is the author of many extraordinary novels including *Turtle Diary*, *Riddley Walker*, and most recently, *Mr Rinyo-Clacton's Offer*. He has also written some classic books for children including *The Mouse and His Child* and *The Frances Books*. He lives in London.

A NOTE ON THE TYPE

The text of this book is set in Bembo. The original types for
which were cut by Francesco Griffo for the Venetian printer
Aldus Manutius, and were first used in 1495 for Cardinal
Bembo's *De Aetna*. Claude Garamond (1480–1561) used
Bembo as a model, and so it became the forerunner of standard
European type for the following two centuries. Its modern
form was designed, following the original, for Monotype in
1929 and is widely in use today.